The Cowboy's Christmas Homecoming

The Cowboy's Christmas Homecoming

A Coyote Cowboys of Montana Romance

Sinclair Jayne

The Cowboy's Christmas Homecoming
Copyright© 2023 Sinclair Jayne
Tule Publishing First Printing, November 2023

The Tule Publishing, Inc.

ALL RIGHTS RESERVED

First Publication by Tule Publishing 2023

Cover design by Lee Hyat Designs

No part of this book may be used or reproduced in any manner whatsoever without written permission except in the case of brief quotations embodied in critical articles and reviews.

This is a work of fiction. Names, characters, places, and incidents are products of the author's imagination or are used fictitiously. Any resemblance to actual events, locales, organizations, or persons, living or dead, is entirely coincidental.

ISBN: 978-1-959988-88-5

Dear Reader,

I love writing Christmas stories, especially when they are part of a series and part of Tule's town, Marietta, Montana. *The Cowboy's Christmas Homecoming* is book three in my Montana Cowboy Coyote series, and it finally brings home a character—Rohan Telford—I introduced off-page about five years ago in *Giving Hearts*. Reunion romances are my favorite to write because there is so much emotion to play with. I always love the drama and the big ranching family dynamics. And of course, cowboys.

This book is especially close to my heart because Christmastime can be a time of great joy and sorrow for so many people, but for me, there is always that promise—even if it seems out of reach—that you can go home again, or create a new home, a new beginning. Joy can be seized or rediscovered in inches if you are just willing to hold on tightly—even when it's hard or seems hopeless. I do believe that miracles can be around the next corner or the one after as long as you keep moving forward.

I wanted to write a series that incorporates two of my favorite types of heroes—cowboys and soldiers. While cowboys have always been a favorite of mine, I don't have any in my family—that I know of. But my father, uncle and brother have all proudly served our country so this book and this series is a shout-out to all of them—Sinclair Jones, Wayne Jones and Gregory Jones.

Thank you for your service, your sacrifice and your stories.

Sinclair Jayne

Prologue

THE SIROCCO WAS threatening to kick back up. The hairs on Rohan Telford's arms and the back of his neck rose as if in challenge to Mother Nature's threat. They could all feel it—his brothers molded from duty, sweat, blood, respect and devotion to a guiding light, now extinguished. They all needed to be someplace else, and the window to leave was closing. But no one hurried this process.

Wolf—their new team leader—was solemn. He carefully folded up each slip of paper, his head bowed, lips tight, expression tense, as if the task were a difficult one. A bullet of resentment shot through Rohan. Wolf wasn't receiving orders from beyond the grave to carry out the final wishes of their fallen team leader, Jace McBride.

Jace had been the best leader, the best friend, the best everything that Rohan had been honored to serve with. Jace had been the best man Rohan had ever met with the exception of his father. He shut down his dark ruminations about home, not allowing his expression to change or his weight to shift. All his brothers were grieving, and he didn't want to reveal his own pain and doubt. Agony rolled over him with the power of the two-ton one-hundred-percent rank bulls he used to ride on the junior rodeo circuit.

Home.

Not anymore. He'd lost that privilege. Shut out his family and tossed away the love and respect of the woman, who'd been his one and only. And now Jace, the leader, the dreamer, the glue that held them all together was gone.

Jace had been in the process of mustering out.

That had shocked all of them. Left them adrift. But even in the process of leaving them, Jace wanted to lead. He'd planned to return to his hometown of Marietta, Montana— also Rohan's hometown, the place he'd been avoiding each time he'd re-enlisted and avoided taking leave. Jace had had plans—for himself, but also for all of them. Jace had still envisioned a future, whereas Rohan had been lost in the now. Next mission. Next target.

Jace had wanted to help his mom, dad and sister bring their small family ranch back to profitability. He had wanted his brothers to join him in Marietta. They would stay together. Create a business. Work the land. Build new lives. Have each other's backs. Rohan suspected that some of the men had been on board with Jace's plan. Or halfway there. Jace was charismatic and persuasive. And Rohan, with a thriving ranch to return to, should he wish, should have been a slam dunk.

But he couldn't imagine returning to Marietta. He was too different. His family was too different. They were happy. His two brothers married with children. His sister, finished with college and bottomed out from her thwarted music career as a once up-and-coming rock star, now worked with his mom breeding and training cutting horses. What did he have to offer?

Nothing.

He'd told Jace he couldn't go home. He hadn't told him why. But Jace had looked him in the eye and said, 'You can always go home. You, Rohan Telford, will go home.' That had been the day he'd led the mission Cross should have.

Rohan's shriveled heart squeezed painfully.

Jace had always had to have the last word.

Wolf held Jace's battered helmet in both hands and murmured something. A prayer? Too late for that. Blood spatter remained on the helmet. Wolf had refused to clean it.

"Each of you will pick one task," Wolf's deep voice resonated, his Texas Hill Country twang mostly under control. "You will complete this task in Jace's name, no matter how many challenges fate throws at you. You will honor Jace, his memory. His intentions. And your brothers."

Everyone kept their heads lowered except Cross. His freaky eyes that looked like lightning shattering storm clouds focused on the helmet—probably imagining it should have been his empty helmet, his blood. Cross had never missed an extraction, and he hadn't shared what had gone wrong.

"No discussing the task until it's complete," Wolf intoned. "No switches. No help. No shirking. We owe it to Jace."

"Jace," all his brothers murmured as if they were in church. Jace had been an Amen for all of them in different ways.

"We've all put our paperwork in to muster out at different points this year. We will meet in Marietta next Memorial Day at Jace's grave for his final send-off. Our brother's spirit must be at peace. Do not let him down."

Wolf's intense navy-blue gaze skewered them all, one by one, until each man—Remy Cross, Ryder Lea, Huck Jones, Calhoun Miller and him—met that dark stare that drilled into their souls.

"Yes, sir. Coyote Cowboys until the end," they all stated, voices firm, not betraying the pain they were in.

The choosing began. Wolf palmed the helmet. Huck had held it initially, but his hands had been shaking too violently. Rohan wanted to comfort Huck. He'd been with Jace when he'd been hit multiple times. Huck had done his best. Kept the enemy off them. Managed to get Jace to an emergency extraction and help, but it had been too late. Not his fault. They all knew it, but Huck—the best with emergency battlefield first aid Rohan had ever worked with—would likely never forgive or forget.

But Rohan stayed put. He'd never known how to solace himself much less anyone else after his colossal life screw-up years ago.

He watched each brother step forward and pluck out a piece of paper. By an unspoken agreement, no one looked at the paper right away. Maybe the tension was too taut. Rohan's limbs felt like molten lead. It was hard to breathe. Impossible to focus. Maybe Jace had been right. It was time to go home. But how? He was so far from the man-child he'd been—full of dreams and swagger, confident of his place in the world and the girl-woman at his side.

No. He couldn't go home. She might still be there.

The longing that tore through him was visceral, and he looked down, almost expecting to see blood, bone, torn tissue. No, he couldn't see Ginny again. Not ever. He wouldn't be able to walk away a second time. He'd hurt her worse than a man should ever hurt a woman.

He dragged in a breath through his nose, pressing his lips tight. Returning to Marietta and flying under the radar enough so that his family didn't know he was there would be an impossible task. Maybe Cross—the ghost—could do it. But maybe the task would be…no. He shut down speculation. He shut down hope. He'd mastered shutting down everything but the mission years ago.

This was just another mission.

Two slips of paper remained.

Random or fate?

Mocking his question, Rohan picked the folded paper on the left. It burned like a flame in his palm. Calhoun took the last slip.

"We honor Jace as he would honor one of us," Wolf said.

"Jace McBride," they said as if any of Jace's favorite

beer—the Montana-based Moose Drool that Rohan's younger brother Boone had air-flighted to them at some exorbitant cost—remained in the empties, grouped in one corner of the airport hangar.

His brothers-in-arms one by one unfolded their slips of paper. The air snarled with tension and grief, but no one spoke or broke expression. No one knew what had been on Jace's list except Wolf and maybe Huck, whom Jace had told about the list and where to find it when he realized he wasn't going to make it back to base that last time.

Rohan tried to read the room, divine what he and his brothers were up against. He couldn't imagine what Jace had felt he'd needed to make amends for. He knew the McBride family—he'd gone to school with Jace's younger sister, Willow, but he hadn't met Jace until he'd moved over to Special Forces eight years ago. That's when he'd become a member of the Coyote Cowboys—a slam that they'd all taken as a compliment. Growing up ranch in the American west. Even though Rohan didn't feel like he could fit back in Marietta or at the Telford Family Ranch that his father had saved and dragged into the twenty-first century, he was a cowboy to his soul. His younger brother Boone had taken his place ranching alongside their larger-than-life father.

His fault. Bitterness soured Rohan's mouth. Boone had grown into a good, strong, ranching family man. He deserved the place by their father's side. He'd earned it, all of it—the ranch, his wife, his children, a legacy to hand down.

Unlikely the ranch could support two sons, one of them with a growing family. Rohan in a burst of selfishness had squandered his birthright and dreams and shot his life onto a new trajectory.

Stop stalling.

Rohan unfolded the slip of paper as if it were an artistic origami swan, deserving his complete concentration. His emotions and tension soared, but he reeled them back in—until he saw the words written in Wolf's distinctive tight, upright, all-caps writing. It took him a moment to absorb the enormity of the words. What the task would force him to do. Him. Not Jace.

The paper fluttered to the concrete. Instinct slammed his boot over the scrap.

Carrying out Jace's wish was the last thing he was suited to do. He couldn't. He'd wreaked enough pain on the Lane family. But then he looked up and saw Wolf lancing him with those intensely dark blues that saw through to the soul he'd once had—not the shredded one. One by one his brothers all looked at him, and Rohan realized that he'd been running from himself and his selfish, callous words and actions for years.

He was out of options.

Time to give, not take. What would Jace do? His brothers had often teased Jace about his goodness, his altruistic nature that put them all to shame. They even wore those stretchy neon WWJD bracelets for a time as if Jace had been their own personal Jesus. Sang the Depeche Mode song from the Eighties to tease him.

"You good?" Wolf asked the question his brothers' gazes all asked.

Rohan was anything but good.

He retrieved the paper and jammed it deep into the pocket of his dress uniform.

"I will not fail Jace—or any of you."

Chapter One

VIRGINIA LANE SWALLOWED a sigh—she'd been doing too much of that lately. She rolled up one of the garage doors of the junk-filled house that her father had enthusiastically purchased with the intention of donating to the nonprofit Harry's House.

'It will be Harry's House Annex,' he'd announced. 'A place and a program specifically for teens.'

Gin pulled her parka closer around her body and surveyed the challenge she faced this Friday after Thanksgiving morning.

She'd been dreading this moment. Delay and hide. It seemed to be her mantra now. Just getting out of bed, parenting her son and getting through each day teaching her two sixth-grade language arts and social studies block classes every day since late September sucked all her energy.

"Mess. Big mess," her twelve-year-old son Lucas flatly intoned in a massive understatement and promptly returned to the travails of Bilbo Baggins.

If only she too could lose herself in fantasy although a long, perilous, no doubt chilly quest with no comfortable hot-jetted bath at the end of the day played no part in her fantasies. What did?

Gin regarded the stacked chairs, tables, boxes, and things she couldn't identify. The spurt of resentment was as hot as it was unwelcome.

Her father was dead.

This, this...junk-filled garage and junk-filled small ranch house on a large lot with a shop at the back had been her father's retirement plan. His legacy. He had devoted over forty years to the high school students of Marietta, Montana, as a vocational education teacher and career and college counselor, and in his retirement, he had intended to devote more time to Marietta's youth—help to launch them into the world.

Her father had sacrificed his comfort and financial security to serve.

And mine.

Dismay swept through Gin. Followed quickly by the cleated running footsteps of shame. She shot a look around as if her father's spirit was watching, although he'd never judge. Ron Lane had been the most giving man she had known. She and Lucas had benefitted from his kindness and guidance and home. What he chose to do with his money and time in retirement was not her business.

Only now it is.

She balled her fists in her gloves and squared her shoulders. Her father deserved her best. With his love, help and encouragement, she'd picked herself up. Made a comfortable life for herself and her son. Now it was her time to honor her father's wishes and memory. She and a handful of volunteers would transform Harry's House Annex into a teen after-school program, building on what he and many other volunteers had started years ago with Harry's House, an after-school program in memory of EMT Harry Monroe, one of her father's former students who'd been killed while helping an elderly couple change a tire along the highway.

Harry too had been giving.

Whereas I am selfish.

Her father said she was too hard on herself, too past-focused, too stubborn. All true.

She dragged her gaze away from the monumental mess—the collection of a life that had quite possibly devolved into mental illness and hoarding. Sorrow settled along with the ever-present grief that clogged her heart. Her gaze shifted to Lucas, her light, standing still and facing north—one of the "quirky" habits he'd developed that she'd decided to ignore so that she could focus on his bigger issues. Lucas needed her, and her father deserved her best, so she had to keep it together.

Feeling ironic, she practiced her smile. Her father had often commented that she no longer smiled, and that even during a 'bad day'—not that her father had ever had one that she could tell—a smile would lift her spirits.

She'd been too busy surviving to think about smiling, and she'd blithely told him that she'd 'put it on the list.'

Her to-do list was likely a mile long by now, and it was long past time to get started. It wasn't as if she had to tackle the annex project on her own. Many of the original Harry's House volunteers were keen to help now that their children were older and would benefit from the expanded after-school program for teens—just not so much the day after Thanksgiving. But she had to get the garage and at least part of the house ready for the first class over the winter break. Local rancher Boone Telford had volunteered to teach a small engine repair and automotive maintenance class that had eight kids signed up.

She'd wrangled a few hearty volunteers for the big cleanup this weekend before a local contractor and a couple of cowboys started the build-out of the garage for the class. They also hoped to get the kitchen and one bathroom upgraded before the winter break.

But that was likely a reach.

"And reach I will," she murmured stepping into the stacked, daunting and smelly mess.

Her father had bought the property at auction. He hadn't been allowed to see inside, but that hadn't worried him. He knew how to fix anything and over the years had built a willing army of volunteers and goodwill. But he'd passed away soon after the purchase, leaving her responsible for the daunting home equity loan and remaining small mortgage on the recently purchased house. With his retirement benefits, he'd been situated fine. But she only had her salary, and until all the paperwork and probate went through, she was responsible for the two mortgage payments, although she knew, her father hadn't intended for the Harry's House Foundation to pay off the remaining mortgage.

Going against her father's intentions curdled her stomach, but she wasn't sure she could be that generous. She had Lucas's future to plan for.

"Do you think we'll find any *Tegenaria domesticas* hiding?" Lucas asked.

I hope not.

Why oh why when Lucas finally had started to speak at nearly four had he focused on spiders? Her father had been thrilled, saying maybe he'd be an arachnologist. The spider fascination had remained, but numbers and mechanical things had been added to his obsessions.

"Spiders usually die off before winter." She spoke with her teacher voice, although science had never been her thing. Words were, though she'd known, even at Lucas's age, she couldn't make a living with poetry. But it hadn't stopped her from imagining herself bathed in sunlight with her journal out, braving the elements, or curled up at the massive fireplace at the Telford Family Ranch and writing poetry about her thoughts, surroundings and love.

The absurdity of that dream—squashed flat—still had the power to burn her cheeks with humiliation at her naïve stupidity.

She'd deserved to be rudely slapped into reality.
But I rise.

"Tarantulas have longer life spans," she remembered, "but they aren't stalking around Montana."

"In winter spiders enter a diapause phase. They can produce a chemical like antifreeze so that they can stay alive in winter. If the spiderlings hatch, they winter in the egg sacs to keep warm. I bet we find spiderlings in all this junk."

Years and years of language and speech therapy had paid off.

And just like that, a bad day got worse.

"Then it's good we have gloves on." Gin shoved her snarky thought away and strove to sound more cheerful.

"We'll need to find a place to put them so we can save them." Lucas actually looked up from his book.

He got the book love from her. And her curly black hair and blue eyes. But the rest of Lucas—like his biological father—was an alcohol-fueled college party mystery, her souvenir from her semester of trying to drown her grief and anger.

"Okay." She forced energy into her voice. "Let's start pulling some of this junk out into the front yard." A tomorrow problem. Also a future Gin problem—finding more volunteers to teach the teens interesting and useful skills. She knew she should sign up. She had taught middle school for six years but mixing her career and volunteer hours and motherhood seemed like an overload of rioting teen energy and raging hormones.

She needed to keep her focus on the now. Clean up. Build-out. First class.

"Noooooo," Lucas wailed, eyes bugging, body tensing, face going red. "We can't, can't, can't throw anyone away. The spiderlings will die outside. The weather report says snow flurries this afternoon and up to six inches of snowfall between ten and twelve tonight."

Ah yes, Lucas, her personal meteorologist in addition to spider expert and numbers little man. And this was after he pulled his head out of a book. He was brilliant, but a struggle for a small-town rural school to challenge and meet his needs, and that wasn't counting the social piece that was a big, fat, lonely zero.

Focus.

"We can be careful," Gin hedged, but really she could hardly have frozen or hibernating spiders hiding in egg sacs in what would hopefully be a shop class in a few weeks. "We need to start organizing these piles of junk," she said, wanting to kick herself for dismissing Mrs. Gramery's life collections so callously. Lucas's thin face crumpled in betrayal. She felt the double kick to her maternal heart.

Future spider killer. Making her kid dig around festering junk on a school holiday. Her sins added up.

"We will be careful," she promised. "And if we find any…spiderlings, we'll put them in a box and…" oh, God, she did not want to bring them home "…ahhhh…we'll figure out a warmish place to keep them."

"Above the dryer?"

No!

Phobias were irrational. It was in the definition, but she still felt sweat break out on her scalp, under the jaunty green beanie that had a large white bobble and reindeer along the side. The beanie had been an impulse purchase even though money was now much tighter since her father had remortgaged their home to purchase the property next door to Harry's House, which meant she now had two mortgages instead of none, and only one paycheck. And one of the houses she technically didn't own as stipulated in her father's will.

Gin problem for another day.

Her phone buzzed with a text, and relief rushed through her. She didn't have to be the spiderling murderer quite yet. The text was from one of the families who'd volunteered to help her clean out the garage this morning for the cabinetry build tomorrow, but they indicated their out-of-town family was staying another day and couldn't make it.

"More people means a faster finish," she murmured under her breath even though she knew she wasn't being fair. It was a four-day holiday for many. A time to enjoy family and count blessings. But for the daughter of a man who'd devoted himself to others—*including me,* she reminded herself staunchly—vacations had always involved helping others.

Now she was the one who needed help to carry out her father's legacy, and this was the second set of volunteers who'd canceled. Her phone flooped in another text. *Make that three cancellations,* Gin thought gloomily, biting back a swear word. What would her father do?

"Get it done."

And with a smile.

Scowling Gin grabbed the first chair in the stack closest to the entrance and tugged it off its perch of chairs. It might be an antique, but she doubted it. If it was functional, it would be saved for the teen hangout room or donated. If not, it would be heaved in the dumpster she'd ordered to be delivered later this morning.

"C'mon, Lucas," she said forcing steel laced with encouragement in her voice instead of the whine that no doubt wanted to bust out. "It's you and me."

ROHAN FOUND THE dog near the summit of I-89.

He'd pulled the rental truck off into a small viewing area, not because he wanted a view of Paradise Valley—he didn't—but because he wasn't ready to drive to the Telford Family Ranch and announce to his parents and siblings and their significant others 'hey look who's home.'

Not that they wouldn't welcome him.

Absolutely they would.

He was the problem. He didn't feel ready to close the past chapter of his life and start a new one.

But he did have one job to do before he figured out his next. He looked up at the dark gray sky dragged down by impending snow and fighting the pull of the struggling morning, as if Jace would be there encouraging him. 'Mount up, Cowboy.'

It had been Jace's favorite ending line—a motivation to remind those in the unit where they'd come from as well as a promise they'd all return to the land. Fifteen more miles, and Rohan would be home. He wished it were fifteen hundred, but even that likely wouldn't be enough to settle him for the task and adjustment ahead.

He could keep driving.

Even as the temptation whispered, he heard rustling to his left and spun, already pulling his Glock 19 from the small of his back.

The dog crawled out of the scraggly, wind-blown pines, low to the ground, eyes—one green, one blue—wide and pleading, and the tan, black and white tail tentatively thumped.

"Hey, you." Rohan spoke softly, his voice low and rusty. He hadn't spoken to anyone in days since he'd left the base for the final time, exit interviews, paperwork, and the closure he hadn't expected until he either died on a mission or retired out in another decade or so.

He crouched down, hand low and extended. He'd grown

up with all sorts of ranch dogs—mostly border collies, Great Pyrenees or cattle dogs. This dog looked like a combination of several breeds and as if it had been living alone and rough for a while. Anger stirred in his gut.

No collar. Several long scars marred the left side of the dog, and its ribs were visible. He watched the dog's approach for signs of aggression. None. But there was fear and hope, which should not make him feel like screaming into the wind imminent with snow.

"Hey," he said again, as the dog flattened even further, shivering—from fear, cold or likely a combination.

He had a few apples, elk jerky, pretzels and a couple of ham and cheese sandwiches he'd purchased at a convenience store in Bozeman where he'd stopped for supplies. He'd determined to drive to Miracle Lake for a spell, hoping to clear his head before he headed to the ranch, or a potentially gut-punch reunion at Mr. Lane's house when he delivered Jace's letter.

She won't be there. She wanted to see some of the world before settling down.

The dog moaned and whimpered, and Rohan's shriveled black heart twisted in his chest. He couldn't carry the burden of one more soul, but he couldn't leave one more life behind. Mumbling who knew what, he picked up the dog and straightened to his full six one. His size had been useful in the military, but a pain in the ass when he'd been determined to excel on the college rodeo circuit and compete professionally for a few years before taking his place alongside his father at their fifth-generation ranch.

He tucked the dog close to his body, and it tentatively licked his cheek. "Let's get you checked out and see if there's space at the local shelter."

There wasn't. But a local vet, who volunteered at the shelter, had been arriving to check on a couple of the injured residents, offered to do a health screening for the dog. No chip. But the unspayed female did have mites, parasites, the beginnings of mange, blisters and frostbite on her paws. She was less than a year old and severely malnourished.

Talon Wilder had not been impressed with the ham that had been regurgitated on her hands as she'd examined the quivering animal.

"It was all I had," Rohan had apologized twice.

And when she'd asked several questions about the dog, all he'd been able to do was shrug and offer up a weak, 'mystery to me' defense.

The dog needed special food, small portions several times a day. Medicine and once healthy, an appointment to be spayed. Over five hundred dollars later, Rohan was back in the rental truck and the dog had booties, a coat, food and water dish, leash and harness, special food, a bag with several medications, a bed and a look of devotion that swamped Rohan with dread.

"I'll put up a flyer," Talon had said sunnily. "You'll be listed as the fostering parent."

"Please no," he'd said as she'd walked him to the truck, carrying some of the supplies.

He was flying under the radar. Or trying to. He needed to carry out the task for Jace and then figure out his next move, and of course visit his family.

"But we don't have space." Talon's expression had drooped and crinkled with worry. "And with the holidays, we often become inundated, even as some families do adopt animals for Christmas. Hopefully it won't take long. Please."

She'd misunderstood him. Easy to do. Not too many thirty-two-year-old men wanted to role-play being incognito in their small hometown where most everyone knew you through your father.

"No need to list my name," he'd clarified. "But I will care for the dog until an adoption can be arranged."

"Thank you for being such a Good Samaritan," Talon had said, although from her tone and expression, he had a feeling he was missing some subtext. "And welcome home, Rohan. Thank you for your years of dedication and service to our country."

"How did you know who I am?" Sure, he'd had to use his credit card, but he'd never met her.

"Several of my brothers and sisters-in-law do business with your father. You are such a source of pride to your family. Your father often talks about his hopes for when you come home." She'd smiled. "He's in for the best Christmas ever this year."

He must have frowned because her smile had slowly faded, and an unasked question lingered in her eyes.

"I'm surprising them," he'd blurted. It was true, but he hadn't meant to say it. "So, I'd appreciate you not mentioning that you saw me. I'm heading to the ranch today." It sounded like he was obfuscating. "I've been keeping this secret for a while. Hoping to keep it a few hours longer."

He'd sounded like an idiot.

Talon had mimed zipping her lips, smiling through the gesture before bouncing up on her toes, her wildly curly blonde hair reminded him of his high school girlfriend Ginny, only Ginny's hair had been a midnight black that had always looked so beautiful against her pale complexion with the cute freckles splattered across her nose like constellations.

Ginny.

Maybe she'd married. That thought should not still burn a hole in his gut. Ginny was smart, beautiful and talented. She'd always wanted to travel, experience the world, write about it through her poetry. Ironic that he, ranch born and raised, had been the one to leave for so many distant shores when he'd felt Montana to his marrow and other than riding the pro circuit for a handful of years, he hadn't wanted to stray far from the Big Sky State.

How was he going to face Mr. Lane with so many years and losses between them? Had Ginny told her father? Probably not though they'd been tight. Mr. Lane had often been called Mr. Marietta because he was so involved in everything. He'd been very protective of his only child and had trusted Rohan.

Rohan hadn't deserved the trust.

"Keep in touch with the shelter about Mystery's health," Talon had said.

"Oh, I'm not naming the dog," he'd said quickly. "I just meant that where she came from was a mystery."

And still was.

"It's a cute name. Run with it." Talon had turned around and returned to the clinic with long strides.

And just like that he had two unpleasant choices—seek out Mr. Lane or head home to a ranch that no longer felt like home and a family that no longer felt like his—something they'd never be able to understand, even if he tried to explain.

Chapter Two

"**G**INNY?" A DEEP voice with a whisper of graveling smoke wafted up from the driveway, still shrouded in the gloom of the morning.

Gin, chair hefted over her head like she was auditioning for a new dystopian streaming series, froze. Impossible. Not Rohan. Never again. Her grief, exhaustion and worries were playing tricks on her.

She squared her shoulders and mentally braced herself, turning toward the sound. Her blood turned to ice, and she weakly lowered the chair back onto the pile.

No. Impossible.

Her brain howled, but her stiff lips couldn't form any words. She blinked but the rangy cowboy in dark denim, heavy denim coat and black wool Resistol cowboy hat continued to walk up the driveway with that damn rolling walk that used to turn her tummy to goo in high school. Her knees weakened, and to give herself something to do, she picked up the cup of hot chocolate Lucas had poured for her earlier even though she hadn't wanted it.

She clutched the warm paper cup as if it were a banister she could clutch to avoid falling into the past. How could he be here? Why was he here? He'd made no moves to find her thirteen years ago. Hadn't kept in touch or asked how she was. He'd never apologized or tried to win her back. No, Rohan Telford had instead dropped out of college and run off to play hero.

No explanation.

Fury seared through her, burning away the shock. There wasn't any room for the hurt anymore.

Hot chocolate sloshed over the cup's rim, wetting her mittens.

It was really Rohan.

Rohan with his arrogance, confidence of his place in the world and that stupid sexy walk of his. A whisper of a smile, which was so familiar it hurt to see, teased his lips.

How dare he walk up her driveway like all the years and sorrow and emptiness had never happened. And worse, he looked better than ever. Dark green eyes. Impossibly long lashes. Sinful mouth, Copper Mountain jutting jaw and high cheekbones that were so prominent they practically created shade when the sun shone. Rohan removed his hat. Same thick, coppery-colored hair with even more blond highlights than she remembered, probably from all his years and miles running around the world's hot spots—saving everyone except them and their never got to be born baby.

"Ginny." His voice was hoarse, deeper but so familiar she ached and that pissed her off.

Rohan was back. Thirteen years too late.

Gin dashed her hot chocolate straight into hometown hero Rohan Telford's beautiful, masculine face.

"WHAT THE..." ROHAN sputtered, biting back a curse as he dragged a folded bandana out of his back pocket and wiped his face. Ginny stared at him, deep blue eyes with sooty lashes wide with shock and more beautiful than he remembered.

Then he spied a kid squatting down in the garage behind Ginny, and his body turned to ice, and he could barely feel the press of the dog close to his calf.

Ginny had a kid?

Their kid?

Fury speared through him. She'd lied to him about something that important?

The kid, holding two pieces of wood scraps, paused whatever he was doing—arranging the wood in some sort of a pattern—looked up at his mom.

"Mom?"

Hands shaking and feeling like he was in a stupid movie he breathed in deeply, finished wiping his face and tucked the bandana back in his pocket. He was lucky she'd missed his new hat because Virginia Madison Lane had always had one hell of an aim.

Mom. Any hope that the kid wasn't hers flamed out. He

choked down his bile. How old? He couldn't tell. Their child would be thirteen. The kid seemed small for that. Delicate. Young. Still his heart beat unevenly, and his mouth was desert dry.

"Ginny." Her name was an accusation as much as it was a question.

The kid, still holding the two wood scraps sidled next to his mom. His gaze bounced worriedly between him and Ginny and then settled on Mystery.

No. He was not naming the dog. Not keeping her. He was here for Jace. He'd check in with his family and then…he had no idea what would come next, especially if the kid…no he couldn't think it. But he had to know.

"You have a kid," he said.

Ginny stepped in front of her son and squared off with him—total Ginny power move—shoulders back, hands on her hips, translucent, milky complexion, smattering of freckles across wide cheekbones now stained with pretty pink. Black riot of hair, sapphire-blue eyes even with the starburst of yellow around the pupil glittered with strong emotion. He'd never seen eyes like hers when he'd fallen in love with her in middle school or in the long slog of years since. Her kid had her eyes, her hair, and the same pointy chin.

Nothing of him.

He wasn't sure if he should be relieved or… He shut down the unproductive thoughts like he'd been trained. He had no right to be jealous, though his stomach curdled, his throat burned and heat prickled up his spine. Ginny had found a better man. Good for her. He didn't have time for this. He had one job to do. Give Ron Lane the letter.

She stuck her chin out farther. "You have a dog…with pink booties and a pink coat."

He looked down at the dog who sat as his feet, tail swishing the ground, eyes nervous but holding the same painful glimmer of hope.

"Ahhh…the pink was the only color the shelter had," he admitted, wondering why the color embarrassed him.

"No camouflage?"

Rohan pressed his lips together. Thirteen, almost fourteen years hadn't been enough to cool her anger. No surprise there. Ginny had always been passionate about everything—poetry, hiking in the mountains, causes, him.

They faced each other, and Rohan had an impression of two gunslingers at high noon in a spaghetti western the local theater used to play for the early shows on Saturdays. He and Ginny had loved to watch them—or hold hands in the dark of the last row and stare at each other and kiss while the movie played.

"Who's the father?" he demanded, voice harder than it should be.

"None of your business." Her eyes narrowed.

"Can I pet your dog?" the boy asked.

"Not mine. I'm caring for her until the shelter finds her a

home. But sure. Put the stick down though. She's had a rough start to life."

"Don't even want to keep a dog," Ginny noted. "Lucas, be careful and keep your gloves on. The dog looks dirty and...mangy. It might have worms and..."

"Found the dog in the woods near the pass. Brought it to the shelter. Vet checked her out and treated her. She has meds." He still felt the need to defend himself, when he had a feeling nothing he could say would change the anger glittering in Ginny's eyes. He could taste the distance that pulsed between them.

Still, if he'd learned a few things from his teenage debacle with Ginny, it was that words and apologies matter, and holding her close was far better than keeping his distance, though she'd likely rack him if he attempted that now.

"Sure we don't have unfinished business?" he asked softly, his eyes on the boy, who crouched down next to the dog. Rohan looked for clues and braced himself for her answer.

The boy started humming as he stroked the dog's ears. The dog's tail thumped faster.

"Why are you here?" Ginny demanded.

"I asked a question." His voice further quieted. The men in his unit would have known it was time to back down. Ginny didn't care.

"So did I," she snarked. Then she turned away. "Like you care," she dismissed.

He took an impulsive step forward, hand already out.

She held out an arm like a crossing guard. Stop.

"You weren't on this hook this time," she said bitterly. "And that's all I'm saying to you."

Disappointment crashed through him. Strange. He felt he was observing himself from a distance. The boy was not his, but instead of relief, he felt empty, wrung out. What was wrong with him? He shouldn't want a half-grown son he didn't know. He looked back down the quiet residential road, many of the homes still dark in the early morning.

He dragged his stinging gaze back to the boy petting the stray dog, both of them not his.

"What's your dog's name, mister?"

Mister. Not dad. Not this time. Ginny had moved on quickly, whereas he, Rohan finally admitted to himself, was still stuck in a past where his wrongs could never be righted.

"That's a mystery, Lucas." He spoke with an effort, each word felt dragged out of his chest. "I found her, sick and injured and hurting, and when I brought her to the vet and said her name and past were a mystery, the vet thought that was a good name."

"I like it." Lucas didn't look at him, just the dog.

Ginny stared at her son—she'd yet to look at Rohan except when she'd hurled the hot chocolate in his face.

"Mystery," the boy, Lucas said. "I read mysteries. Writing us a mystery."

"My dad used to say, 'A boy needs a dog,'" Rohan remembered. "Maybe…"

"No." Ginny uttered the syllable, shutting down any speculation. "Absolutely not."

He accepted her anger that bled from every pore, but it was the pain in her eyes that held him rooted. He wanted, no, needed Ginny happy, whole, loved in a way he'd never be again.

"Why'd my mom throw her hot chocolate at you?"

Back to that. Rohan shifted, uncomfortable. He waited for Ginny to explain. She didn't. He looked into the garage as if seeking inspiration, but he only saw what looked like an episode of *Hoarders*. What was Ginny doing in such a dump? It made his heart hurt to think of her here. She needed to be safe, comfortable, taken care of even if it was by another man.

"We were friends in high school," he awkwardly offered.

"Friends don't throw things."

True. Rohan looked at the boy more closely. Something was off about his tone or intonation. He'd yet to make eye contact. The rhythmic way he stroked the dog had a pattern to it—one. One two. One. One two three. One. One two three four. One. One two. One... The dog quivered under Lucas's touch.

Ginny blinked several times and stared out at the street shrouded in gloom. Somehow her determined jaw cranked tighter.

"They don't," he agreed. "She's still mad." And had a right to be.

Mount up, Cowboy.

Jace's words. Encouraging everyone even when a mission seemed hopeless.

Rohan knew there was no way back to Ginny. But giving up and walking away again seemed even more impossible. But if she was happy… Again, he looked at her body language, her lithe form that was more angular than it used to be, the garage packed with crap.

"Lucas, you got any of that hot chocolate still?" Rohan spied the large thermos in all the clutter. He didn't like to drink sweet things, but he wasn't ready to quit even though he knew that once he delivered the letter to Ron Lane, Ginny would all but shove him out of her life again.

"Yes," Lucas said still not looking at him. "You want some?"

"Yes, please."

"No."

He and Ginny spoke at the same time, and the kid's gaze ping-ponged between them.

"He's not staying," Ginny said, her voice diamond hard.

"If you've got enough, I'd be much obliged. Not used to the cold." Yeah, he used that pansy excuse.

Ginny's outrage almost made him smile.

"You got whipped cream?"

"Yes." The boy's face slightly animated, but his voice was still flat.

"Bring it on."

Ginny flung her arms out and practically growled and suddenly, Rohan was not sorry he'd come. He couldn't help the quick look at her left hand. No ring.

Dumb idiot.

He stomped on the leap his stupid heart took. That door was long ago slammed and there would be no happy ending on this mission. He needed to deliver the letter. Check in with his folks. Touch base with Cross and Huck Jones who'd mustered out before him. Had they completed their missions, yet?

"You look like you could use some as well," Rohan said, noting the boy's cup was nearly empty.

"Yes, sir." The boy ran over to a small table that held a small cooler and two large thermoses. "C'mon, Mystery."

The dog looked at him. Followed the boy.

"You might have just found your Christmas present for your son." He lowered his voice—she'd always loved his voice. His smile. And his walk. Maybe he could work with that though he didn't deserve even an ounce of her forgiveness.

What are you doing, Cowboy?

But he couldn't seem to help himself. Even furious and aloof, she warmed him, woke him up inside, and he was so tired of feeling empty.

"One more mouth to feed and more chores are not what I need." Her expression scrunched in distaste.

Worry shot through him. Did she need financial help?

He could do that.

"Answer me. What are you doing here, Rohan?" Ginny stepped closer to him, and he could smell lemon verbena—her soap and lotion since he'd first met her, and it made him dizzy with hunger as memories slashed through his mind. Ginny laughing, running out her front door smiling, arms open to hug him like he'd been gone days instead of a couple of hours. In his truck, her thigh pressed to his, head on his shoulder, hand tucked tight as she sung to the radio. Or Ginny at Miracle Lake, writing poetry, sharing it with him. Riding with him on Telford land, lying next to him alongside the offshoot of the Yellowstone River that cut across his family's ranch. He'd loved to hold her, feel her breathe.

All the memories he'd tried to lock away broke open in a kaleidoscope of color, sound and emotion, and he had to close his eyes to try to orient himself.

"Please, Rohan." She sounded resigned. "What game are you playing?"

"No game." Her air of exhaustion hit him. What was wrong? Ginny had always been bursting with energy, ideas, passion.

"I don't want you here."

That was obvious. He'd been braced for her rejection since he'd drawn his task from Jace's helmet. No matter what he'd imagined, this was worse. Ginny with a son. Ginny hurting in some way he didn't yet understand.

"I know," he said. So many other words wanted to come

out. *I'm sorry. I've missed you. I've never stopped thinking about us. I...* So many regrets tugged at his tongue, but he bit them back.

"I need to see your dad." He told her the reason why he was here, even as he realized that he'd been lying to himself when he'd first plucked that task from Jace's bloodied helmet.

He'd wanted to see Ginny.

And even though he didn't deserve her forgiveness, he needed it so that he could move on.

"He wasn't at the house when I drove by. Neighbor told me you'd be here." Somehow he almost sounded normal.

"You bastard," Ginny whispered and then took a swing at him. Stunned, he caught her wrist. Her palm was flat, fingers splayed.

She was shaking and her eyes filled with tears. Sorrow tore through him. And something else as he felt the delicate softness of her skin. Her scent cut through the dirt and mildew and other unpleasantness wafting out of the garage, sparking heat in his chest.

"That's not how I taught you to hit, always tuck your thumb," he reminded her.

She stared into his eyes, and Rohan could feel the same connection he'd always felt to her. His thumb stroked along her wrist, and her pulse hammered in her neck.

"Get out," Ginny said. Her gorgeous blue eyes sparked fire.

He should heed her wishes, but even as she spoke, her cheeks bloomed a gorgeous rose, and her eyes fluttered. She swayed toward him and even through her layers of clothes and his, the ghost image of her warm, silken body imprinted on his skin, and he felt whole in a way nothing and no one had ever made him feel.

Home wasn't Marietta. Home wasn't his family. The ranch. Home was Ginny, and when he'd lost her, he'd lost himself. And to an outsider, it looked like he didn't have a shot, but Rohan had often faced impossible odds with a rank bull, or bronc or finding a sniper's nest in a canyon to keep his team safe.

"Ginny," he whispered, both lost and found.

If she'd pulled her wrist away, maybe he would have had a hope of stopping what felt inevitable.

"Rohan, please." Her voice was a warning that sounded more like a plea, not a no.

He barely had the bandwidth to check on the boy, whose back was to them as he poured out hot chocolates. Rohan angled his body so he blocked Ginny's if and when the kid turned around.

"Ginny, you have no idea how…how…I'm so…" The words and intention and moment overwhelmed him. She'd been the wordsmith, never him. He was and had always been about action.

Chapter Three

HEAT POURED DOWN her throat and expanded in her chest, searing away the numbing chill of the morning. The sad garage bursting with the mildewing former treasures of a long life ended faded, leaving only Rohan and Gin. His hard body pressed against hers, his lips a direct contrast—soft and coaxing as he kissed her.

He still held her wrist and his thumb stroked a hypnotic circle. She breathed him in—mint, and then his scent of pine, sandalwood and a hint of leather that was so familiar, tears pricked her eyes. His other hand, warm and calloused, cupped her face, angling her closer and the tentative brush of his lips deepened with intention.

"You're so beautiful." His words were a hoarse whisper against her lips, and her heart pounded so loudly she was certain he could hear it. A low moan that sounded too much like pleasure escaped her throat and shocked her back to reality just as Rohan whispered her name.

What was she doing?

She was a mom. Rohan was so far in her past she shouldn't be able to see him, and she definitely shouldn't be kissing him again. Had she learned nothing from her 'semester of wilding'?

"Stop." She scrounged up some sense from her staggeringly weak will. She tugged at his hold on her wrist and took a step back. "Stop," she whispered again, her gaze fixed on him. She felt dazed, like she'd been picked up and plunked down into an alternate reality.

This could not be happening. She'd kissed Rohan. No. He had kissed her. She rubbed her wrist on her jeans, trying to get the feel of him off her skin. She touched her lips that still buzzed.

"What? Why?" She tried to dredge up anger or something to hurl at him, but she was still hung up on the kiss. She felt like she'd been zapped back into her body by a defibrillator. And all she could think was that she wanted him to kiss her again.

No.

She wouldn't open herself to that kind of pain again.

"You can't come back all swaggering hot-body cowboy like thirteen years never happened." She wiped her mouth with the back of her hand feeling rather childish, but she had to interrupt the end-zone victory dance of her nerve endings. She'd kissed more than her share of men during her rebound when she'd tried to rid her body and heart of its Rohan fixation, but his kisses had been the only ones she'd treasured and remembered.

"I know how many years have passed."

His voice sounded like a diesel engine starting, and she

hated how she could still read him. He sounded gutted. Unfair. He'd walked, leaving her alone and devastated.

"I know you don't want to see me, Ginny."

"Gin," she corrected. "And that is the one thing we can agree on." She crossed her arms.

"Tell me about the boy."

"Lucas?" She watched her son carefully still pouring the hot chocolate into two cups—so they were exactly even while he talked quietly to the dog. That was new. Normally he tonelessly hummed.

Her father had wanted to get Lucas a dog. He'd thought it would help him to focus on something outside of himself. He'd thought a dog would be a companion since friends proved elusive and would teach him to care for another creature. But she'd resisted, worried the dog would become one more duty she'd have to tick off each day. A rare, fleeting smile stole across Lucas's face revealing a dimple that she'd never had, and her stomach lurched guiltily.

"Tell me." Rohan stood next to her, also watching Lucas, who squirted whipped cream on the hot chocolates and then some on his finger that he let the dog lick off.

"Use the wipes to wash your hands, Lucas." She couldn't help the reminder. "Nothing to tell," she said stiffly.

"You said...you told me..." Uncharacteristically—at least how she remembered him—Rohan paused and seemed to struggle with words. "You told me that you'd lost our child."

Oh. Of course. That. Always their history like an anvil on her foot trapping her.

She winced. "I did," she said, bracing for the familiar dark ache. "He's another man's biological child."

She strove for a sophisticated tone, not wanting Rohan to know that she was embarrassed by how she'd acted out after the double loss of their baby and him. But most humiliating, she'd lost herself. She'd always imagined herself as strong, independent, smart, confident. Boozy college party slut, as her roommate had teased her, hadn't been a role she'd ever imagined playing.

She swallowed and waited to see how Rohan absorbed the news.

Why do you care?

She was an idiot. Was she hoping to make him jealous? Beyond ridiculous. She wasn't seventeen anymore.

Rohan hunched a little, and his cheeks hollowed even more. His vivid green eyes seemed like the only color in the gray morning as the pregnant sky threatened snow.

"The father in the picture?" He sounded strange, like an actor in the wrong play.

"No." She couldn't meet his searching gaze.

Anger brewed. She hated all this uncertainty. She'd been fine this morning, daunted by the scope of the annex project that her father had inadvertently dumped on her. She'd been worried about finances, time, commitment and Lucas. But this morning she'd known who she was and her role. She'd accepted the obstacles in her path and had a plan. But now she felt awkward, unsure what to do with her hands, her expression, her voice, her body.

"Here's your hot chocolate, mister." Lucas walked carefully, one foot in front of the other like he was on an invisible balance beam. "Mystery and I made another one for you too, Mom."

"Thank you." Gin reached for the cup. "I promise not to...spill this one."

Lucas's eyes shone as he looked up, up, up at Rohan whose dark cowboy hat set off his features—stark cheekbones, hollows, hero chin—to perfection. It was like he'd wandered off the set of *Yellowstone*, and Gin really wanted to kick him for looking even better than before.

"Thank you," Rohan said, his expression warming as he looked at Lucas. "I got two kisses."

"One," Gin stated even as she realized he was referring to the candy perched on her whipped cream, just starting to melt at the edges.

"No." Rohan's voice sounded like dark melting chocolate. "Two."

"Stop it," she hissed, glaring at his teasing, only to realize that he did indeed have two chocolate kisses perched perkily in his mountain of whipped cream—bigger than hers so it was clear where Lucas's loyalties lay.

She pressed her lips together as she felt the heat of the blush that stained her cheeks and swept lower along her collarbone, which was thankfully not exposed. She inconveniently remembered how Rohan loved to flirt and tease her and explore how far down her blush would descend. He'd been so playful when they'd been young—nothing like the soldier he'd become she imagined, judging by the shadows in his eyes and grim, stoic demeanor.

Why was she remembering his playful side?

It was like he had some magic memory potion. She wasn't forgiving him. Not ever. There was no going back from what he'd said and done.

And then he had the audacity to pluck one of the red-and-white kisses from his whipped cream and hold it out to her. It would serve him right if she spit on it. Or bit his finger taking the kiss. And then she saw Lucas's glowing expression as he stared up at Rohan—a cowboy—one of her sweet boy's fascinations, but she, his mom, made every excuse to not get riding lessons for Lucas or visit one of the handful of dude ranches in the area because she never wanted to crack that door open on her past.

Rohan's fault.

But no, she shared the blame because she couldn't seem to rise out of the ashes of her past, even for her beloved son.

"Oh, to be a phoenix," she muttered, earning a hard look from Rohan. Oops. She'd said that aloud.

"White chocolate's my mom's favorite," Lucas imparted.

"I know."

Gin didn't know who was more surprised—her, Lucas or

Rohan when she leaned into Rohan and took the chocolate from his fingers.

She tried to shut down the intimacy of the brush of his fingers against her lips. Epic fail. Rohan's touch had always disarmed her whether he was being sweet, caring or passionate. He'd taught her how her body could work. And then she'd done her best to forget every one of his lessons.

"Your mom once taught a poetry class at the rec center using the taste of melting chocolate," Rohan said.

"She's a teacher," Lucas stated flatly. "She used to write poetry. I found her journal. It didn't make sense. I asked my grandpa to explain it, but Grandpa said I should put it back because it was private and that I should never look through anyone's private things."

"Smart man," Rohan said.

"Your name was in it."

Gin choked on her hot chocolate. Rohan's palm rubbed between her shoulder blades.

"Okay?" he asked softly, bending solicitously toward her.

No, of course she wasn't.

"She doesn't write poetry or anything anymore."

She felt kicked to her soul and knocked flat on the icy driveway—a one, two, three knockout punch. Totally exposed. But she had to pull herself together.

With the huge project ahead of her, a dearth of volunteers and now Rohan's arrival, the Christmas season—her first without her father—was starting off with a howl. Rohan should have stayed gone in the desert or jungle or wherever he'd been deployed over the years.

"Lucas." She drew in a deep breath and used her best teacher and mom voice that had never failed her. "Mr. Telford just stopped to say hello and must be on his way." Her voice sounded as cold as the air enveloping them and also slightly robotic like Lucas's.

"We have a lot to do today, so please continue sorting, and I will join you in a minute."

"Exactly?" He brandished the watch her father had bought him—the too big, too gadgety in her opinion, sports-oriented watch but it had a timer on it that allowed for fractional seconds—something that thrilled her numbers guy.

"Maybe not exactly."

"How many extra seconds?"

She did not let her shoulders droop. "Set the timer for five minutes," she relented. "No more than that." She was firm because Rohan was getting out of here and not coming back. "Come get me if I'm a second longer." She tried to smile though her face felt frozen, and her lips *still* buzzed with that kiss.

"Mister Telford has a buckle. I bet he has a lasso in his truck," Lucas speculated, and that should not shoot heat through her body.

"Not anymore," Rohan said.

There was a beat of silence. And another. She could practically hear Lucas's beautiful, but unusual brain click through the possible comebacks.

"Your mom made a request, Lucas."

"It wasn't precisely…" Lucas trailed off, clearly seeing something in Rohan's face that should not be there because Lucas was not *his* precious child.

"Yes, sir." Lucas turned away, tapping his usual one, one-two rhythm unconsciously on his leg, and the dog, who'd been sitting on his feet, followed Lucas into the fluorescent-lit dump.

Gin turned her ire on Rohan.

"I can handle my own child. Years ago you made your feelings abundantly clear."

Judging by the myriad of expressions that chased across Rohan's face, she'd scored a hit.

"Why did you want to see my dad?" She just needed him to go. She needed to regroup. She couldn't deal with his shock, questions, sympathy when she told him Ron Lane wouldn't be able to help anyone with anything anymore.

He looked down at his boots as if the answer would be there. Then he took a sip of the hot chocolate, and she was pissed that she noticed that some of the whipped cream clung to the corner of his upper lip. Years ago that would have been an invitation. Now she took a step back.

"I have something for your dad, Ginny. I need to explain."

The blood froze in her veins.

Should have splurged on renting the space heaters.

It was like the ridiculous non-sequitur thought was trying to save her from the hit of Rohan's unexpected and unwanted reappearance in her life, and his casual, callous request to talk to her father. There was nothing anyone could ever tell her father again, including her.

"Why?" she asked coolly. Did Rohan have some ludicrous thought about grasping at redemption about his callous indifference years ago?

Too many years too late.

Rohan looked uncomfortable, dipped his head again to look at the toes of his boots so that she saw the graceful dip at the top of his Resistol. The hat looked new—not the dark tan felt hat with the double dip she'd been so enamored with as a teen.

He looked up, his eyes a deep glittering green, and for a moment they had a sheen like he was about to cry, but he blinked and the illusion was gone.

"You remember Jace McBride?"

"Yes." She was confused. "I knew his sister Willow in high school. So did you."

She and Willow had lost touch as Willow left to compete on the rodeo circuit. She was as celebrated for her barrel-racing skills as her strawberry-blonde beauty. They'd just begun to rekindle their friendship this past fall at the rodeo, but there had been a small film crew doing a documentary on small-town rodeos that had taken to following Willow around because she was getting married to an almost-famous bull rider that weekend, so the friendship had stalled. So had Willow's marriage. She'd wanted to give Willow privacy, and then her father had unexpectedly passed.

Gin had pulled back from her friendships, curling up into survival mode.

"I served with Jace."

"I'm sorry for your loss," she said stiffly. "Willow and her family had been devastated. Gutted," Gin said. "But she was determined to honor her brother's memory at the Copper Mountain Rodeo no matter what cruel fate littered her path with."

"Of that I have no doubt."

"I do." Gin felt stung, and the loose control she had snapped.

"I think a brother who sticks around and helps his family when in need would be more of a prize." Her voice rang with hurt and anger, and her phone, tucked deep in the pocket of her coat, buzzed with a text—probably another cancellation. She'd already noticed that the dumpster delivery had been canceled and been rescheduled for Monday afternoon.

Rohan didn't flinch. Why would he? She'd long ago lost the power to hurt him. Why couldn't she too let go?

She should be a better person. Her father would expect that. He'd never held a grudge. Not ever.

"Sorry." She forced the word out. "My father was a good man too. The best. He always told me to assume best intentions, and I…" She'd taken to assuming the worst.

As she struggled to get through her apology without tears, Rohan was reaching into his back pocket to pull out a square, red envelope.

The color of blood.

Rohan froze. "Was?"

GINNY BLINKED, HER face crumpled in grief, but she seemed determined to battle back.

His Ginny had always been a fighter.

Not yours anymore.

She'd stopped fighting for them, and he'd let her quit. He'd instead fought for his country and his self-respect.

The envelope felt like it weighed more than his gear he'd hauled in and out of hot spots on missions.

"Was?" He could barely choke the question out again.

She nodded, brushed at her tears. More fell.

"Ginny, I am so sorry," he said, the inadequacy of his words burning his chest. With his gloved fingertips he lightly followed the train of tears. "So, so sorry."

"Me too," she whispered looking at her son instead of him.

He too watched the boy as he'd gone back to arranging the scraps of wood in some sort of pattern instead of doing what Ginny had told him to. The dog followed Lucas, the pink booties incongruous in the dinge of the garage.

Ginny wrapped her arms around herself so tightly it was as if she was trying to hold herself together, and he remembered another time she was trying so hard not to cry, and he hadn't comforted her then either.

"When, Ginny?" he asked, taking a step toward her, the desire to comfort driving him. She stepped back and held out a shaking hand.

"He passed suddenly in late September, just a month into his retirement."

"How…?" Not that it mattered. She'd lost her father. The horrible irony hit hard. Ginny, who was devoted to her father—and he to her—had lost the only parent she'd ever known, and he had two loving, supportive parents he didn't feel ready to face.

"Aortic aneurysm."

"I'm so…"

"I know." She dashed at more escaped tears, her movements clumsy.

Everything screamed at him to leave, let her grieve in peace, but he'd been running for years—it took him coming home to see that. It was long beyond time for him to man up and make up for a lot of things.

"Jace wrote a letter to your father." He held it out farther.

"Two months too late for that." Ginny squeezed herself tighter, which lifted her slight breasts, that he'd been trying somewhat successfully to ignore.

"Jace made a list of things he wanted to do when he returned home to Marietta."

"Oh." Ginny blinked a few times. "That makes his death even sadder although I'm sure the young who pass early always leave so much undone, so many dreams unrealized. Even my father—" She broke off. A shadow chased across her face and her gaze bounced around the garage full of junk and her son creating some kind of art or mathematic art from the junk.

She shivered, and Rohan once again stifled the urge to hold her.

"You need a couple of space heaters or some of those outdoor patio heaters to work in the garage, especially with the boy."

"Thank you for your unasked for obvious insights, Rohan." She sounded tired instead of annoyed, and her shoulders slumped, which kicked his protective instincts up again.

"What was on Jace's list?" She asked the question dully as if only half interested.

"We—the brothers in his unit—all chose randomly. The tasks were written out and folded up. Secret. We each took an action item from Jace's list and agreed to come to Marietta to carry out the task."

"So, you came home for one of your soldiers."

The bitterness scorched him.

"And then good deed done, you'll head back to blood,

guts and glory."

"You're better than that," he said softly. "You never embraced sarcasm before."

She winced and drew in a deep breath. "This is hard, Rohan, to see you again." Her honesty shocked him. "Too many painful memories."

"Good ones too," he prompted, choking up and feeling desperate. His times with Ginny had a magical, golden hue, and when he'd been so far from home, and in dicey situations, he'd often comforted himself with thinking about her, about them. Before.

"I don't think about those."

He rocked back. The good memories sustained him.

His reaction to her unwelcome and shocking pregnancy and then the later loss tormented him. Why had he frozen up like that? Why had he lashed out in disbelief? He still couldn't wrap his head around how he'd failed a woman he'd had no trouble admitting he was in love with and who was his one.

"I do," he admitted, his voice sounding far away.

He deserved to be forever shut out of her life, but he didn't like it. Not at all. And for the first time, a perverse voice inside him bitched that he didn't need to abide Ginny's reality. He was a cowboy and a soldier. He solved problems. Made things better. Saved people. He hadn't been able to save their child. But maybe he could save them.

The idea stole his breath but had taken root. He just

needed to nourish it.

"I think when I lost you, I went numb," he admitted, wanting to give her honesty, something he hadn't been able to do when he'd emotionally abandoned her while he processed their news.

She made a dismissive sound. "I'm not rehashing the past. And I don't want to read any letter for my father." Her voice was decisive, her eyes dark blue and turbulent.

"It was one of Jace's last wishes."

Ginny seemed to steel herself, and she turned away from him. "I know all about last wishes," she murmured, so softly he could barely catch it.

"Your dad never gave up on anyone." Rohan felt desperate.

He owed Jace so much, and Ginny even more. Maybe this letter could help her find some peace. Maybe he could somehow find a way to ease the wound that festered between them. Help them both to move on.

"I'm not my dad."

"Please, Ginny. This letter is for your father." He waved it at her.

Red flag to a bull. Ginny had always been stubborn. Before, she'd never given up on anything or anyone.

Except me.

"A letter to a dead man from a dead man." Her laugh was metal cold.

An instinctive denial rose up in his throat. 'Only too late

when you're dead.' It was something his father used to say. Something Jace used to say. And then the Coyote Cowboys. It had been like a standing retort, an answer they'd cling to when optimism was in short supply. But Jace was dead. And so was Ron Lane.

"Take the letter. We can read it together if you wish," he rashly promised as Jace had no doubt expected MR. LANE to read it alone.

Ginny looked at the block letters spelling out her father's name—the name his students had called him. She paled as if the letter were haunted.

"No. Absolutely not. Even you have to see how crazy that is. The...audacity of...loss. It's too late Rohan. Too late for everything." She pressed her fisted hands over her mouth, but not before an almost hysterical burble of laughter burst out.

"Go, Rohan. Go do all the oh-so-important things you wanted to do without me. Go live the amazing life you planned when you headed off to the University of Nevada Las Vegas on your rodeo scholarship instead of going to Montana State with me. I didn't trap you. I trapped myself while you ran free. Then you threw everything away—us, your family, the ranch, your scholarship, college and dreams to go play hero." She slashed at the space between them and, turning her back on him, she walked away into the filthy, freezing garage.

Chapter Four

Rohan drove down Collier Avenue feeling disoriented.

How had such a simple task—to carry out his Coyote Cowboys' vow—become so personal?

And how had he screwed up so spectacularly after less than an hour in town? He had an abandoned dog and a bitter ex.

She still despises me.

He absently rubbed his thumb on his aching sternum. The dog, instead of curling up in the back seat, rode shotgun, sitting up and staring at him like he held an answer for anything. Absently he reached out and stroked the multicolored head.

Seeing Ginny had really tossed him in the dirt. He'd been determined to do right by Jace no matter the cost; Ginny had upped the stakes. He'd known he'd hurt her badly. He hadn't known that she would still feel raw.

So do I.

There was no way back.

He stopped his rental truck in the middle of the street. Was that still true? He'd thought it many times over the years. Nursed the hurt and aching futility when he'd been thousands of miles away. But he was back in Marietta. No plans. No idea if there was truly a spot for him at the ranch—of course his family would welcome him home. He'd always have his own room. Love. But did they need him? Could he build a life of meaning on his family's ranch though he was so changed?

Did he want to?

Had he subconsciously been hoping to see Ginny, to learn that she was unmarried? Had he secretly imagined testing the waters?

Iced over more than Miracle Lake in the middle of January.

Miracle Lake. The place of so many firsts for them. First time they'd held hands. Kissed. Said 'I love yous.' The place where he'd first brushed her springy hair back from her forehead. Bundled up and watched a meteor shower that had turned into a sunrise. He'd taught her to ride on the ranch, but Miracle Lake had been their spot where they'd done so much else together. It had become their talisman.

He felt like driving there now—recentering himself for the next…battle. His lips cracked into a wry smile—still the war analogies.

Had Ginny been back to Miracle Lake? Did it remind her of him?

Could Miracle Lake provide one more miracle for them?

Rohan stared through his windshield at the rows of houses facing off. Only a few shone with Christmas lights.

Something deep inside him flickered in response. Christmas was the season of homecoming, giving, family, renewal. Could he find the courage to forgive himself for the past and move on?

That would start with an apology. The boy he'd been hadn't had a clue how to find the path back to Ginny, to his family. He'd run about as far as he could go. Jace's death had been the end of the road. His vow and the letter were the first steps back. He reached behind him and slid the red envelope out of his pocket and looked at it. It didn't matter what was written in the folded missive. He'd made a commitment. He intended to honor it—'no matter how many obstacles,' Wolf had said.

He thought of Ginny and Lucas alone, facing a garage filled with junk. Didn't matter why. Ginny needed help. He had strong arms, a strong back, a strong will and a need to help her. The cowboy code.

"Ready to ride on a rescue mission?" He turned to his silent companion, who continued to regard him as if he were some kind of hero.

He didn't feel like one, but he could change that. Rohan wasn't a quitter. He'd been in more impossible situations. They just hadn't ever felt so personal. But he had a debt to pay to Jace. And a bigger one to Ginny and the child they'd made and lost.

He shifted the truck into drive. A loose plan rattled around in his head and solidified when he saw the sign for

Big Z's. Determination hardened his jaw, and he felt his body settle into what he thought of as mission mode. He checked his watch. Big Z's should be opening soon.

Fifteen minutes later, dog dogging his heels, he was the first in the checkout line with extra gloves, heavy-duty trash bags, tools, a stack of trash cans, tarps and several space heaters and a propane patio heater.

"Rohan Telford." Big Z's owner Paul Zabrinski came around the corner to give him a hearty handshake, a man hug and to slap his shoulder. "I hadn't heard you were coming home this Christmas. Boone does most of the ranch errands into town. He said nothing. You on leave for Christmas? Can't believe your dad didn't say anything when I saw him last week. Is it top secret?"

Paul, always friendly, was joking, but Rohan was still inwardly cursing his bad luck that Paul had opened up the store instead of an anonymous employee; but really, he should have known. The Zabrinskis had always been hard workers, who never asked anything of their staff that they weren't willing to do themselves, and the morning after Thanksgiving was still considered a holiday by many—not in retail or in ranching, though.

"It was a sudden opportunity." He spun out his story. "Wasn't expecting leave," he continued—because he'd put in his papers months ago, and had yet to tell his family. That would have made Jace's death and leaving a career he'd loved more real. "Hoping to surprise my family."

Paul stared at him like he'd said he was hoping to be the first tourist on Mars.

"They don't know you're here?" He looked at the items in the basket. "Are you…sorry, Rohan, not my business."

Rohan felt awkward. He'd kept secrets for years. But Paul was someone he'd known most of his life, and he wasn't running classified missions for the government any longer.

"I'm helping out a friend," he said. "Then I'll head over to see my folks."

"Of course." Paul smiled. His expression still held a tick of bafflement, but like the seasoned businessman he was, he smoothed the tension by looking at the dog. "Looks like you're bringing home a friend. What's her name? A biscuit okay?" Paul reached into a jar on the counter.

"Found her up at the pass looking worse for wear," Rohan said. "Took her to the shelter, and she's had a checkup, some meds and now she's riding shotgun—no chip."

"Got a name?"

"Mystery," he dragged out feeling like the dog deserved a name, and Lucas had liked it.

"That's appropriate." Paul came around the counter and held the bone out to Mystery. Mystery looked up at Rohan, and he felt a touch of something warm infuse his chest as he looked at the dog's soulful mismatched eyes.

"Go ahead," he said softly.

Mystery politely took the offering.

"I got a community board you can put a lost notice on if

you want," Paul said. "But she looks like she's been living rough for a while."

"The shelter has her picture and will put her on their website," Rohan said, reluctant already at the thought of handing Mystery over. "I'm fostering her for now."

That too didn't sound or feel right. By Paul's knowing expression, he seemed to twig on Rohan's feelings at the same time he did.

"I'd appreciate it if you could keep my homecoming secret for a little longer."

"Of course." Paul sounded polite, but doubtful. "For how long?"

"I'm going home this afternoon, or early this evening. Need to help a friend on a project and then I'll head home to get some Thanksgiving leftovers before Boone scarfs them all." He tried to inject a touch of humor into his voice.

He still felt so unsettled and out of step with everything and everyone.

"Okay." Paul rolled with it. "Then you probably don't want to make any more stops in town," he cautioned.

"Thanks, Paul." Rohan tipped his hat and paid.

Rohan pushed his cart out the door, Mystery on his heels after giving a final sniff of the floor looking for crumbs, just as Rohan's brother Boone walked in.

Boone staggered back as if they'd crashed together, and while Rohan mentally cursed his foul luck, Boone clutched his chest and stared at him like he was a hallucination.

"Rohan." Boone reached out and touched him.

"Not a mirage," he said, imagining Paul's reaction to this unplanned reunion. Boone's blue eyes—so like their mother's—were wide with wonder.

"Holy, shshshsh—" Boone broke off and took a quick look around like their mom was going to pop up brandishing a bar of soap.

"What are you doing here? Mom and Dad said nothing."

"That's because it's a surprise," Rohan asserted, feeling defensive.

"A surprise?" Boone yipped like the puppy he'd received for his tenth birthday. "A surprise?"

Rohan braced himself for one of the huge hugs Boone liked to give—the kind that felt like a bear would give as it lifted you off the ground. But Boone made no moves, just stared at him like he was a ghost.

"Are you home on leave? For how long? What are you…?" Boone's brows crinkled when he saw the two baskets of supplies.

"Make yourself useful and help me load up my truck." Rohan strode out of Big Z's needing privacy, the cold air and some space to pull himself together. Was it really so weird that he was home? It wasn't as if he didn't regularly communicate with his family.

He was just so accustomed to secrecy and 'need to know.' Not even his unit had always known where he was. And he'd yet to text either Cross or Huck to tell them he was hitting town.

"How'd you get here...oh, this is a rental." Boone kept pace with him, and it was a second hit to realize that Boone was all grown up. Married. A father. Boone had still been in middle school when he'd left for the army. He'd come home for Boone's wedding—barely made it—but Boone had still seemed like the kid he'd remembered, vibrating with enthusiasm and good cheer, crazy in love with his wife, Piper, and not afraid to show it.

Now Boone seemed calmer, more thoughtful. Boone kept his hand on one of the space heaters as Rohan reached for it.

"Rohan, what's going on?"

"What's it look like?" He reached for the jumbo box of Hefty trash bags. "I'm back. Why are you making such a big deal about it?" Rohan then lifted the stacked trash cans and placed them in the bed of the truck.

Boone stared at him, mind working. "Back, back or back on leave?"

Rohan wasn't sure how to answer that.

"Why didn't you tell us?" Boone's stare was hard with accusation.

"Why's it matter?"

Something indefinable skittered in Boone's expression, and then his eyes hooded. "We just weren't expecting you."

We. You. That pretty much summed up his lurking fear—that he'd left it too late, had been gone too long. He was no longer a 'we' with his family. He'd long ago lost his we status with Ginny and now he no longer was a we with the Coyote Cowboys.

I'm alone.

What else did he expect? His panic when Ginny told him her news and their hideous breakup after she lost their child had alienated him from everything—her, his family, himself. He wasn't the man he thought he was. He'd joined the service seeking…something, and his years in the army had changed him so significantly he no longer recognized anything of himself from the boy he'd once been.

Would his parents see the son they'd loved? Boone was looking at him like he was a stranger.

"There a problem, Boone, with me being home?" He swung around and faced his brother, who looked stunned.

"No. It's just…what is this stuff? What are you doing? I still can't figure out why your homecoming is so top secret?" Boone's eyes bulged with another question, and Rohan's irritation cranked.

"Why are you so hung up on advanced notice?" He blew out a breath and jerked the space heater out from under Boone's hand and loaded it in the truck. "I have my reasons." His voice was harsher than usual, and he tried to adjust. "Just respect that."

Rohan noticed the dog cowering, shaking—from cold or his harsh words. His heart pinched. "Sorry."

"Not a problem," Boone muttered, and Rohan remembered that the few times when Boone's obsessive dogging of his footsteps and litany of questions had finally aggravated him enough to snap—usually when he was trying to get alone time with Ginny—he'd feel so guilty by Boone's crushed expression that he'd apologize in the same manner.

"Who's this?" Boone reached down to let the dog sniff him for a moment before stroking it. The unbobbed tail cautiously swept the snow as the dog inched closer to Boone.

Smart move on the dog's part. Rohan felt too volatile, like all the emotions he'd shoved aside during his service had come roiling to the surface this morning.

"It's a mystery," he said wryly.

"Hi, Mystery," Boone said, misunderstanding, but maybe ultimately he hadn't. Rohan watched as Boone reached in his jacket pocket and pulled out a dog treat and held it out. Mystery looked at Boone's pocket and his hand hopefully.

"Definitely more where that came from." Boone smiled. "How'd you get a dog in the service? I thought they were all highly trained and jumping out of planes or sniffing buildings for bombs."

They were. "You watch too much TV. Will you keep my secret?"

"What? How am I supposed to do that? For how long? Why?" Boone's eyes were huge, and for a moment he looked like the little brother that Rohan still pictured in his mind.

"I got something I gotta do today and then I'm coming to the ranch. I promise."

"Do you need help?" Boone asked, his troubled gaze bouncing between the dog, Rohan and the bed of the rental truck holding the trash cans and space heaters and more of his purchases.

"I just need the morning. Maybe the afternoon," he said. The feel of the red envelope in his back pocket was a reminder that his promise to Jace had yet to be kept.

He didn't know what Ginny needed. This delivery and some time to sort out the garage might be the end of the road for them, and he tried not to think of the symbolism of that.

"Rohan." Boone took off his hat, shoved at his full head of coppery-brown hair, wavy like his but with fewer sun streaks. Then he shoved his hat back down on his head. "I just don't understand…"

"Nothing to understand. I'll be home this afternoon. Or evening. Promise."

He didn't want to think about how he was going to pull off arriving at the ranch and shouting out a cherry 'Hello. Guess who's home'—as if fourteen years hadn't changed everything.

One emotional quagmire at a time.

"Do you need help?" Boone's expression lit with determination.

"I'm good," Rohan lied, and reached out a hand to shake on the deal.

Boone pulled him into a hard hug. "Welcome home, brother," Boone whispered, his voice cracked with emotion, and Rohan couldn't speak at all.

Chapter Five

GIN GLARED AT the text. Another volunteer was dropping out for tomorrow's work party. Usually, Marietta had many eager hands willing to jump in, but maybe that had more to do with her dad. He'd had so many friends. He'd never met a stranger. He'd always been the first to raise his hand to help.

But this project—the annex to Harry's House, which would be an after-school hangout for teens, offering tutoring, classes, a safe community space so that the original Harry's House could expand its program for younger children—was her father's legacy. After he'd done so much for the town, she'd imagined the town would be eager to do something for him, and for Marietta's teens.

But she'd never had her dad's charisma and charm. She'd always been more introverted, bookish, lost in her imagination, intense and independent. Decent traits for a teacher, but maybe not so much a community organizer. Perhaps she'd been too ambitious to try to have a soft opening and one class over the winter break.

But it had motivated her to get off the couch and out of her paralyzing grief.

"So suck it up, buttercup," she bossed herself.

She was determined for the annex to become as important to the town as Harry's House. Like her father, Harry Monroe had been quick to raise his hand and jump in to help. He would have been proud of Harry's House, just like she wanted her father to be proud of the annex, even if she had to do it alone.

Not that she would. This rough start was a bump in the road. She needed to focus on the goal—not be distracted by setbacks.

"One piece of trash or junk at a time," she promised herself.

She worked for a while, chilly with the garage door open, but afraid if she shut it, she and Lucas would be overcome with whatever had been brewing in the garage over the years. She glanced around. She'd barely made a dent. She should text Colt Wilder and Remington Cross to tell them not to come in this afternoon. No way would the garage be emptied enough for them to begin the work of attaching the supply cabinets they'd reclaimed from other jobs and refinished for the annex. And without the dumpster coming, she couldn't pile the trash outside for three days. The neighbors would rightly complain.

She also noted she would run out of trash bags before noon. One more thing on the list. Gin stretched up on her toes and reached up, hoping to get her blood flowing, then she bent over, touched her toes and just as she stood back up, a truck pulled into the driveway. Relief coursed through her. Finally, someone was coming to help.

Gin walked forward smiling.

Until she saw Rohan pop out of his truck. His green stare sliced through her sharper than the stiff breeze blowing off Copper Mountain.

"What are you doing back?" It pissed her off that her heart did a happy hop before it settled in a nervous rhythm that made her breathless.

Rohan pulled a stack of five large hard plastic trash cans and brought them into the garage. He walked right past her, and she got a whiff of pine and sandalwood that nearly buckled her knees it was so familiar—he still used the same soap or cologne he had in high school.

"Rohan, you don't need…"

He walked back to his truck and retrieved five more heavy trash containers.

She crossed her arms, fighting the opposing forces of relief and resentment.

"Why are you getting involved?"

He separated the trash cans, placed them in a line, and put a trash bag liner in each one efficiently, while she stewed and tried to think of something to say to make him go when she needed his help so desperately.

"Told you. I made a promise to Jace."

"What's Jace got to do with it?" she said mystified and inappropriately piqued that he wasn't back for her.

"Read the letter." He angled a hip toward her. "Still in my back pocket. Then we'll both know."

The letter. Dread balled in her tummy. And Rohan's prime ass, temptingly within reach, woke something she wanted to keep slumbering. The two opposing visuals would have been funny if she'd been someone else. She'd been avoiding thinking about the letter, and she'd definitely tried not to notice that she could see the square outline in the back pocket of Rohan's Wranglers.

"Just tell me." She strove to sound authoritative, but instead her voice was husky, and she could practically hear the invitation in it.

Rohan stilled and looked at her. The heat in his eyes curled her toes, but then he banked it. "I don't know what it says."

Mystery had settled next to Lucas, who'd finished with his wood arranging and spiderling search and had now moved on to arranging dominoes that he'd found in one of the piles of detritus. She tried not to think of the germs. She'd wash his mittens later today.

"But I do know Jace, and he wouldn't have written a letter that held little meaning."

She jerkily nodded. Her still-unresolved feelings for Rohan shouldn't tarnish the memory of a good man who'd died in service for his country, but what difference could a letter do now? She bent her head and squeezed her eyes shut. Rohan just inadvertently woke so many memories. Maybe if she said a prayer for Jace, a prayer for her father, she'd find the strength to stumble through this painful reunion without disgracing herself.

"Hey." Rohan was close. "Jace can't be here. I can. Jace was a better man than I could dream of being. He never would have come home to give your father a letter and then driven off again without helping out with whatever project your father had going. I need to honor Jace. I made a vow. Like it or not, I'm here, an extra pair of hands for you to use."

She was a pervert as her mind immediately dragged up what Rohan could do with his hands. She wanted to kick herself. She was done with sex. Done with Rohan.

"This is for Jace," she clarified, steeling her spine to look into his eyes.

"Yes."

The monosyllable arrived after the slightest of hesitations. Humiliatingly, disappointment slapped her. She was acting like a naïve, romantic idiotic teen girl again. It wasn't like she wanted Rohan in her life.

"You're right." She kept her voice cool and casual, and wished she'd spent more time in the high school theater instead of on the volleyball court or the passenger side of Rohan's truck. "I don't like it."

HE COULDN'T BLAME her.

But while Rohan might have personal failures as a partner, son and briefly a potential parent, he did know how to get the job done.

He shrugged and turned away from her stiff, hands-on-hips posture and instead focused on the boy, worry tugging at him.

Rohan pulled on a new pair of leather gloves and joined Lucas and Mystery. Ginny followed him.

"Hey, buddy." Rohan squatted on his haunches next to Lucas. "I bought you some work gloves. This garage is dirty, and there might be splinters or nails or other sharp objects, and your knitted mittens won't stand a chance against sharps."

He heard Ginny's sharply inhaled breath.

"I can take care of my son," she hissed, keeping her voice low and contained, but he'd definitely struck a nerve.

One more strike against him.

Lucas held out his hand like Rohan should slide on the glove.

"You put them on," he encouraged, ripping off the tag with his teeth.

Lucas's gaze—eerily beautiful like his mother's—skittered around his face, lighting on his left shoulder.

"I can help." Ginny pushed around him. "What do you say, Lucas?"

"I can do it." Lucas took the gloves and then tucked

them against his body. "I'm looking for dominoes. I want to make a Christmas train."

"Lucas, we're here to work," Ginny said, also squatting down beside him. "Remember we're going to make the Harry's House Annex into a teen community after-school program, for Grandpa? It was his dream for his retirement."

Lucas slowly drew on one of the leatherwork gloves, but his attention was on the ten dominoes he'd set up in the start of a grid pattern.

"Grandpa's dead," the kid said, sounding like he was on autopilot.

Rohan felt his heart thud to his cowboy boots, which still felt tight. He'd worn tactical boots for all his years in the service, but Wolf, who'd stepped up as the temporary team leader following Jace's death, had ordered the custom-made boots for all of them to celebrate the five team members mustering out following Jace's death. They'd been designed by some outfit—Kelly Boots—in Whiskey River, Texas, where Wolf was from.

So that's why Ginny and Lucas were digging out this dump.

"I don't have enough." Lucas looked at him.

"Enough what?" Rohan tried to shake off the crowding memories.

"Dominoes to make a train," Lucas said. "Grandpa used to make a Christmas train—a real one only smaller—with me, but he's with angels. I need to find more dominoes."

Thankfully the boy had tagged on that last bit of conversation or else Rohan would have volunteered to set up a Christmas train—whatever that was—and he could just imagine how Ginny would have felt about him coming into her house and playing dad with her son. He might be struggling with the concept of being 'home,' and 'safe,' and living up to his promise to Jace's spirit, but he preferred to keep his head on his shoulders and hot things out of his face.

"That sounds like a lot of fun. You think there are more dominoes in these piles?"

"Might be."

"What would be the best way to find them?"

"I'm looking now."

"If we start picking up what we know is trash, and loading them into the bins, seems more likely that the dominoes will fall out than if we sit and look for them hiding."

Lucas's air of defeat morphed to curiosity. He looked at Rohan's work gloves then the ones he'd been handed. Rohan made no move to help with the gloves, because the idea seemed ludicrous. The kid was eleven or twelve—at least he looked it—and it still burned that Ginny had replaced him so quickly. He hadn't touched another woman for almost two years after they'd broken up because it had felt like cheating. Even then everything had been casual hookups. But Ginny had made a baby with another man.

Where was he now?

Lucas's face twisted up as he worked his hand into the

glove and then he held his arm stiffly, fingers spread wide and made a puttering sound.

"Too stiff?" Ginny pulled the glove off Lucas.

"The man said I need it."

"Rohan," Rohan tagged on.

"You don't need them," Ginny said. "They would be helpful, but…"

"I got an old pair of gloves in my gear," Rohan remembered. They were worn from hard use in the field, but he'd packed them for home by habit.

He went to his truck and returned.

"Try these," he offered.

"Thank you." Ginny sounded stiff and disapproving. "But really, Rohan, I can handle this."

"I know."

He definitely didn't know what he was doing as far as parenting, but new leatherwork gloves were stiff and uncomfortable, and his tactical ones were Gore-Tex and soft from years of use.

Ginny huffed a sigh. "Let me…"

"I can do it," Lucas said. "Miss Sims said I need to try to 'dapt."

"Adapt," Ginny said. "And you do work hard at it, I know."

"Not really." Lucas looked at his mother, his expression frank.

Rohan's snort of laughter surprised everyone, including

Mystery. Three sets of eyes skewed his way.

"Learning to adapt. We got that in common," he admitted because if there was one thing he was going to need to do in these next few days, weeks and months it was learn how to adapt. The army shrink had cautioned him—so had the mounds of paperwork he'd had to read and sign, as well as everyone who'd lined up for his exit interviews.

Life on the outside was going to take time and effort. And he was going to need help, which had burned. Special Forces soldiers never lined up to say they needed help. Jace had said they'd be their own support system.

Then the words he'd so casually uttered sank in. Gutted him. If their baby had lived beyond its second trimester and had been born, he would have had something in common with his child—shared genetics, disposition, appearance, skills, maybe.

His eyes met Ginny's, and he knew, just knew she was thinking the same thing.

She shot to her feet like she'd been launched. "If you're really here to work, let's get to it." Her voice was brittle, and the window into the life he'd lost slammed shut again.

ONE GOOD THING about seething, she got a lot of work done. Gin practically had an internal Hemi engine as she stalked around the garage sorting things into piles of trash, recycling, items that could be donated and, surprisingly, used in the annex when it was up and running. How dare Rohan show up and pretend like nothing had happened. How dare he try to bond with her child. How dare he be so helpful. And hot.

He let her stew and stomp while he too filled up the trash bags, tied them off and loaded them in the truck. If she'd been a more reasonable and forgiving person, she'd probably marvel at how efficiently they were working together, like the team they'd once been.

But according to her father, she'd excelled at holding grudges—not that that should be a badge of honor. When her mother had reappeared ten years after leaving her and her father, asking to see her, her father had, of course, been encouraging. Gin had refused. She preferred the parent who had stayed and loved.

Gin was so worked up trying not to think about Rohan and their past, while her father's ashes waited for the spring to be scattered in a stand of ponderosa pines somewhere near Miracle Lake, that she was careless. While balancing a too large armful of tattered and filthy rags and material, she kicked a paint can, stumbled, dropped her load, bruised her knee, and in a clumsy attempt to stabilize herself, clutched a dangling rope. Unattached, it slipped off the beam and tangled between her feet.

"Dang it," Gin barked, trying to hop over the rope and the pile of clutter, but her front foot skidded forward sending her into the splits, which she'd been unable to do even in high school. "Eeeep!"

She twisted, hoping to fall on her butt, but knocked into a trash can, tipping it over. Gross and ouch. She braced for the fall, scrunching her face, not wanting to see or smell the gook she'd fall into. But she never hit the ground. Instead, she felt Rohan's strong arms around her, lifting her back up.

"Okay?" His gravelly voice vibrated against her back.

For a moment she swore he held her against his chest, but no, she'd better be imagining that. She pulled away, rubbing her gloved hands down her face. Yuck. She was likely filthy.

"I'm fine. Totally fine without you or your help." She was appalled by the anger rattling around inside of her and the harshness of her voice, but she couldn't shut up. "And Lucas doesn't need you either. Don't try to play the good guy with my son," she snapped. "It's way too late. You left me. You left everything behind."

She felt like she was vibrating. This wasn't the time for a showdown. She should have hurled her insults years ago instead of helplessly sobbing all the way home, and he'd not chased after her. She was horribly aware of Lucas staring at her wide-eyed, two newly discovered dominoes in his hands. Rohan's eyes shimmered with hurt, and she felt a flash of triumph, which quickly plummeted to shame when his stoic expression settled like a weighted blanket.

How could she still be so raw so many years later?

"Ginny." Rohan's voice was deep and tortured. "I can't just…I can't…I'm so very…"

She held up her hand hoping to ward him off. She needed her anger. She had so much to do and owed her father so much. She couldn't let Rohan reawaken her dormant heart and kindle a spark of forgiveness. She couldn't survive losing him again, and she had to think of Lucas and her father's legacy.

"Ginny, you have no idea how many times I have…" As if under a compulsion Rohan stepped forward, almost as if he was attached to a string she jerked. Her stomach bottomed. He couldn't touch her again. He couldn't kiss her. She'd tumble faster than any of Lucas's dominoes he was digging from the years of refuse.

"Don't apologize." Her command sounded like a gun going off.

"A million times I've wished I could…"

Blinding LED headlights illuminated them, and Gin felt like she'd been both rescued and trapped.

"Another volunteer," she gasped in relief and kicked the trash she'd dropped out of her way to escape Rohan and whatever errant confession he wanted to drag out backward, kicking and screaming from his flabby conscience.

She made a beeline for the truck, not caring who drove it.

"Thank you for coming," she called as the engine cut.

Then Boone Telford hopped out of the Ford F-250.

Both boots slapped on the snowy pavement. A smile cut across his handsome face. "Look at you two having a reunion without me. Just like old times seeing you facing off. Hope I didn't interrupt anything."

Typical Boone, Rohan seethed, *interrupting.* It was like he was a tween dogging his every step again.

"Why are you here?" Rohan wondered at his kick of temper.

Boone, the big idiot, tucked his thumbs in the front pockets of his Wranglers, his fingers framing a silver and gold buckle for Copper Mountain Rodeo bulldogging champion from this past year, and grinned. Wait, Boone had won that recently?

Rohan stepped closer. "You're still competing?" he demanded, nearly disbelieving. "I thought you quit when you caved and did the whole wife and baby thing."

He immediately winced at his words and tone that clashed together like boulders tumbling down Copper Mountain in a dangerous landslide.

"I still got it." Boone smirked. "Won partners in roping with Luke Wilder a year ago too. I just compete at a few local rodeos bulldogging or roping. No more bull or bronc riding."

"Telfords." Ginny pointed at them both with a wagging

finger. "I'm here to work. Take your family reunion and who's the manlier cowboy out of my garage."

"Your garage?" Rohan stared at the horror. She couldn't possibly be thinking of raising her boy in this dump. What about her father's house? He thought she'd said something about…

"Aw, Gin, I'm sorry," Boone said, grinning and interrupting Rohan's train of thought just as he'd done when they'd been kids. "I just had to put this big idiot in his place since he snuck into town, no warning, and stopped here before going to see Mom and Dad. He's keeping his visit home a big secret." Boone made a motion with his fingers to zip his lips.

"Visit," Ginny harumphed as if that proved something.

Rohan felt the need to defend his honor. He'd made a vow to Jace. He hadn't known Mr. Lane was dead or that Ginny still lived in town. His mission to Marietta had suddenly become more complicated and maybe retreating to the ranch was a better option for now.

But then he looked at her kid still picking up small, random piles of trash, shaking them and then delighting in a random domino dislodging, dropping the trash on the ground to seize the domino instead. Rohan didn't know much about kids—just from when Boone and Riley had been kids, but they'd only been a few years younger. He didn't know what normal was, but he could tell Ginny had her hands full either way. She was fiercely loyal. She didn't have backdown in her. He'd always liked her strength, her fearlessness, her passionate sense of right and wrong.

And he'd done her horribly wrong all those years ago. He couldn't leave her to sort through this mess alone.

"You didn't tell your parents you were coming home?" Ginny stared at him in disbelief. "Don't let me stop you, Rohan Telford." She swept one arm wide toward his truck. "Scoot."

Like he was Mystery.

"I'm helping you clear out the garage." He'd already explained why.

"So am I." Boone's curious gaze swiveled between them. "I have coffee. Sodas, sandwiches from the Java Café, cookies and muffins. Heard from Colt that the other volunteers bailed on you so I headed in early and ran into this lost cowboy at Z's."

"Chocolate chip?" Lucas asked, pausing as he shook another pile of papers.

"Of course, bud," Boone said. "What are you looking for in all those stacks of things?" Boone asked striding over to the child. Lucas spoke too softly to hear, but Boone nodded.

For some reason, Rohan's heart fisted in his chest.

He knew he was being ridiculous, but he couldn't shake what felt like feral reactions to Boone's easy relationship with Ginny and her son. She wasn't his. What was next? The urge to mark Ginny by peeing on her? He knew Boone adored Piper and was as honest and loyal as a man could be. His reactions and impulses disconcerted him.

"Colt says today and tomorrow are the only days this week he and Remy can do the garage build and start on the kitchen."

"I know." Ginny kicked at an old desk. "I didn't come over here before today." She hung her head. "It was too hard thinking of my dad and all." She looked at Boone, her eyes swimming in tears. "It's irresponsible of me, I know. But I didn't know it was this bad."

"Ahhh, Ginny." Boone hopped over a pile of junk, his arms open to hug her, and Rohan had to fight the instinct to slug his brother. "No worries. I'm here. Colt and Remy are bringing reinforcements. We'll get the cleanup and garage build-out done."

"Thank you."

"I'm here too," Rohan said, feeling like an annoying afterthought. "Less talk more work," he added to his brother who laughed in his face and then added the insult of a wink and a snappy salute.

Rohan let it go and focused on clearing out the garage, following Boone's example of hooking more trash bags on the walls, and organizing and labeling the contents with the ever-present Sharpie he kept in his pocket. He'd be lying if he didn't admit that he pushed himself extra hard to prove his worth, but while he told himself it was to show Ginny he wasn't a totally selfish four-letter word, he also felt the need to flex on his little brother, who spent the first five minutes texting like a self-absorbed teen would.

"You aren't telling Mom and Dad I'm here?" he demanded in a low voice. That was all he needed, his parents being hurt he didn't come home first.

"Not everything's about you."

When he and Boone hefted out several rolls of carpet and unrolled them on the frozen dead grass to see if they'd be usable with a cleaning, the morning was beginning to brighten and warm. A few more trucks pulled up and Boone whistled.

"The calvary has arrived."

Chapter Six

THE CALVARY ENDED up being two local ranchers and their wives, Beck and Ashni and Bowen and Lang Ballantyne. Soon after, Colt Wilder, who had already committed to working on the shop cabinet install with a friend of his who'd recently left the service, arrived with his thirteen-year-old son, Parker.

"Colt, you're already doing so much," she expostulated, nearly tripping over Mystery who greeted each new arrival with determined sniffs and a sweep of her tail, leaning into the strokes and head scratches before returning to Lucas's side.

"Needs doing." Even though Colt had volunteered on many projects in town including quite a few at Harry's House, she still felt like she didn't know him much. He had an intense stare and a smoldering stillness that made her uneasy—probably because she was a chatterbox when nervous, and Colt seemed to limit himself to action punctuated by a few one-syllable words now and then.

"Hey, Lucas, I have an idea." Parker hopped out of the truck and joined Lucas. "Have you ever done a dump run?" Parker made it sound like it was a fantastic adventure.

"We're going to be the captains."

Lucas stared at Parker like he was a god and followed him out of the garage to hear the plan. She tried to quell the spurt of hope at the idea that Lucas would have the opportunity to interact pleasantly with a peer. She'd taught Parker last year for the language arts and social studies block. He was a good kid, not only smart, but also kind, well liked and responsible. He often volunteered to tutor at the elementary school—that must be how Lucas knew him.

Another man drove up with a teen girl with edgy, shorn black hair with red tips and a few green streaks.

"You like?" She spun around while Parker stared at her hair. "For Christmas." Then she shook Lucas's hand like an adult and smiled at him. "I'm Arlo."

"Your head looks like a Christmas ornament," Lucas stated, staring.

Gin winced and walked over to the kids to smooth things out, but before she could, Arlo's laugh stopped her. Arlo ran her hand through her hair so that it stuck up.

"I didn't think of that. I was going for Christmas. Maybe I should see if I can get some silver streaks."

"Sick," Parker complimented. "We three are a team organizing the dump runs for the trucks. You got the masks?"

Arlo held up her hand where several respirator masks dangled from one finger. "Shane sprayed an essence of peppermint so we won't smell the cat pee and whatever else the house or garage is rocking. You got the safety glasses?"

"Roger that."

"We're going to look like superheroes—you in?" She looked at Lucas, her eyes shining with enthusiasm, and something pinched low in Gin's belly. She couldn't remember a time when Lucas had been included.

But anxiety clawed. During the pandemic Lucas had had such a hard time with the masks—even the cloth ones—so she'd mostly kept him home. No way could he manage the N95 mask and goggles. He was too sensitive to pressure and textures.

Arlo and Parker donned their masks, and she pulled out her phone. "Ready Harry's House Superheroes?"

Parker helped Lucas with the mask, and instead of fussing or pulling away because he hated anything to touch his head, face or neck, he let Parker mask him up even as he waved and twisted his hands nervously at his sides. Then Parker worked the glasses over his face. Arlo adjusted one of the side straps.

"My dad glued foam on your glasses so they wouldn't feel hard," Arlo said. "Comfortable?"

"Roger that," Lucas said, and Gin almost burst into tears when Parker gave him a thumbs-up. The kids squished together and Arlo took a selfie.

"Wait, we need the dog in the picture. Way more clicks for Harry's House."

The kids followed Arlo and crouched next to Mystery. Lucas slid one arm around the dog, which made Gin feel both happy and awful. Her dad had been right. She'd been limiting one of Lucas's options to connect because she'd been afraid—not only of the work and responsibility a dog would entail, but also because she didn't want to care for something and then lose it.

She closed her eyes as they uncomfortably pricked. She was letting her own fears hinder her son's happiness.

"I'll post it on the Harry's House socials…Dad," she said as a tall, very broad man with flowing dark hair that brushed his shoulders finished a call from his truck and strode up the driveway.

He stopped in his tracks, and his face had the oddest expression before he gave a short nod. Then Arlo ran, quickly hugged him before tugging Lucas and Parker out of the garage and around the corner toward the house. She should go with the kids…Lucas would need her guidance to help him navigate whatever job the kids expected him to do because he'd get distracted and wouldn't be able to follow their quicksilver directions. It was a challenge to redirect Lucas. They'd get frustrated. He'd get lost.

"You supervise here. Cross and I have the kids," Colt said to her, and Gin stopped in her tracks. She knew she could trust Colt. He was an assistant scoutmaster of the Boy Scout troop that Lucas had moved into this year, but her father had done all the scouting meetings, projects and campouts with Lucas. She still hadn't figured out how she'd manage Scouts. Despair settled in her tummy.

"Remy Cross," the giant introduced himself and for a moment, Gin felt like Colt had split in two.

She must have been staring as she shook Remy's hand because there was an awkward silence that expanded, and he tugged his hand back, and she flushed, noticing the shiny wedding band, but she hadn't been thinking of him like that at all. It was just the eerie resemblance between the two men, one of whom she'd never seen in town, and he was a hard man to miss.

"Cross." Suddenly Rohan was there, and Gin had to take a step back while they did some bro-hug thing that reminded her of wolves greeting each other. She was proud of herself for not rolling her eyes—she'd been cooped up with middle school girls for way too long.

"You're here. You tight?" He looked at Rohan as if checking for injuries. "You set up?" His gaze strayed to her.

"Just arrived this morning so getting there." Rohan did not look at her.

"Wasn't expecting you until after Christmas. Oh. That's right, you've got family in town. Anyone here?"

"Guilty," Boone shouted out.

Rohan introduced his brother and the Ballantynes who he knew from the summer teen rodeo circuit and then he slid his arm around her. Gin nearly jumped out of her boots. "This is Ginny Lane."

"Virginia. My friends call me Gin," she said pointedly.

"Not this friend." Rohan kept his smile, but there was an

undercurrent in his tone that she'd never heard before, and her temper kicked in.

She was tempted to push him away, hopefully off-balancing him, but that would be childish. Besides, she probably didn't stand a chance. This adult version of Rohan felt alien. Gone was her long, rangy cowboy, and in his place was a much more filled-out frame, harder than she remembered, and she had an unwelcome fantasy of letting her hands wander under his shirt to see if he had abs and a chest that looked as defined as she imagined they might be after thirteen or fourteen years as a soldier.

Of all the men here, why was she perving on the one who was totally unworthy? Well, it wasn't as if she'd let herself truly fantasize about another woman's husband, but she could mumble an admiring 'yum' under her breath and move on with her day. But no. It was Rohan who lit her fire.

"Roll out," Colt said. "Cross and I will start ripping up carpet and flooring inside. With this many trucks we each do a dump run or two and we'll have the garage and house cleared and get a good jump on the garage build, maybe start in the kitchen."

"We'll catch up later." Cross looked at Rohan with a definite question in his eye. He even angled his chin at her. Rohan stood close enough that he could have planted a flag on the top of her head.

"Nothing to gossip about on this end," she stated to Remy.

"Hmmm quick denial. Good to know."

The former soldier stalked off toward the house—even his boots didn't crunch in the snow.

"Did you not see his wedding ring?"

"OMG." Yup. Too long with middle school girls.

She pushed at his chest, but even though she daily hit her father's home gym, at dawn, hating every minute of it—Rohan didn't even rock.

"Too much testosterone in here," she muttered under her breath and joined the new arrivals—the two women who chatted as they sorted through the piles.

"I'll join the others inside with the partial demo. Taking my hormones with me, Ginny." Boone winked.

"Not you too. Only Rohan called me that, and he doesn't anymore."

"Ginny and I will handle the garage," Rohan said, and she wondered why he was messing with her.

"Your funeral, brother," Boone teased following the other men out.

The four of them developed a rhythm that made the morning pass quickly and efficiently, although Gin found herself frequently sneaking glances at Rohan even as she scolded herself for noticing his existence. But wow, the way his Wranglers cupped his butt and the long, powerful length of his legs. And his broad shoulders—even through his thick, fleece-lined flannel—did something ridiculous to make her tummy flip.

No. Don't look.

"Those cowboys sure are tempting," Ashni Ballantyne whispered to her, and Gin felt herself blush.

She'd enjoyed listening to Ashni and Lang discuss heading to the Scott Family Tree Farm later in the day to pick out a couple of Christmas trees for the ranch. It sounded so fun and family-oriented, but it made her miss her father more. The three of them had always found a tree at the Scotts', and it sounded like all of the Ballantynes lived in the one large ranch house, which made her feel the absence of her father more.

Cutting down a tree with just Lucas sounded daunting physically and emotionally.

"I've had it bad for my cowboy since high school," Ashni said. "Lang drooled over Bowen when he was on the teen summer rodeo circuit. You were with Rohan in high school too, right? I remember you from some of my summer visits."

"Oh. We're not together," Gin said quickly and found herself staring into curious dark eyes that looked full of stars. "Not for a long, long time."

"Really?" The way she drew out the word sounded both teasing and theatrical.

"We were high school sweethearts," Gin admitted. "But we went our separate ways after graduation."

That was a politician-worthy spin.

"Oh. My mistake." Ashni winked. "Just doesn't seem all that separate, but you do you."

Gin went back to work, loading up Rohan's truck with things that could be recycled. That would get him out of the garage for a little while.

She thought she'd recovered some of her composure when Rohan returned from his first trip and quickly went back to work.

"Okay?" Rohan busted her and walked toward her all fluid swagger, his expression concerned. "Tired? Take a break. Sit by the heater. Boone brought some sandwiches." Rohan unfolded a metal chair that she'd found earlier that morning, took off his flannel and folded it so the cold metal wouldn't seep through her clothes.

Too embarrassed to admit she wasn't tired, only perving, and too undone by his easy concern—it felt so familiar—she folded onto the chair, feeling like a silly Victorian woman with the vapors, desperate to steal a moment alone with a hero.

"You ladies want to take a break—there are muffins and sandwiches from the Java Café."

Ashni and Lang looked around. "Maybe in a bit," Ashni said. "We only have a few hours as Beck's granddad and his mom have the baby, and we're all heading out to the Scotts' to get some Christmas trees this afternoon."

Rohan paused. "Sounds fun."

"I know." Ashni smiled. "I love Christmas. We're all going to be together this Christmas. My parents are coming for two weeks, and Bodhi and his wife Nico will arrive next week. Granddad is so fired up that everyone will be at the ranch this Christmas."

"Wow, even Bodhi's married."

"Heck yeah," Lang added. "The Ballantyne men don't mess around. They know a good thing when they see it."

"They do," Rohan said softly after a couple of beats of silence. "I'd forgotten Boone told me the three of you got married at the Ballantyne Bash over a year ago. It's good to see y'all happy. I remember meeting you a couple of times, Ashni, when you came to watch Beck compete during the summer. And you—" he pointed at Lang "—rode like the wind. Surprised you didn't do it professionally. What was that name Bodhi used to call you?"

To Gin's shock Lang stuck her tongue out at Rohan. "You just keep on forgetting, Cowboy."

Ashni giggled, and Rohan's lips quirked in the beginnings of a smile. "It'll come to me."

"You do that, and you'll have a bruised body part that Gin won't thank me for," Lang warned.

"Me? I have no say about any of his body parts," Gin said quickly.

Rohan laughed, and even though she was embarrassed, it felt good to hear him enjoying himself. Earlier this morning things had felt so fraught.

Gin tried not to feel like the odd woman out. Ashni and Lang were part of a large, loving, extended family and married to attentive, adoring cowboys, and Gin couldn't help but remember she'd once thought that was her future.

But, she reminded herself, she was lucky. She had a solid, secure career she enjoyed and a son she loved. Her father had always supported her decisions and had been a buffer against the world. The three of them had been a tight family, and even though she often felt alone, she had friends and a community and a legacy to nurture.

"Maybe you should change what you do and don't have a say over." Ashni used air quotes around 'say.' Gin's mouth dropped open, surprised by the teasing, but warmed to be included in their circle of camaraderie.

She was the problem, always holding herself back. Always feeling like she didn't fit in.

Her father had always encouraged her to resume her friendships, but she'd used Lucas as an excuse. Her father had continued to gently push Lucas into social situations that were so painful to watch while Gin always tried to shield him. He'd wanted Lucas to step out of his comfort zone, and Gin now realized that those lessons had also been directed at her.

She too needed to stop protecting Lucas so much and probably herself.

"Boy or girl?" she asked Ashni.

"Girl. She's eight months old. Beck's so proud you'd think he invented fatherhood."

Gin smiled. That was cute. She didn't know Beck that well. He'd always been the youngest Ballantyne and had hung out with his two older cousins during the summers when they'd been in town visiting their granddad. They'd often been at the fairgrounds working on their rodeo skills along with Rohan, and where Rohan went, Gin had followed when she could.

"He's already holding her in his arms and having his horse trot around the arena," Ashni added. "You and your son should come tree hunting with us," she offered. Her dark gaze danced with warmth and welcome. "There's plenty of room in the trucks—or you could ride if you want." Ashni shivered. "Lang and Bowen are planning to ride out."

"I'm a female centaur," Lang joked. "My grandpa sold my horse when I went to college even though I was on a rodeo scholarship so I didn't ride for years, and now that I'm on a ranch, I have a hard time getting out of the saddle. You and Lucas should definitely come. I can teach you both to ride if you don't know how. It's not as much fun to buy a tree from a lot."

But it was easier—especially for a single mom, facing her first Christmas without the rock of her father.

Boone came around the corner, easily toting three rolls of carpeting on his shoulder. Lucas followed with one small roll, balancing on his shoulder just like Boone's. His face shone with pride, even as it was scrunched in effort.

"Don't go stealing my brother's girl," Boone said to Ashni. "Gin, you and Lucas should definitely come tree hunting, but with us. The fam's going out this afternoon—we're trying out a sleigh my dad and I have been refurbishing for the past couple years. Maiden voyage."

"I—" She broke off, stunned to have received two inclusive offers to join two different families on a very family-oriented activity that sounded like something out of a children's Christmas book. She felt a bit like a bug pinned in a collection. "That sounds so wonderful Boone," she started politely, "but—"

"It's settled then." Boone hoisted the carpet rolls into his truck and helped Lucas get his into the bed as well. "You got a strong one there, Gin."

Boone picked up a white bag. "Here are the cookies," he said to Lucas, who peered suspiciously in the bag.

"Are there any nuts?"

"Nope. I told them no nuts for you." Boone grinned down at her son. "Oatmeal, white chocolate chip and regular chocolate chip. Nothing crunchy. Choose your poison."

"They aren't poison," Lucas said, staring at the cookies again. He stuck his hand in the bag.

"Only one, Lucas," Gin said firmly, "and you can only touch the cookie you intend to take."

He jostled the bag and looked in again.

"Big decision," Boone stated. Boone looked over her head—probably some silent sibling communication thing with Rohan, but then she realized Rohan had a box of sandwiches he was holding open for her. It was such a mirror—her and Lucas being offered food, that she wanted to make a joke to combat the warmth that burbled in her chest, but she couldn't rip her heart wide open again.

"Is it a real sleigh like Santa's?" Lucas asked.

"Lucas, we shouldn't…" she began, not wanting to get her child's hopes up, but he so rarely expressed an interest in doing anything with someone else. And she had to admit the thought of being bundled up in a sleigh or walking through an evergreen forest and gathering greenery and twigs and pinecones to make a wreath for their front door and finding a small tree without having to wrestle it home on her own was more seductive than it should be.

Even though her father was gone, she knew she had to decorate the house, build new traditions to help both Lucas and herself. He needed routine. He needed connections. She did too.

"You should." Boone winked at her. "Definitely."

Gin looked up hopelessly into Rohan's face.

"Sorry," she mumbled. "Boone's making things awkward again."

"I'm not sorry," Rohan said, shocking her back into silence. "You and Lucas should definitely join us."

He took a turkey, ham and cheese half and she chose half of an egg salad sandwich.

He downed his in a few bites while she stared up at him, trying to think of a proper response.

"It's your homecoming," she whispered. "I can't intrude on family time."

"You could never intrude, Ginny."

The rest of the garage and the people working in it faded away. There was only Rohan looking stern and a little pale and his cheeks more hollowed out than she remembered and shadows in his eyes where there'd never been any, and she realized suddenly that his homecoming might be as hard for him as it was for her.

He had the family. The ranch. The confidence. Everything.

But he'd become a soldier.

She'd always wondered why and also why he stayed away so many years.

He didn't look happy. And that bothered her even though she'd cut him out of her heart.

"Mom?" Lucas's voice cut across her worried questions. The mask hung down around Lucas's neck like the other kids'. The goggles perched on his head. Mystery sat by his side. "A sleigh. Can we go?"

She still held the egg salad sandwich, and her stomach churned uncomfortably, both with hunger and stress. Lucas's eyes sparkled—something she rarely saw. Boone and Rohan exchanged a look—Boone's challenging, Rohan's much harder to gauge.

"I dare you, Ginny." Rohan's voice sounded rusty, but the look he gave her was pure cocky cowboy dare as he leaned forward and took a bite of her sandwich. "I double dare you, Virginia Lane," he whispered, his breath warm against her chilled cheek.

"WHY DIDN'T YOU go home before seeking out my father?" Ginny finally asked into the silence pulsing in Rohan's truck.

Rohan had been braced for an inquisition once Boone had masterfully maneuvered him into driving Ginny to the ranch while he took Lucas into town first to pick up a to-go order of hot chocolate at Sage's Chocolate Shop. There had been an implied chocolate treat and the kid—he still couldn't wrap his head around the fact that Ginny had a son—had climbed into Boone's truck along with Mystery.

Lucas going separately clearly bothered Ginny. She looked worried and had started in with the reminders like Lucas was five or six. And he'd tried not to think about what might be wrong with the kid or what Ginny thought might be wrong. Boone had been Boone—quick with a grin and to wave off worry.

"Ain't my first rodeo with kids or with Lucas, Gin." Then Boone had tipped his hat. "Besides, I'm picking up Piper and our little monkey. She had a client this morning, and I did some shopping and so there won't be room in the truck for you. See you both at the ranch."

Rohan pondered Ginny's question. Did he go for honesty or easy? Words tangled in his throat. He wanted to apologize about so much but wasn't sure a twenty-minute drive was enough to begin to cover all of his regrets.

"I..." he began.

Maybe the Japanese tradition of hara-kiri had it right. It was the ultimate apology, spilling your guts literally. He'd never imagined there could be a path back for them, but after learning about Ron Lane's death and a morning of watching Ginny navigate single motherhood while facing a monumental project, he didn't think he could slink off to nurse his own wounds. Ginny's light had dimmed. Her confidence too. And when Lucas had stated that she no longer wrote, he'd felt gutted. Words and ideas and images tumbling out of her mouth or onto the page was such an essential part of Ginny.

How could it be all gone?

His fault?

The other man's?

Her father's death?

He knew he was forever changed from his time in the service and his regrets over his immature and selfish reaction to their unexpected pregnancy. But he'd always imagined her unbowed by life, confidently striding into the next challenge, pursuing her next idea. He'd loved the way she'd sketch on napkins, write down ideas, or words for use in a future poem, which sometimes she would share with him when they'd be alone on the ranch or at Miracle Lake.

"You and your family were always so close." Ginny had pivoted on the seat to stare at him, her gaze as accusing as it was curious. She huffed out a bitter laugh and ran her hand through her hair. "I always envied you your family. Mother who did the whole mom thing." She rolled her eyes and waved her hand. "Baked cookies, packed your lunches and made those delicious dinners, and she volunteered for so much at the school, and grew that amazing garden and still did the books for the ranch and had a small horse training side hustle, and you had siblings. Your family dinners were always so lively."

His chest felt heavy. "They were," he admitted remembering. Ginny had often come to dinner once he could drive. She'd bantered with his siblings, talked recipes or planting tips or books with his mom, helped with the cooking, writing recipes down. She'd glowed at the table, and he'd felt like the luckiest cowboy.

"So what happened?"

You. Me.

"I don't know," he said inadequately.

"What's that mean?"

"And there she is," he murmured, charmed even though she was poking him for answers he wasn't sure he had. Or maybe he just didn't want to share.

"Yeah, here I am, and I want to know why you're shutting your family out."

"I'm not. We're driving to play happy family and chop down a tree for Christmas and ride in a sleigh, which is utterly surreal considering two weeks ago I was—" He broke off.

"Ooooh, top secret, Soldier." She crossed her arms and

swiveled back to face forward. There was a chill even though the cranked heater blasted. He preferred when she labeled him cowboy.

"*We* are not playing happy family," Ginny said stonily. "You are helping me and Lucas to get a Christmas tree, and he is going to have a ride in a sleigh because Boone is a generous man."

Boone. No mention of him. Rohan knew he was being unreasonable.

"I can be generous."

"Don't bother."

"You've changed." He spoke without thinking.

"So have you."

Ginny peeled off her coat and tossed it in the back seat, and he caught a glimpse of the gentle swell of her breasts outlined in the periwinkle cashmere sweater. His mouth dried, both from the view and the memory that the sweater had been a gift from him to her for her seventeenth birthday. He'd bought it at a department store in Bozeman with money he'd earned from repairing machinery at neighboring ranches. He'd never spent that much on clothing before or since.

She hated him. She hadn't spoken to him since he'd awkwardly tried to comfort her about losing their baby, no doubt saying something lame, and she'd turned on him like a rank bull, screamed, thrown a chemistry textbook at his head and cursed him out before running out the door. He'd been so stunned by her anger and the death of their baby and the riot of emotions he couldn't process that it took him a few minutes to regroup and by that time she'd driven off, and he'd had practice.

But she was wearing the sweater that had cost him most of his savings and had been from Scotland, which at seventeen sounded exotic and fancy.

He knew he shouldn't read anything into her wearing the sweater. She hadn't known he was coming home. But she hadn't burned it.

Rohan drove carefully down Main Street toward the highway, keeping his jumbled thoughts to himself. Ginny had been the one with the words and the emotional intelligence. He'd been more of an action man, which had endangered his life as much as it had saved it.

Her posture was rigid, her crossed arms closed her off, but her breasts rose higher, pressing against the thin weave of the sweater that still looked elegant and beautiful, sweetly caressing her small curves.

"You're lucky." Her eyes squinted at the highway ribboning out before them. "You still have all your family, but maybe I'm the stupid one. Maybe you don't care about family and still don't want one of your own."

He was stung. He'd been eighteen. His first semester of college. But snapping back wouldn't help. Ginny wanted a fight. He recognized the signs and that settled him.

"I'm utterly changed," he said.

That got her attention.

"I don't recognize myself," he admitted, controlling his expression so she wouldn't see his spurt of triumph that for once today he was playing it right with her. "I think I've been avoiding the ranch more over the past few years because the changes in me soaked in deeper. To my bones." And as he spoke, he realized it was true. And Ginny deserved the truth. No more hiding behind the image he thought he should project—stoic, know-it-all cowboy. "I no longer felt like myself, like the boy I'd been and the man I'd started becoming before the service. I no longer feel like Taryn Telford's son."

She faced him now, defensive posture easing a smidge.

"I'm don't feel like I belong."

"You belong," she whispered.

He risked a look at her. "I'm unrecognizable."

"I recognized you."

Her tone kicked up a flare of light in his chest like a struck match.

The tight hold she had of her body loosened and she reached toward his hair, no doubt wildly messy from his hat and the exertion of the morning, but she froze, withdrew her hand, and he felt the absence of her touch keenly. Ginny had always been so tactile. And she'd loved his hair.

"But I know what you mean," she admitted, back to staring blankly out of the windshield. "I don't recognize myself most days."

Her long neck looked fragile, and her swallow was audible over the blast of the heater.

"Why?" he whispered, hurting for her, hurting for him.

She didn't respond.

"Ginny," he said, urgently. He wanted to pull the truck off the highway and hold her and say…what? What could begin to close this distance? Words tumbled around his brain like rocks in a rock polisher his parents had bought him for his birthday one year.

He wanted to miraculous heal then but had no idea where to start.

At the beginning.

It was something Jace would have said. His father too.

He drove another mile, thought about one approach after another, but nothing seemed to fit.

"You're still damned beautiful." His voice rumbled in his throat, thick with emotion, and while part of him wished to call the revealing words back, he couldn't deny their truth.

Ginny made a dismissive sound.

"I may not have said this earlier," he said cautiously, "but, Ginny, I'm so sorry you lost your dad."

"Yeah, me too." She blinked furiously. "Everyone's sorry."

"Was he…had he been…"

"Nope." She could still decipher his clumsy verbal attempts as if fourteen years hadn't passed. "He was happy, healthy, always busy. He had big plans for his retirement."

A shadow crossed her face and she gulped in air. "He died suddenly, immediately. Aortic aneurysm, like I said before. Nothing anyone could have done."

Another mile rolled past before he could trust himself to speak. That didn't mean he had nothing to say. He had plenty. He just wasn't sure what was the best path forward. Maybe she didn't want him to offer his help. It would probably be smart to get the lay of the land first, so to speak.

"What about Lucas's father..." Yeah, he wanted clarity on that.

"I don't want to talk about him."

"In or out of the picture."

"Why?" She turned to glare at him, her spectacular blues squinty and glittering like newly cut sapphires.

"You aren't him so you have no right asking."

True. But they had a history. Surely that should count for something.

"Ginny, I need to know that you are safe, taken care of."

The burble of laughter sounded angry. "Right," she mocked. "My safety is your priority. I'd driven hours to tell you I'd miscarried our baby, and you couldn't get me out of your dorm room fast enough."

Rohan had whiplash from her jerking them both back to the past, and her skewed memory. He'd lost his deposit from the dent in his wall from the hurled chemistry text.

"The things you said to me," she accused.

He couldn't remember his words—probably something

stupid his shocked brain had dredged up and let limp out of his mouth, thinking to comfort. All he could remember was the sound of air rushing in his ears, and an overwhelming pain that they'd lost their baby, just as he'd started to process how their lives were going to change.

"It was the things I didn't say that got me in so much trouble," he admitted. He hadn't said he loved her. He hadn't said he was sorry. He hadn't said they should get married anyway and that he'd transfer schools. He hadn't promised he'd always take care of her.

"This was a mistake," Ginny hissed, her hand on the door handle. "I don't want to talk to you. Boone's the biggest idiot."

Only instinct had him pump the brakes instead of slam on them even though he hadn't driven in icy Montana conditions for years. Heart in his throat he grabbed her arm as the truck slowed. Glancing in the rearview mirror, he maneuvered to the side of the road.

"What the hell?" Terror for her nearly closed off his throat.

"I don't want to go into any of this with you."

But that was just it, he finally accepted. Into it—the messy, the painful and the humiliating, they must both dive. But not when he was driving. And not when she felt trapped. He took in her defiant form pressed against the truck's door. Her eyes were huge, and her breath panted out. She looked scared and angry and on the verge of panic.

He breathed in slowly, counted, held, out. Twice more.

Something Mr. Lane and his father had always taught him echoed in his head. 'Actions speak louder than words.' Rohan's actions and his lack of words hadn't matched what had been buried in his heart when they'd been young and in love and so far out of their depth.

But they were both adults now.

"Ginny," he said carefully. "There are many things I want to say to you."

"It's over thirteen years too late," she said. "Let's just leave it."

"I can't. I won't. But now is not the time. Still, I need to say them, and I believe you need to hear them, just as you need to read the letter Jace wrote your father."

Her eyes narrowed again. "You think you know what's best for me?"

"No." He was relieved to see the fight back in her. "You've always been smart, independent and driven." Only a few of the many reasons he'd fallen so hard for her. "But sometimes we all get lost and need a little push."

"So I can push back?" Calculation gleamed in her eyes, and his heart kicked up.

"Please do."

Chapter Seven

ROHAN PARKED HIS truck near the house and drew in a deep breath. He'd tried not to notice the changes as he'd driven up the long gravel drive. The fences were now white and in good repair. A long row of ponderosa pines lined the entrance, giving the ranch a more majestic appeal. As they neared the house there were a few clusters of quaking aspens as well as some empty whiskey barrels along the fence line, likely an indication that his mother planted annual flowers in the late spring.

He played with the key chain to the rental truck, realizing he didn't have a key to the house anymore.

"Big moment," Ginny said softly as he made no move to get out. To Rohan's shock, she covered his cold hand with hers.

"I'm not sure exactly what's bothering you," she said conversationally. "But I do know that when something is hard, it works better to just jump in or on, which was your advice to me in high school in case you've forgotten." Her lips kicked up in the first smile he'd seen.

"I've forgotten nothing," he said.

Her eyes went a deeper blue, and her gaze searched for

what he didn't know, but he hoped she saw his sincerity. Her smile slowly slipped.

"Everything's hard," he admitted. His voice sounded low and rough, like he'd swallowed a patch of the gravel drive. He was so tired of holding everything in, especially with Ginny. "Harder than it should be."

"Is it the adjustment of leaving the military or something more specific to your family?"

The kindness in her eyes burned through the pain of decisions he'd made years ago before he'd even realized he was deciding anything. He felt utterly exposed, and yet unexpectedly safe. Looking down he saw their fingers were linked. So many memories of holding her hand. Ginny had been his sounding board as much as his father had been until he'd lost them both.

"I lost you." The truth but not what he'd been planning to say because he hadn't had a plan. "And then I lost myself and finally my family."

Compassion bled through her troubled gaze. "You're not lost, Rohan. You're home. You're with family." She nibbled on the pad of her thumb, and it was such a familiar gesture when she was worried that he nearly pulled her against his chest despite the large console between them. He ached to hold her.

"It might take time to adjust, for all of you, and effort to find your new balance and path. But you are home." Her eyebrows drew together, and her fingers tightened on his hand. "It's hard to adjust for some vets. Colt Wilder—he was there today with…your friend—he helps vets settle in, get jobs, services. I know you have the ranch and your family, but counseling and…and someone to talk to." Her words spilled out of her mouth quickly, and her cheeks were stark white with a slash of color, and it took him a moment to realize that she was worried. For him.

He was almost afraid to believe it—afraid to hope, but he held on to her hand, and to the tendril of hope. Her words and her worry were a prayer washing over him, and like a divine joke, he heard the rumble of Boone's truck.

"Rohan, let's go see your family."

He still didn't move. He wanted to absorb this moment, feel her hand in his, smell her fresh scent, see the sparkle in the depths of her eyes and hope.

"It's like the first summer plunge into Miracle Lake," she said briskly, tugging on her hand to free herself. She swung open the truck door and pulled on her gloves before looking back at him over her shoulder. Challenge and humor glinted in her expressive eyes. "Cold as death, but totally invigorating. Cowboy up, Soldier. Time for your conquering hero's welcome home."

He climbed out of the truck, feeling eighty. Ginny had never lacked courage or honesty, and it was time he embraced the same—ironic as most people probably though he was the brave one, but he'd run about as far as he could go.

He walked around to her side of the truck to stand beside her, in case it was icy, but his father had always paid attention to safety details.

Rohan inclined his head, indicating that she should precede him.

"Such a gentleman." She rolled her eyes. "Seriously Rohan, these are your parents." Her palm flattened on his chest. "They are practically legend for their kindness, generosity, love and work ethic."

"And that's the problem." The words jumped out before he could crank his jaw back shut.

"*That's* the problem," she repeated, astonished, just as the front door opened. Ginny whipped her hand back down to her side and spun around. She wobbled a little in the slush, and he instinctively steadied her.

"Surprise," Ginny called out into the expectant-feeling silence.

"Rohan? Rohan?" His mom's voice rose the second time, crackling in disbelief, and then she shrieked and ran at him.

She full-body hit him, not hard enough to stagger him, but then her arms hugged him hard. She repeated mom things over and over, her hands running down his arms. "You're home. You're really home. You didn't say anything. No warning. You're home. I can't believe it." Again she full-body pressed him, her cheek only reaching to his heart. "My son." Her eyes shone with tears as she gazed up at him.

"Hi, Mom." It was the most inadequate response ever, but all he could choke out of his tight throat.

His mom's tears flowed now, and he hugged her back, patting and rubbing his mom's back awkwardly while he finally lifted up his gaze to see his father, standing still, hand on his chest, in the doorway of the old ranch house that had been added on to and updated over the generations. He braced himself. His father, Taryn Telford, had always been his ideal—one he'd utterly failed in coming close to the mark.

His father walked toward him, much calmer than his mom. His warm blue eyes searched his, looking for what clues, Rohan had no idea.

"Good to see you, son," Taryn Telford said, his voice husky with repressed emotion.

His dark hair was still thick and shaggy, lightly threaded with gray. His body remained rancher lean. And as he moved, Rohan could see no lingering signs of the severe injury his father had suffered a handful of years ago at a livestock auction when an inexperienced stock hand had let a bull escape, which had gored his father.

"It's good to be home," Rohan said, covertly checking out his parents for signs of aging. He'd been unable to obtain leave when his father was injured and had missed his older half-brother Whitman's wedding a few years ago. He'd barely made Boone's but had had to fly out the next day when his unit had received the go orders for another covert mission.

Ginny had said the initial welcome would be the hard part, but Rohan suspected his struggle had just begun.

THIS ISN'T AWKWARD at all.

Gin had felt plenty judged over the years, especially when she'd come back home—the high school co-valedictorian—nearly failing her freshman year of college and returning home, pregnant, no named father and her long-time high school sweetheart also dropping out of college to join the army instead of attending the college rodeo finals, where he'd been favored to take All-Around Cowboy.

She'd weathered all that. With her father's help she'd rebuilt her life—commuting to earn her degree and placing Lucas in the college childcare program when he'd been two. She'd completed her masters, had been up for teacher of the year twice, and served on several educational committees and Harry's House board of directors all while raising a special needs son.

She had nothing to be ashamed about.

And yet she still felt her knees shake when she turned to face Taryn and Sarah Telford.

For the most part, she'd managed to avoid them. But she knew they'd blamed her for Rohan leaving school and joining the service. Taryn had approached her father one night, asking to see her, wanting answers—what had sent his son running into the arms of an army recruiter instead of registering for classes for his second semester of college. Her father had had no more clue than Taryn Telford. And then when her pregnancy had become obvious, he'd come back. Her father had still protected her from the kind but searching eyes of Taryn Telford, assuring him that Rohan was not the father.

That had always been a bigger sorrow for her. She would have still had a connection to the man who'd always felt like the love of her life. But no, they'd both shredded that tie. She'd turned to parties, alcohol and barely remembered hookups, and Rohan had served his country—often on the other side of the world.

Why?

She'd never asked herself that. She'd been too miserable, and then too embarrassed and later relieved. But years had passed, and she was a grown woman, and Rohan was home and maybe she should take the opportunity he seemed to want to take to finally close that painful and confusing chapter of their lives.

Boone arrived.

"It's good to see you, Mr. Telford," she said quietly when the excitement had settled a little and Rohan's parents had each turned to look at her even as Lucas jumped out of Boone's truck, Mystery right on his heels. Boone unstrapped his blonde toddler daughter, Reid, from a car seat, and then he walked around the truck to help Piper down.

Piper waved at her, her baby bump just beginning to show.

"Mister," Taryn snorted and smiled. "Taryn."

Rohan's mom finally peeled herself off of Rohan and took Gin's hand and pulled her into a full-body hug.

"Hello, Virginia, it's so good to see you again."

"You too, Mrs. Telford."

"Please, we were practically family."

It shouldn't hurt, but it did. Her father had said the truth would set people free. Not exactly her experience, but she wasn't a person of faith the way her father had been. And she was far more flawed.

"Call us Sarah and Taryn. I was so sorry to hear of your loss. Your father was such a good man, well respected. His loss is a loss for all of us."

"Thank you, Sarah." Gin hugged his mom back and smiled at his dad. "I go by Gin now."

Not Ginny. Too many memories. But she would not look at Rohan to see if he took her point. She would definitely not look. She looked.

"Some things never change," Sarah noted softly, and Gin inwardly cringed at her obviousness.

Grimacing at the crunch of snow, Lucas made his way to her side. Both Taryn and Sarah looked at Lucas, her and then Rohan. She felt the heat prickle her scalp before washing down her cheeks, neck and chest. What was worse in their minds, knowing she'd been a partier abandoning her morals in an attempt to forget or thinking that she'd kept a grandchild from them?

"Change is inevitable," Gin said feeling more awkward

by the moment. She and Lucas didn't belong in this homecoming tableau.

And then it went silent again. What was up with all the Telfords? It was like everyone was trying too hard to be on their best behavior. Or it actually reminded her of high school theater, opening night when someone missed their cue, and everyone got momentarily thrown off. She'd been the fixer then. And apparently even over a decade later, she still needed to step into that role.

"Rohan was on his way home to surprise you when he saw me and Lucas at the Harry's House Annex about to tackle the first big project, and Rohan being Rohan, he stopped to help." Her smile felt like she'd stretched it with a coat hanger. "And then Boone brought snacks, rounded up other volunteers, worked through to the early afternoon and then invited me and Lucas to pick out a Christmas tree with all of you and have a sleigh ride."

When would she shut up?

Both his parents pivoted their attention back on Rohan, while Boone fidgeted with his keys. His curious gaze kept bouncing between the major players—his parents and Rohan—but nobody else stepped in to fill the silence. Boone looked at Piper.

"Welcome home, Rohan." Piper stepped up and hugged him. "I was thrilled when Boone said you were home for a visit. I hope you can stay at least for Christmas. It will be the most blessed one ever."

Piper smiled and then stepped back and slid her hand into Boone's. Reid stared at the strangers and envy slid through Gin. This family could have been hers. Should have been hers. Their child would have been Parker and Arlo's age now, even though she'd tried not to think of that this morning during the work party.

"How long are you home for, son?" his dad asked.

"Dear, let's just savor the moment." Sarah gave Rohan another hug, and then stepped back to slide her arm around her husband's waist.

"C'mon in, all of you. I have coffee cake in the oven for after we find our Christmas trees." Her gaze warmly lit on Lucas, who was squatting beside Mystery trying to teach her to shake.

"Riley's inside still working on her chili entry for our annual tradition." Sarah smiled. "Boone and Piper's is already filling the house with delicious smells. Miranda and Witt made their entry last night because he's on call this weekend, but now everyone is here." She wiped her eyes. "Home. Safe where we all belong. Together."

"ROHAN!" THE FRONT door banged open and Riley ran, slipping, but agilely recovering, with a hop and a skip. She hurtled into him just like she had as a kid.

Usually, he'd pretend to stagger a little—it had been part

of the game, except she was so much thinner than she'd been when he'd seen her last that he held on tightly, but carefully, not wanting to bruise her. She'd moved back home from LA over two years ago. He knew she'd come home emotionally wounded and ill, but when they'd texted or FaceTimed, she'd always been smiling, full of local news and happy to be back on the ranch working with horses and their mom again. But it had worried him she'd hardly ever mentioned music. As a kid she'd always been singing, making up songs, writing things down. She and Ginny had bonded over lyrics or couplets and Ginny had always been a supportive sounding board for the much younger Riley.

"Okay, let me breathe now."

Riley let go and stepped back. She looked so much like a younger version of their mom that it took him a moment to find his voice again—not that he had to. Riley peppered him with questions.

"Why didn't you tell us you were coming? How long are you home for? Can you stay through Christmas?" She looked at their mom. "Don't worry, Mom. I'll get everything fixed up."

But it was the last statement that snagged his attention.

He looked at Riley, who smiled hugely. "I don't really need a studio and Petal can bunk with me. It will be fun. The single girls. Petal and I can hit Big Z's for man-color paint after we find our Christmas trees." She laughed, but it sounded a bit forced. "I can't imagine you'll love the lavender Petal and I chose for your old room. That would be one hit too many for your soldier cowboy man card."

"What about my room?" He'd been unable to track everything Riley had said, but then he was distracted when his older, half-brother Witt walked out of the house with his wife, Miranda. He had his arm around her, and she was visibly pregnant and moving slowly but smiling in welcome. His cousin—their adopted daughter, Petal—held her other hand and looked shyly toward the gathered group. Petal carried two-year-old Cannon, whom Rohan had only met through video calls.

It thumped him then—not only how long he'd been gone, but also how out of touch he'd let himself become. Two marriages. Two nieces. A nephew. Three more babies on the way. Riley back from her world-touring rock-star turn.

"My room?" he asked again into the sudden tension.

"Not a problem," his mother said quickly. "We have plenty of space always. Easily sorted."

His warning radar pinged again. He remembered feeling something about Boone was off after he'd adjusted to the initial shock of his reappearance. Boone had questioned him several times about why no notice and how long he was home.

"What's up about my room?" As ludicrous as it sounded, he felt the need to get everything out in the open. Never once had he questioned that he'd have his room at the ranch if he ever needed it.

"No big deal." Boone grinned and waved his hand as if sweeping the question into oblivion where it belonged. "So should we giddyap with the vintage Christmas tree hunt and launch the sleigh's maiden voyage now or do we want to get Rohan's digs sorted first? Tired, brother?"

Rohan looked at all of them. His father went to speak but said nothing. Witt shifted, frowning, and Miranda patted his arm. Piper caught her breath and smoothed her daughter's messy hair. His family had always been tight, had each other's backs, and never had he felt so much on the outside.

"I wasn't planning on going tree hunting this year," Miranda said. "I can stay back and help you, Sarah, with…"

"Absolutely not." Witt finally spoke. "You are supposed to be off your feet as much as possible, and paint fumes, I don't think so."

"Twins," Miranda said, brushing her belly with her palm. "They're starting to cooperate more. I'm feeling better," she told her husband.

"Let's keep it that way."

"But there are other ways I can help, Sarah," she added softly.

"I can help as well," Piper said quickly. "If you think you can handle two monkeys, Petal."

"Of course." Petal waved at Reid, who wiggled to get down from Boone's arms.

"What's going on?" Rohan asked more forcefully.

"It's nothing, sweetie," his mom said, and Rohan's jaw dropped. Sweetie? Like he was twelve. He was a Special Forces...nothing. Not anymore. And he didn't feel like a cowboy yet, either. He looked at Ginny to see if she was laughing at the endearment, but she wasn't. She looked as uncomfortable as he was feeling.

"Just a glitch," his mom said. "Easily handled with a few deft waves of my magic wand."

"So who wants first ride in the sleigh?" Boone the peacemaker stepped into the burbling tension. "Mom? Dad?"

"We'll stay behind this year," Taryn said, his arm around his wife. "Let you young people reconnect and have fun."

His mom nodded and smiled, but he thought there was a tinge of regret.

"Why don't we all go?" Rohan spoke into the undercurrent of tension. "It's always been a family outing."

"I really..." Ginny started then lapsed into silence, looking guilty.

Everyone's attention swiveled to him, and Rohan took a deep breath.

"I guess a surprise wasn't such a great idea," he said tasting each bitter word.

He'd been anxious about coming home, but he'd thought that was just him, not in reality a problem, yet he hadn't been a tight part of the Telford clan for almost fourteen years, now.

Everyone spoke up, objecting to that conclusion, like he'd known they would. Polite. Loving. Even when in a socially awkward situation he'd thrust them all into with his habitual secrecy.

"I should have let you know," he admitted. "It was last minute." Lie. "And my training." He shrugged and tried for a smile. "I can sleep on the couch. Or the floor. I've slept in worse." Not a lie. "So, let's see this sleigh and go murder some evergreens. We need six trees this year."

"Six?" Boone blinked.

"Yes, six." He felt reckless. Angry though he couldn't pinpoint why. "One for Ginny and Lucas's house. One for Harry's House and one for the annex. One for Mom and Dad's and one each for your house and Witt's."

"Oh. Ummmm," Boone said. "About that…"

"Finally. About that." He took an aggressive step forward, tired of not being in the loop even though he knew, absolutely that this was his own fault. And acting like a jerk wasn't helping.

What would Jace do?

Not make everyone uncomfortable.

"Rohan." Ginny's hand was on his arm, and he looked down into her face.

She smiled at him and then looked at Boone and her scrutiny speared his entire family.

"Rohan's been traveling for several days, and then he

stopped to help me this morning and worked flat out. Say what you want to say because y'all are acting kinda weird, and that's not what he needs from his family during his Christmas homecoming."

The hope he'd felt earlier in the truck expanded in his chest. Ginny was still hurt and mad, but that didn't stop her from defending him.

"Sorry, Rohan." Riley hugged him again hard, and her voice ached with tears. "We are so happy, so thrilled that you are home on leave. We're just shocked."

Now was probably the time to correct the 'home on leave' impression, but something held him back.

"But happy. Joyful," his mother said. "We have a full house right now, but I am queen of logistics so that is *not* a problem," she added.

And then the explanations tumbled over each other. Boone and Piper were remodeling their house—busting out a wall to expand—another bedroom, playroom and bathroom. Witt and Miranda's house had been damaged by a tree falling. Essentially his entire family was housed at the ranch house.

"You're bursting at the seams," he noted.

"I can check to see if the Graff has a suite," Witt offered. "That's where I stayed when I first moved to town, how I re-met Miranda." A ghost of a smile touched his mouth. "With my call schedule it's convenient to the hospital, Petal's school and Miranda's shop—to check in only," he added.

"Yes, Doctor," Miranda said demurely, her eyes laughing at his protectiveness.

His mom, dad and Riley each voiced a protest he was on board with.

"Unnecessary. You should all be together, especially at Christmas." He wasn't aware that he'd taken a step back until he felt himself bump into Ginny. Her hand splayed on his back. "Family should be together."

"You're family too, Rohan," his father said. "We will make it work."

"Easily and happily," his mom added.

"Exactly." Riley nodded her head. "We'll have it sorted by tonight and with style. I haven't had a slumber party in a long time." Riley fist-bumped Petal as if a teen girl would happily give up her privacy.

Rohan felt the need for action. Too much standing around. Too much talking.

"So, four trees." He had to get this show on the road, or he was going to lose it, whatever it was. He'd promised Ginny and Lucas a sleigh ride, and they were at least going to get that.

"Five," Piper finally spoke up. "We're participating in a fundraiser Christmas tree auction this year. We haven't picked a theme yet, so that is up for debate—maybe homecoming," she said softly.

"Brilliant, baby." Boone kissed her. "Only one of the many reasons why I married you."

His family's tension began to ease, and Rohan pretended his did too. Maybe Ginny would be right. This awkward part wouldn't last. His way of being with his family—a habit of eighteen years would come back. He'd find himself and rebuild his life on the ranch like he'd always imagined.

Mystery was tentatively meeting the other ranch dogs while Boone was bossing everyone about who would take the first shift in the sleigh, or one of the ATVs or snowmobiles. It was then that he noticed Lucas silently crying, which looked kinda freaky.

"What's up buddy?" he asked, crouching down next to Ginny who was coaxing Lucas to use his words.

What was up with that? The kid was only a year or two younger than Petal, and she always seemed chatty and with it, almost like an adult when he'd FaceTimed his family.

"Gramps let me hold the saw last year, and he said this year, I could help cut."

"I know we all will miss your gramps, Lucas," Rohan said. "But I gotta admit to you, I haven't cut down a Christmas tree in a lot of years, and I'm going to need some help. Will you be my partner this year? Show me how you and your gramps did it?"

"For reals?" Lucas sniffed and wiped at the few tears with the back of Rohan's tactical gloves. Rohan's heart gave a funny lurch.

"For reals." He'd never said such a ridiculous thing in his life.

"Okay," Lucas said after a pause, and Rohan looked at Ginny, wondering if she'd be mad that he'd overstepped again.

He couldn't read her at all. Her eyes looked so navy—dark and fathomless, and then he saw the glitter of tears on the tips of her lashes, quivering. He had a mad impulse to kiss them away and barely stopped himself.

Instead of pulling away or standing, she stayed crouched in the snow looking at him until one tear slipped down her cheek. He caught it with a finger.

"Let's go find us some evergreen Christmas trees," he whispered.

Chapter Eight

"It's like we're in a Christmas movie," Petal said, as the snow drifted down in fat flakes as they stood next to the sleigh posing for pictures.

Gin couldn't argue with that assessment. She was also trying hard to focus on her maternal role so the sleigh ride wouldn't seem romantic. After much jockeying for position, she and Lucas were riding in the sleigh with Riley, Petal and the two little kids—Reid and Cannon—and then Riley had insisted that there was plenty of room for Rohan too.

And that meant touching.

She carefully poured out hot chocolate into the small thermos cups that thankfully had lids. She tried to ignore the two hot chocolates Lucas had had earlier in the day. She didn't want to be the buzz-kill mom. Lucas had been moving a lot this morning with Parker and Arlo, loading up the trucks for the dump runs. Who was she kidding? She was the buzz-kill mom—always worrying, bracing for the next social disaster or emotional meltdown.

She'd already seen the weird looks Rohan had shot her when she—no doubt in his mind—over-reacted to something Lucas was or wasn't doing. So what? Rohan and his uninformed opinion was nothing to her. Except her father had calmly urged her to ease up over the past couple of years—stop trying to make Lucas fit in another mold. 'He is who he is,' her father had said with a smile, 'and who he will be. Stop shooting for the mythical normal.'

As a teacher she knew there was a huge range in children's development. But she also saw how the so-called misfits were treated, and some nights she couldn't sleep as anxiety about Lucas's future beat at her. And now she had no father to provide the warmth, humor or perspective.

"Hey, slacker." Rohan gently bumped her with his shoulder as he rounded the sleigh to help Boone hitch up the horses. "You're falling down on hot chocolate duty."

Gin looked at Riley standing next to the lined-up cups. She brandished whipped cream.

"Oops."

"You got caught dreaming." Riley made a kissy face.

"Oh. No." She had to shut that down, willing her cheeks to not blush. "He… We…" What exactly was she trying to say? "Ah just stopped by at the annex and saw…"

Riley rolled her eyes. "Give it up, Gin. Rohan comes home after years away and before he heads home, drives down memory lane and 'happens to see you.'" She made air quotes. "Yeah. Nothing to see there."

"But…" She paused. She didn't want to mention the letter—the one she wouldn't read. "It's not like that," Gin insisted, feeling her cheeks burn.

She finished pouring the drinks, trying not to watch Rohan, but how could she not? The way he moved in the snow and how he took his gloves off to stroke a horse's neck and scratch its ears. She even stared as his lips moved as he spoke softly to the horse and remembered how he would whisper private things to her. And then there was the happy visual of how his butt filled out his Wranglers when he bent down to hitch up the two horses. Rohan was irresistible eye candy. She spilled some hot chocolate in the snow and kicked at it. Riley smirked.

"You never seen a cowboy before? This town is full of them."

But none of them had drawn her attention before or since Rohan.

Riley squirted the whipped cream and then wielded a bottle of red and pink crystalized sugar sprinkles.

"Lucas doesn't like sprinkles," she said quickly. "The texture."

Petal took the can of whipped cream and the sprinkles from Riley and held it high above her head, and mouth open, she squirted some in her mouth and then shook out sprinkles. She laughed.

"Oh, try them Lucas," Petal said, her face blissful. "They're crunchy, and with the whipped cream it's a party in your mouth."

Frowning, Lucas looked at the hot chocolates and then at Petal wielding the bottles like an overeager gunslinger.

"I'll try," he said taking a cup and holding it out. "Please," he added. "Thank you, Petal."

Gin stared at her son—he was trying something new. And he'd said 'please' and 'thank you,' something she was forever prompting him to do.

"Let's load up," Boone said after the two beautiful grullo quarter horses had been hitched to the sleigh. The horses' coats gleamed gray in contrast to the lightly falling snow. The horses tossed their heads as if eager to be off and the few bells sewn onto one of the straps jingled, which delighted the two little ones.

Boone and his dad ducked into the barn to return for some blankets and as Gin helped Lucas, she asked him if he wanted his noise-canceling headphones. Lucas paused, looked at the two little ones being handed into the sleigh by Rohan and then the bells and then Petal.

"Not yet," he said, settling down in a corner of the sleigh across from Petal, who held one of the kids on her lap and was already sharing her hot chocolate. "Petal said we are going to sing Christmas carols."

Great. Gin hadn't sung since high school choir and youth group at the church except in the shower. Rohan had had a beautiful voice. For Lucas, the choir programs had been torture. He'd stood on the riser, hands over his ears, mouth closed and every year she'd heard a few audience members speculating or quietly laughing about 'that kid.'

She fingered his headphones in her purse. "Okay." She

tried to smile like she wasn't worried. "Let me know."

She still stood outside the sleigh, looking at the two steps up. She wasn't sure where to put her hand, and didn't want to look ungraceful, and in truth she was more than a little nervous about the ride, and about how Lucas would take it, but he was looking all around, his eyes shiny with wonder and curiosity, and she wondered when exactly she'd turned into such a dud.

"You're overthinking it." Rohan's voice tickled her cheek and his strong hands gripped her hips, and easily lifted her into the sleigh, before he followed her in.

"I notice I didn't get an up and personal assist," Riley noted, hopping up after Rohan had settled next to Gin like he belonged there.

She stuck her tongue out at her brother.

"That's why," he said.

Riley laughed and pulled her nephew Cannon on her lap. "Piper, there's plenty of room," Riley said.

"Are you kidding?" Piper laughed. "I can ride with reunited lovebirds and a bunch of kids or sit up high next to my man. Hmmmmm. The dilemma."

"Darn straight." Boone lifted his wife onto the seat. "Behave," he said to the bundled-up group in the sleigh.

With a quick tap of the reins, they were off.

"I do overthink," Gin admitted.

"We have that in common," Rohan said, his green eyes more serious than she'd expected. "Maybe we could make a pact this Christmas. Less thinking, more doing."

Her mind immediately slid into the sexual zone, and she kicked it out, but the moment seemed more intimate than it should considering that they were surrounded by his family.

"What does this promise entail?" She tried to keep her tone light, but it was hard to breathe. "A pinkie swear? A to-do list?"

"Enough of lists," Rohan said. "I have lived my life and career with lists. And now Jace's list. But the pinkie swear works." Rohan held up his hand, his pinkie straight up.

Gin worried everyone was watching them, wondering, but wasn't that the point of this childish promise?

She touched her pinkie to his, and his finger curled around hers.

"I promise…" he vowed in a deep voice that shot through her body like a flaming arrow.

He was waiting for her to speak. What did she want? What changes did she need to make as the promise of the holidays whispered and the new year beckoned?

"I promise to try to find joy in the small moments."

"Joy," he repeated, a question in his eyes, and for a moment he looked so sad that Gin worried she too would become teary when she hadn't cried in years before her father passed.

"I knew this Christmas was going to be so hard because of my father passing, but already, I feel more like I can do this—get Harry's House Annex ready for the first class, keep it going for my father's legacy."

The warmth in his eyes pushed her on. She still hurt for his awkward homecoming. "Thank you, Rohan, for helping today, and for including me and Lucas in your family outing. This can be my reminder to seek out joy and connection, not just tackle work and hard things."

And then as Rohan continued to hold her pinkie and look at her, Riley and Petal began to sing 'Joy to the World.'

It took a moment for Gin to find her voice—a rusty, faltering, half-whisper, to remember the words, and then Rohan's baritone joined in. Petal googled the words on her phone and handed the lyrics to Lucas, and when Gin heard her son's still-childish voice pipe up, she sang out into the chilly air as the horses trotted across one of the pastures toward the foothills on the ranch.

"Timber!" Petal shouted falling backward off a stump, spreading her arms wide and swishing the snow.

Now the snow was really coming down and Rohan paused, marveling. It had been how long?

"Try it, Lucas." Petal stuck out her tongue to catch the flakes.

Lucas was doing the tapping thing again on his thigh, the same peculiar pattern, his face scrunched in concentration as if listening to something far away.

"We can be angels," Petal encouraged and held out a hand to be hauled upright by her adoptive father.

It still seemed unreal that his sullen half-brother Witt, who'd turned his remote teen persona into high art, had not only married the cheeriest chatterbox in the high school, but was a father and had moved back to Marietta as well. Witt had come to live with them when he'd been twelve after his mother's death. He'd been highly academic, scornful about life on the ranch, irritated by his fascinated siblings and determined to leave them and Marietta behind forever when he'd headed off to college. But now he had a thriving orthopedic practice at the local hospital, and Boone had informed him while Rohan had stalked off to the wrong barn to retrieve the horses—which still stung—that Witt had bought land contiguous to the Telford Family Ranch. Boone too had property, and he'd enthusiastically discussed the nonprofit he'd created for at-risk youth to learn ranching and rodeo skills in the summer.

"I'll give you a tour of the ranch tomorrow."

Boone's promise still rang in his ears—a tour of his family's ranch.

"You ready?" Witt asked him.

Rohan startled back into the present and realized Witt held the netting so that they could wrap up the first tree that had been chosen. His lean features were stamped with seriousness, and Rohan wondered what had brought him back and why he'd stayed. He'd made no effort to reconnect with Witt on the calls home, he thought guiltily.

"Been a while since I've seen snow."

"Big adjustment coming home."

So Witt. Factual. Succinct. Witt efficiently wrapped the tree and the net slid out of Rohan's gloves.

"Took me a few months to get my head straight."

Rohan blinked. Witt was sharing?

"Take your time. Telfords play the long game."

"Yeah." Rohan wasn't sure what to make of the advice from his older brother, who now seemed to embrace the ranch life. He was lean and fit and comfortable with the tools and equipment.

"Miranda helped my re-entry." Witt watched Ginny wandering around with Lucas and Petal and likely discussing tree possibilities.

"Wait, are you giving me romantic advice or something?"

"It's my big-brother moment. How'd I do?"

Rohan wasn't sure if Witt was joking or not.

"Miranda will expect a full report." Witt tied off the net, pulling the branches of the tree in tight.

It would have been easier if Rohan had held on to his piece of the net, but he was so shocked by Witt's conversation. "Cut the next piece of netting. Temp's dropping, and I want to still have all my toes after this family bonding outing."

Rohan cut several more lengths of netting to wrap the trees. He and Witt loaded the first tree onto the trailer hitched to one of the ATVs, and then wrapped two others without conversation.

"I was a jerk in high school," Witt said after they loaded two more on the trailer.

"You were a jerk longer than that," Rohan said, thinking of Witt's sulky silences and closed bedroom doors, and how his arrival had booted Rohan out of his oldest sibling spot. "But I didn't make it easier on you," he admitted.

"People—women—are more forgiving than you can imagine," Witt said. Again his gaze strayed to Ginny, Lucas and Petal. "I've been home in Marietta five years now."

"More big-brother advice?" Rohan wasn't sure how he felt about that.

"Gin's a complicated woman, strong and determined, and community-focused. Her kid's got issues, but don't we all?"

Rohan was tempted to ask about the issues, but he felt Ginny should be the one to tell him—if she felt the need, and he knew then that he really wanted to regain her trust. Be a part of her life again, even if he had no idea how he was going to manage that. Jace would tell him to get off his ass and make a plan. Take the first step.

"Besides, I turned out okay," Witt said flatly.

Again, Rohan had no clue if Witt was making a joke or stating what he felt was a fact.

"Jury's out on that," he teased and shoulder-checked Witt as he walked by. "Let's go wrestle more trees, brother."

WHAT WERE ROHAN and Witt talking about? They both looked so serious. Well, Witt always looked like that. She didn't know him that well—he'd been at college when she and Rohan had been dating, but since she'd started picking up a weekend shift at Miranda's boutique at the Graff for some extra money, she and Miranda had become friends, so she'd seen a bit more of Witt. Miranda had also encouraged her to talk to Witt about Lucas as she saw some parallels in their behavior and take on the world. So far she hadn't found the courage to do that, but knowing that Witt probably was on the spectrum, and yet was a successful doctor and happily married and a father, did give her hope. She was just too afraid to have it extinguished.

She and Riley followed the kids as they examined each tree. Lucas so far hadn't 'found their tree.' Petal had started the snow angel game on one of the stumps, and the two littles enthusiastically threw themselves off the stump over and over. Lucas looked doubtful.

"Just fall, Lucas," Petal encouraged.

"Fall, fall, fall." Cannon jumped next to him. "I catch you."

"I will too if you want," Petal added, "but we'll mess up the snow angel's wings."

"Thank you, you two," Gin said. "Lucas, you don't need to make a snow angel if you aren't feeling it, but if you'd like to try, I'll do it with you—hold your hand or I will catch you."

Lucas shifted on the stump, clutching his hands together, muttering, clearly nervous and undecided. His tapping was more pronounced. Her father had taught him that instead of the excited hand flapping.

"Hey, Lucas, ready to help me find the tree for the annex while you look for the perfect tree for you and your mom?" Rohan walked up, brandishing a saw and looking like a model in a ranching catalog. "I'm not your gramps, but I knew him well. He was one of my teachers in high school, and he helped me with my college applications."

"I'm going to college," Lucas puffed up. "My mom's working extra at a store to help get us there."

Gin nearly groaned as Lucas repeated that tidbit—in the exact words she'd used soon after she'd taken the second job when she'd realized how much the two mortgages would eat up of her monthly income. She wished she'd realized what her father had done, but really, what would it have changed? He'd always been giving—including to her and Lucas. She didn't dare look at Rohan to see how he felt about that information—not that it was any of his business.

"How big?" Rohan fell into step with her. "Cross said the house is getting a major facelift. Is a tree practical this year?"

She relaxed. This was a much safer subject than her suddenly more insecure finances. "Yes, it is. We are going to have a soft opening for kids to see the space and Boone is going to teach the first class."

"In what?"

"Engine repair, car maintenance, and in the spring he's going to open up the shop behind the annex for some trade work—electrical and welding—and then he's going to restore a classic truck that he and my father bought at an auction. Boone really has been working more with at-risk teens, both with his foundation and now with the annex."

She did a double take. Rohan had a really weird look on his face. Surely that wasn't news. She remembered that Rohan had had a gift repairing anything mechanical. He'd been a TA for her father, and he'd often worked odd jobs repairing heavy equipment on neighboring ranches. He'd often brought Boone with him.

"Boone's really grown up. You taught him so much." She wanted to lighten the mood that suddenly seemed heavy between them.

"Yeah," Rohan said. "Boone's impressive."

She wondered what was bothering him—something she'd said? Rohan had had endless patience with his younger brother always tagging along. And Boone had worshipped him, wanted to do everything Rohan did.

"If you want to have a friendly competition with your brother, we'll need more volunteer teachers for classes once the annex is complete," she teased. The look he shot her curled her toes, even as she realized she had no idea how long he was home.

Was he going to run back into danger again? The thought made her stumble. Of course he caught her elbow. He stared into her eyes, and she stared back and something passed between them, more than the puffs of chilled air.

"Maybe I will," he shocked her by saying. Then he stalked past her. "Lucas, I see a possibility up ahead."

She watched as Lucas ran after Rohan, hopping in each one of the man's large boot prints.

The two of them discussed the tree and were joined by Boone and Petal while the little kids and their grandparents and Riley engaged in a quick snowball fight before Sarah and Riley separated and began cutting and collecting swatches of greenery and twigs in a large canvas tote.

It was so painfully perfect. The happy family. The snow. The holiday activities. The camaraderie. The traditions being passed down.

"Lovely, isn't it." Sarah paused by her.

Gin nodded, not trusting her voice to speak. She watched as Rohan lay on his back under a tree while Lucas sprawled on his belly next to him, listening intently. Petal took pictures. Witt held the tree up; Boone squatted on his haunches next to Rohan and Lucas. Mystery and three ranch dogs bounded through the snow, excited by all the activity.

This is what my life should have been.

"It's like something you'd see in a snow globe," she whispered.

The vision hurt as much as it felt magical.

"If you're on the outside looking in," Sarah noted. "But maybe you don't want to stand outside any longer, Ginny."

Gin stared at the woman who had served as a mother figure when she'd been a teenager as she'd had no memory of her own to guide her.

"Want to help me gather some greenery to make some wreaths for the ranch and Harry's House and, yes, your father's beloved annex dream?" Sarah held out pruning shears.

Gin's hand closed over the tool, and she turned to follow Sarah up a hill and a little deeper into the stand of trees, but it took several attempts to blink away her tears.

Chapter Nine

"You and Lucas are welcome to stay for dinner, Virginia," his mom said warmly.

"Oh, thank you, Sarah, but I need to get back," Ginny said quickly, not quite meeting his mom's eyes. "We need to get the trees in water and up at Harry's House and the annex, and I've got papers to grade."

"It's a holiday weekend," Sarah protested. "And your first without your…"

"I know. I know. Thank you." Ginny's voice was firm, and she looked like a racehorse about to bolt. She bit her thumb and then quickly stuck her hand in her pocket. "Sorry, Rohan. I should have driven."

"I'll drive you and Lucas home," Rohan said firmly.

"Wait, wait, Lucas." Petal paused as she measured out food for each of the ranch dogs while Lucas filled up the water bowls. "You need to download BeReal first. You can be in the group with me, Parker, Arlo and Montana."

"Why?"

Petal's eyes bugged. "It's fun to see what your friends are up to," she said. "Remember when I snapped a picture of us in the sleigh, and it looked like a Christmas card?"

Lucas squatted down and pet Mystery. "I don't have friends or a phone."

The whole room quieted, and it seemed to Rohan that everyone held their breath, except Ginny who made a weird sound as if her lungs had sprung a leak.

"Oh, Lucas," Ginny began.

"You have me," Petal said. "And Parker. And Arlo. And Montana's just a year younger, but she's super smart and artistic. And you have Mystery."

"I still don't have a phone," Lucas said.

"Let's go, bud. Thank you, everyone," Ginny said brightly. "We had a lovely day. Thanks so much for including Lucas and me."

And Ginny was out the door.

"You're coming back for chili dinner, right?" his mom asked, blue eyes worried.

"Of course," he said, but he could feel the pull toward Ginny and Lucas more strongly. "I'll drop Ginny and Lucas off. Help with the tree, and then I'm going to check in with a couple of buddies from my unit, but I'll be back for chili, and don't worry about the room. Couch is fine."

"But…"

"It's fine. Besides, Boone gave me an idea."

"I did?" His brother looked uncomfortable.

"Weird. I know," Rohan said, and it felt good to tease his brother, not play so much defense. "Mystery, let's roll." He tapped his leg, and the dog, finishing off its small portion of food, ran to his side, and Rohan looked around the room—his mom and Riley in the kitchen with Piper making corn bread and a salad. Boone on the computer looking over something with their dad. Witt scrolling on his laptop looking at his patients for the next day. Miranda playing an I Spy game with the younger kids. This was home. This was what he had given up. This was what he had to build a bridge back to.

But first, he needed to forge a path back to Ginny. Right the wrongs he had done.

Ginny and Lucas waited by his truck.

He opened her door to the truck and helped her up. She hadn't yet put her gloves on so he could feel the warmth of her palm, the strength of her fingers. He'd always liked it that Ginny was tall and athletic. Not fragile. And she'd been game for anything—hiking, kayaking on the Yellowstone River, riding, bouldering, pickup basketball or touch football with friends.

"I'd forgotten how…nice your family is."

"Nosy and loud," he'd inserted into her hesitation at the same time she spoke.

"Nice," Ginny reasserted. "You buckled?" she asked Lucas.

He nodded, turned away from them. Rohan lifted Mystery up into the truck, not sure if the dog yet had the strength to make it. After the tree hunting, Mystery had been limping and had seemed exhausted, and so she'd ridden back in the sleigh, curled up and serving as a canine foot warmer.

Rohan headed away from the ranch, cranking up the heat, and wishing he didn't have an audience because there was so much he wanted to say to Ginny, and no idea how to begin. He drew in a deep, pine-scented breath.

"Thank you. I had fun."

"Yeah." He tried to relax his expression and his body, but he was wound up tight—tighter than he'd been on missions.

If Jace hadn't died, he wouldn't be in the truck with Ginny. And if her father hadn't passed, he wouldn't be here either.

Fate was a mercurial bitch, and it was laugh or cry. But he'd learned one thing as a cowboy growing up, which had been reinforced as a soldier—run through the opening. Ginny required honesty.

"Today was overwhelming," he said. "Everyone on the ranch. Happy. Witt even tried to give me big-brotherly advice twenty-some years too late."

Ginny turned to stare at him. "What was it?"

Rohan waved off Witt's advice, but he felt like an engine warming up. He hadn't talked this much in a long time, and it felt good. "And Boone's all grown up—married, a dad, working hip to shoulder with my dad on the ranch, and volunteering with teens, just like my dad used to help out local 4-H groups."

"Did it feel strange to be back after so many years away?"

He stared straight ahead as he neared the junction to

leave Telford land and turn right to meet up with the highway into town.

"I felt like an outsider," he finally admitted. It had been his fear, but he hadn't expected it to manifest so fully. "I remember something your dad said to me once." He pulled up the memory. "That if you stare your biggest fear in the face and embrace it, it loses power."

"That sounds like something he'd say." She glanced back at Lucas, who seemed to be ignoring them. He pet Mystery in that rhythm that Rohan had noticed, but Mystery moaned and laid her head on Lucas's thigh.

He wondered if he could ask about the boy.

Ginny clenched her hands together on her lap as if nervous. Being with her had always felt effortless, but she had been the one to make it easy. She'd been warm, accepting, trusting, full of ideas and love. And when things had gotten hard, he hadn't picked up the slack. He hadn't tried. He'd run.

"Today was…worse than I imagined," he said softly. "It was good seeing everyone so happy, but…everything's different. Even the ranch. So much has changed—different barn and arena for the horses. New equipment. New practices. A partnership breeding bulls with the Wilders. Boone has started a nonprofit for at-risk kids. Riley and my mom have started breeding and training cutting horses. The ranch is organic, and my dad's traveling some as a stock contractor."

"You've been gone a long time, Rohan."

Her voice was soft in the late afternoon. The snow had stopped, but there'd been enough of a fall that the tires sounded muted on the gravel road. Everywhere he looked was white, and the sky a light gray.

"Maybe too long," he mused. "Boone offered to give me a tour of the ranch."

He meant to make it sound like a joke, but it fell flat.

"Take it," she advised. "Baby steps. It will get easier if you stick with it." She turned away and stared out the window.

IT WAS STUPID to feel like crying.

She'd shed enough tears—over losing Rohan, their child, the future she'd envisioned as a poet, the ideal of a perfect son, and now her father. What a waste. She had so much to be thankful for. She was alive, healthy, had a child she loved, a career, responsibilities, people depending on her, her father's legacy to build. Now Rohan was back, which reminded her of how empty her life felt sometimes—like a gaping wound. She had to pull herself together.

"I know you came back to deliver the letter from Jace." She should just take it, but something had stopped her, and she realized—looking at Rohan's starkly beautiful profile, which would have looked historically epic on a coin—what. If she took the letter, Rohan would leave. He wouldn't fight for them, but he'd fight for his fallen brother's last request.

The epiphany chilled her, yet exhilaration skidded down her spine.

"How long are you home for?" She needed to create boundaries.

"I'm out."

"Out?" She breathed the word as if she had no idea of its meaning. "Out as in finished with the military?"

He nodded.

"Done?"

"Finished," he affirmed. "Turned in my papers."

"No more playing hero."

"I'm not a hero."

She sighed. She was being a bitch. "I don't mean to be insulting," she said softly, looking at her fingers twisting in her lap. "I just…the way you left… The danger. I wanted to…" she glanced back "…hate you, but I was so frightened you'd get injured or worse."

She hadn't wanted to imagine a world without Rohan in it even if she could never have him.

"I steered clear of your family, but word gets around even though your dad is modest. I heard about your medals and commendations and promotions. Everyone in town was so proud of you."

She'd been proud too in the heart she'd hidden away. Of course Rohan would be successful at everything he did. "But I was scared. Your mother too was always terrified that she'd be working in the vegetable garden and look up and see someone from the military walking up to her front door."

"Always thought that was the way I'd go out," he admitted.

Fury roared through her. How could he be so casual about death? "How can you say that? Think that? How dare you hold your life and your family in such little regard?" Gin's voice rose, and she quickly gulped in a breath to calm down. She looked back at Lucas, but no, of course he didn't pick up on her rising tension. Instead he drew out the extended version of pi in the condensation of the window.

"You had everything to live for—a loving family, siblings, a ranch, a destiny and a birthright handed to you, opportunities, a place to belong and you just wanted to throw it all away?"

He stopped paused at the T in the rural road, even though no other vehicles were visible. He stared at her, as if he'd never seen her before.

"You were golden. Smart, athletic, charismatic, so swaggeringly hot that I practically had to trip other girls to clear a path for us when we went anywhere together." She huffed out a breath. "You had everything." Her voice broke. "And now you tell me you had some kind of a death wish?"

"I don't think I thought of it in those literal terms," he said finally, making no move to continue to drive.

"Well, that's how it sounds. Selfish and a waste. Did you give one moment to think how gutted your family would have been if you'd bled out on the other side of the world? How I would…" She snapped her lips shut. She'd given him too much of herself already. "You ran away from us to be the martyr on the cross."

He enclosed his hand around hers. "Your warrior blue eyes blazing fire, scorching me clean. When you're passionate about something your energy crackles and snaps so that your hair almost seems electrified and becomes an onyx crown. Putting the peasant in his dumb-ass muddy place."

His hand was so warm and strong, and in the truck, his scent teased her nostrils, and she wanted to draw him more deeply into her body.

"Who's the poet now?" She needed to break the spell he wove so effortlessly.

"That was you, always you."

"Was," she repeated dully. One more thing she'd lost. No. Like Rohan, she too had given away pieces of herself in the ashes of their breakup. But she was an adult, a mother, and she had to stay rooted in the present.

"I'll take the letter when you drop us home."

She wouldn't read it. But she would watch Rohan walk away and know that it would finally be their end. Closure—something her father had urged her to seek with Rohan many times, but she'd never ever felt ready to fully say goodbye.

Tonight, when she said thank you, goodbye and closed her door, it would stay closed. She felt proud of her determination, but then something in Rohan's gaze changed, warmed, and she realized he still held her hand.

"Let go," she whispered, wishing her voice sounded more forceful.

She tugged at her hand a little, but he didn't release it. She quickly looked back at Lucas—still ignoring her. That had been the hardest part about parenting. She loved him so keenly it hurt. She'd wanted his unfiltered, unconditional love. She'd wanted him to be her companion, and yet half the time he didn't seem aware of her. She'd dragged him to expert after expert, trying to get a definite diagnosis and a plan, and while the speech, occupational and physical therapies had helped Lucas reach many of his milestones, emotionally he'd often remained just out of reach.

"I'm serious," she said. "Let go."

"You're holding on to me," he said.

She narrowed her eyes and mustered her middle-school teacher expression, which only made Rohan smile, and she'd forgotten what a devastating smile he had. Her tummy flipped, and then she realized that he was right. She had flipped her hand around and had linked her fingers with his.

"Very funny. Don't make me cut myself when I slap those incredibly sharp cheekbones of yours."

"Hitting's bad," Lucas said, shocking her that he was paying attention at all.

"Sometimes," she said conversationally "it seems like the only way to make a point."

Rohan lifted their linked hands to his mouth and brushed his lips across her fingertips.

"I prefer to make my point using a different method."

"You really don't have to do this."

Ginny had been trying to get rid of him since they'd hit town. It felt like the theme of the day, but perversely, he dug his boot heels in. He'd set up the Christmas tree at Harry's House and another at the annex with Lucas acting as a directional diving rod. And now Rohan lay on the battered oak floors of Ginny's house, screwing the trunk of the tree into the holder. Ginny held the tree while Lucas stood on the couch and judged the tilt. Mystery plopped down beside him.

It hit him then how tired he was as well.

"It's fine," Ginny said even as Lucas waved him left like he was a jet taxiing to the gate. "Really, Rohan. You've done enough."

Didn't feel he'd even started down the road to redemption, but with Lucas in the room, he could hardly fillet their past for the closure he felt they both needed to finally move on, although Rohan had no intention of going anywhere.

He finished the tree and popped to his feet.

"Thank you," Ginny said. Her voice had a final tone he didn't like.

"You still wear the cowboys on the bucking bronc socks," he noted.

"Ahhhh..." For some reason Ginny blushed. "Sometimes?"

"And pink nail polish. It's cute." He'd been hella distracted by the hole in her sock and the cute toe threatening to punch all the way through. She'd been trying to play it cool with him all day, and that touch of imperfection softened her and reminded him of her tenderness.

But he couldn't get derailed. He needed her to read Jace's letter, and he needed to know that she and Lucas were taken care of now that her father had passed.

Like I should have done before.

But a couple of things had come up today that worried him.

"Tell me more about the annex," he invited.

"Rohan." She shoved her shoulders back. "It's not like I don't appreciate your help. We got so much more done today than I anticipated with the annex, but...but..." She paused and crossed her arms. "I'm happy you are home safe, but I think it's better if you find another...cause in town to support."

"Why's that?"

Her mouth dropped open. "Because," she sputtered. "It's obvious." She waved her hand almost jerkily around, and if he hadn't been so tense, he would have laughed.

"It's not obvious to me," he said, enjoying the way her

eyes rounded. He'd shocked her, which was better than indifference. She wouldn't push back so hard if she didn't have some feelings for him. He could work with anger, feelings of betrayal. Indifference was the killer.

But he could also tell he'd pushed hard today, and she was at the end of the rope. He felt the same and he still had his two Coyote Cowboys to catch up with and a family dinner before he could have some time to be alone and assess.

"I'm home. I have time. Does the board of directors of Harry's House have an application process? Are there enough volunteers that they'd pass on a skilled and willing volunteer?"

"Why are you doing this? Jace again?"

"Yes," he admitted. "But it's more than that."

"We have too much history between us," she said.

"Today went well."

"I'm exhausted," she confessed. "The day felt like a mine field."

"It will get easier. Tell me about the money. You seem stressed, and you've mentioned finances a couple of times today."

"Absolutely not," she said and looked at Lucas who sat on the floor petting Mystery. "My life is none of your business anymore. Besides, it's not your thing."

"What thing?"

"Volunteering. Community. Building things. Working

with kids. Marietta. You left it all behind and stayed away for years and years."

"Well, I'm back, Ginny." He picked up his hat from off the coffee table, placed it on his head—it felt good. He called for Mystery. Said goodbye and tipped his hat toward Ginny. "See you tomorrow."

"What?"

"You heard me. Have a pleasant evening."

Chapter Ten

"Why are we not at the Wolf Den?" Rohan demanded, already regretting reaching out to his two former teammates. They'd agreed to support each other, but neither of them had been navigating family or a crash-and-burn relationship on re-entry. It felt hella awkward admitting he was struggling even to two buddies he'd been willing to die for but discussing it in a fancy hotel bar that looked like a historic Irish pub felt impossible.

"Or FlintWorks?" Boone and his dad had taken him there once on leave when he'd come home. He'd liked the casual, slightly industrial vibe, the live music and the beer on tap. The Graff was upscale, and he felt like he'd strolled onto a movie set.

"Seriously, why here? I'd rather be gored by a rank bull than spill my guys in the fancy Graff Hotel bar surrounded by a bunch of tourists pretending to be extras on *Yellowstone*."

"Gut spilling, huh?" Cross said. "Good thing I brought backup."

Cross looked toward the lobby as Colt Ewing—who he'd learned was now going by his birth name Colt Wilder—

strolled through the fancy double doors into the hotel's lobby, turning a lot of heads. He was big, and even though he'd left the service a handful of years ago, a decorated sniper, he still pulsed with an intense edge. They'd crossed paths on a few missions, and Rohan had respected the fierce skill combined with quiet confidence. Colt had always gotten the job done with no boasting and even less conversation.

"Why'd you invite him?" Not that he minded exactly. He'd been reintroduced to Colt this morning when he and Cross had been installing refurbished cabinets and shelving in the garage at the annex.

"What's with the twenty questions?" Huck asked, kicking his legs out under the table they'd moved so that all of them could face out toward the lobby and have the wall at their backs. "You wanted to talk. Talk."

Any words he might have had dried up.

Colt angled the chair next to him and sat.

A beautiful blonde sashayed up to their table. Her unusual blue eyes sparkled with a sexy combination of flirt and mischief. She held a tray with four large mugs of beer on tap—probably Moose Drool in honor of Jace.

"First one's on the house, soldiers," she said, and Rohan nearly choked on his spit when she leaned down and kissed Cross on the lips. "Hey, gorgeous, want my number for later?" She handed him a beer, cocked a hip and smiled at Cross.

"Got it memorized." He caught her wrist and brought it to his lips.

"Get a room," Huck muttered.

"We need the whole house," Cross said easily, smiling, and Rohan stared at him. He'd worked with Cross for years and could only remember seeing him smile a couple of times—and that had been in warning.

"She's why we're here," Cross said. "Baby, meet Rohan Telford, one of the men in my unit. He just mustered out, and Huck, Colt and I are the welcome-home committee. "Rohan, my wife, Shane Knight Cross."

Rohan was glad he hadn't taken a sip of his beer yet. He definitely would have spit it out.

"Wife?"

"Wife. I don't waste time," Cross said. "Locked her down fast."

"Who said I didn't lock you down?"

"Anytime, and you can throw away the key, babe."

"Alien abduction," Rohan posited, not sure why he hadn't twigged that Cross was married when he'd seen him again this morning—probably because he'd been too tied up in knots over Ginny to pay attention to anything or anyone else.

Shane laughed and playfully pointed a finger at him. "Don't get smug, Soldier. Your time will come." She lifted the arm not holding the tray high in the air. "Timber." She let her arm fall back slowly to her side.

Rohan blinked. Was Cross's woman teasing him?

"Riley's brother, right? Riley plays in here some weekends. Rohan, nice to meet you," Shane greeted and smiled warmly. "Welcome home."

It was such a casual, expected thing for her to say, but it hit him all wrong. He didn't feel welcome, yet he knew it was his own head messing with him. His guilt and the feeling that serving had changed him so much had created a self-fulfilling prophecy.

"Thank you," he said while Cross and Huck scrutinized him.

"Anything to eat, cowboys?" Shane asked.

"No." Rohan knew this needed to be a short. "Family's expecting me for a chili cook-off supper."

"The three of us will have a bite. We've been hard at work on the annex all day. Making progress but we worked up an appetite," Cross rumbled, leaning back in his chair, legs spread out, one arm slung behind him in a deceptively relaxed pose. His gaze quartered the room as did Colt's.

Will we ever learn to relax like civvies?

"Surprise us," Cross invited.

"Love to," Shane said. She turned her attention to Colt. "How'd bodyguard duty go?"

Colt didn't change expression exactly, but somehow Rohan felt as if Colt tasted something sour.

"I was too effective, according to Kane. He loves the fan adoration. Luke appreciated my interpretation of a wall. Bodhi Ballantyne surprised us all by showing up and called me a killjoy, but his cousins Beck and Bowen didn't seem to mind. And the documentary's field producer offered me a job."

It was the most Rohan had ever heard Colt speak, even though none of it made sense. Shane laughed. "The field producer must be a woman with very good eyesight."

Colt brooded into his beer.

"Yeah, life's so hard for you," Cross said.

"The field producer lost her glasses, actually," Huck added. "Legally blind I heard."

"Epicurean surprises coming up—and you—" she pointed to Colt "—don't let Hollywood go to your head. You promised me spice racks at the annex for my cooking classes this spring to rival Martha Stewart's. And don't forget the raised beds for the veggie garden and the flower drying and arranging class Miranda's teaching next summer."

"Yes, ma'am. No, ma'am." Colt pretended to tip an imaginary hat.

"What was all that Hollywood about?" Rohan demanded, feeling more and more out of the loop. Even his friends were acting…like normal cowboys but speaking an incomprehensible language of domesticity.

"Documentary about the history of small-town rodeos in the American West," Huck said. "Marietta's Copper Mountain Rodeo was one of the featured rodeos. I got roped into an interview in September when the crew was here getting most of their rodeo footage. I was competing and supposed to walk a certain wild child barrel racer down the aisle for a wedding that never happened."

"Oh, it happened." Cross took a quick swig of beer. "Jace would have laughed at how you completed your penance...I mean duty."

"What language are you speaking?" Rohan demanded. "You're in a documentary about rodeos? Competing? Walking some random woman down the aisle? Since when?"

Huck shrugged and grinned an 'aw-shucks it's nothing' grin that had had panties flying off across the globe.

"The producer and director said I was a natural. The film is pretty much complete, but they wanted to ask a few more follow up questions, and they were out at the ranch where I work yesterday. Sure, my interview will make the final cut." Huck grinned. "Your dad and brother were interviewed as well. I met them in September during the rodeo and also at some pick up shots."

Rohan felt even more out of step.

"Hey, bro." Huck seemed to be warming up. "You never told me your dad was Taryn Telford. He still holds the record for highest score as a bull and a saddleless bronc rider. Six times Montana Champion All-Around Cowboy. Your brother Boone still bulldogs and ropes. Won Copper Mountain bulldogging past two years."

Like Rohan was not aware that he'd never once measured up to his father in saddleless bronc skills. And now his baby brother had surpassed him.

"Why you rodeoing? You had in-field medic skills better

than the medics. I figured you'd head to medical school or become a PA or RN."

"I considered it." Huck took a swig of beer. "But I love being outside too much and always had cowboy fever. Competed as a teen before I joined up, but money was too tight." He was quiet a long moment. "I mustered out early—before any of you because of—" his voice changed, went all mock professional and snooty "—*severe PTSD, interfering with higher-level cognition skills and decision-making, which could interfere with my job functions and duties*—or some professional BS like that. Trauma." He scowled. His face went dark—likely with memories of Jace being hit, and his futile effort to save him.

"Got a medal, head shrunk and an early exit, along with a pat on the back, job well done, son. I headed home to Wyoming to help a…friend, and…decided to ride for kicks and glory for a year."

Sounded like a chunk of the story was missing, and not a good part judging by the shadows in Huck's eyes. "And then I headed to Marietta for Jace, all cowboy goody-two-boots ready to take one for the team and wound up in a film, married with a stowaway already on board, gonna be a daddy early March and talked my way into a job as an assistant foreman at the Ballantynes' Three Tree Ranch. Comes with a sweet ranch house with a killer view."

Rohan waited for everyone to laugh. No one did.

"You've been competing in rodeos?"

"That's your takeaway?" Cross stared at him.

Hell, yeah that was his takeaway. He stared at Huck. He'd always liked him. He'd been quiet. A hard worker. Dependable. And now he was a cowboy. A rodeo star. Working on a ranch. Family man. Living the life that Rohan had ditched in a fury of self-flagellation.

Still, he'd developed new skills. His service had had meaning, an atonement.

"What's your deed for Jace?" Cross asked.

"We're not supposed to talk about it," Rohan reminded him, taking a sip of beer that tasted as wrong as everything felt.

Still it was only his first day. He should cut himself some slack. Jace's letter burned a brand on his ass through his Wranglers. He'd tried to be so smooth tonight, leaving Ginny on a high note, that he'd forgotten to hand over the letter.

"We can once the deed is done," Huck said. "What'd you get?" Huck's happy smile irritated him. He seemed too content, and yet he'd only mustered out a few months before him.

"Classified." He stood up, his beer mostly untouched. "Later." He growled the word and left the glimmering glamor of the bar and beckoning elegance of the restored hotel. None of it felt real.

He didn't feel real.

Rohan pulled up to the front of the equipment barn. Snow wasn't predicted tonight, but the overhang of the building would offer some protection from the weather as Paradise Valley forecasts weren't easily predictive.

He climbed out of his rental truck, his body feeling cold and stiff, not fully online with his nervous system.

Is this what it feels like to be an old man?

Mystery whined, shifting her weight on the seat and looking at him imploringly.

Her needs he could at least meet.

Rohan picked up the skin-and-bones dog, still in her booties and coat, and put her down. She quickly did her business and hastened to his side as if afraid of being left behind.

"I know what that feels like," he said ruefully, eyeing the front door to the ranch house, he'd been bracing to be flung open—his family crowding out. But while the house was lit up—white Christmas lights trimmed the roofline all the way around, and the carriage lights blazed a cheery red—the door, painted a glossy green, remained closed.

"Let's get some chow." He checked his watch. Mystery was due for her meds and another portion of food.

He didn't want to bring his duffel into the house. All the possessions he'd had for the last fourteen years away seemed pathetically small compared to everything his family had acquired and accomplished in the years he'd been away.

"One step at a time," he parroted Jace. Wolf had likely said the same thing, and if Rohan had stuck around instead of bolting on Cross, Huck and Colt, they too might have had words of advice. He hadn't asked them how the first days had been, the first weeks. He shouldn't have had to. He was home.

It was natural to feel unsettled. He'd been away a long time, and today had been a deep dive. Rationally he knew he'd adjust to his family, and they to him. He'd find a place to live, a job that felt right. He had his family. His Coyote Cowboys. He looked down at Mystery.

"And man's best friend." He scratched the dog's ears, and she leaned into him. "Although I think you've stolen the heart of a young boy, who might just need you more than I do."

His boots crunched in the snow, and he didn't bother to muffle his approach. Maybe that was all it took—taking a step like a civvy.

The door opened. Riley stood there. "Welcome back," she whispered.

"Hope you didn't wait on dinner for me," he said cautiously, bracing himself for a full-body slam like this afternoon and her entire life.

"Of course. You're the top chili judge."

He stared at his little sis, all grown up. Worry clouded her eyes, and he hated that. He'd put that there. But also he knew she'd been hurt during her rock star stint in LA, and he hadn't been there to protect her, nor had he been there when he'd come home.

"I missed you, Riley," he said honestly.

"Me too," she answered, and then she stepped into him, hugging him hard. She smelled faintly of horses and orange and cinnamon. "So much."

She finally stepped back, wiping her eyes. "I'm letting the cold in."

She had no idea he meant it literally. He followed her into the kitchen, and even that looked different. It was a great room now with a vaulted ceiling, but the large farm table set for supper was the same. Everyone had been standing around talking when he entered the room, following Riley, and they all went silent and stared at him.

The silence and stillness felt awkward, and Rohan finally understood that it was his responsibility to smooth his rough edges, his mission to fit back in with his family. He had to own his homecoming just as he had to own the mistakes he'd made with Ginny and build a bridge of peace and forgiveness between them, even if he was uncomfortably aware that he desperately wanted to build more. He'd made a promise to Jace and the Coyote Cowboys, and he wasn't going to renege or complain just because the path was stony and tangled by roots tripping him.

He'd run away trying to right his wrongs. This time he meant to stay.

Chapter Eleven

"You are a lifesaver," Gin said as Shane climbed out of her Jeep with Arlo the next morning. Each carried two to-go drink cups from the Java Café and met her and Lucas at the entrance to Big Z's.

"I get that a lot." Shane smiled and handed her a twenty-ounce hot something hopefully loaded with caffeine.

"Peppermint mocha with whip and sprinkles," Arlo said. "Sinful."

"Thank you," Gin breathed. Calorie-laden coffees around the holidays were as close to sin as she intended to get.

Lucas sniffed the cup Arlo handed him.

"No sprinkles," Arlo said. "They don't have the crunchy good ones."

Lucas lifted the lid, stared and sniffed again.

"Can you guess?" Arlo asked, and Gin wanted to hug her for not giving Lucas a look of middle-school-girl disdain.

"Uh-uh." Lucas's tongue snaked out to stab at the whipped cream.

"Peppermint hot chocolate. See the crushed candy on top? Are we really going to paint, Ms. Lane?"

"Yes we are," she said, taking an appreciative sip of her coffee. "Three bedrooms and a living room that will become classrooms or activities rooms." She still couldn't believe how much Colt and his crew of volunteers had accomplished in the house in one day. Her group had definitely stepped up getting all the trash and usable items out of the garage.

She was starting to feel less anxious.

"What colors?" Arlo asked.

"That's why we're here just as Big Z's opens. We need to choose," Gin said looking at Shane's glow. "I don't know how you do it—you work late, but still are up early enough to grab us coffee, and you're glowing."

"Love will do that," Shane said as they entered Big Z's. "Speaking of which…" Shane bumped her with her hip. "Remy and Huck had a beer last night with Rohan Telford from his former unit and said that he'd seen the two of you together in the morning at the annex and that you both seemed to have a history with a capital H."

Gin nearly spit her coffee. "I thought women were supposed to be the gossipy ones."

Shane's aquamarine eyes sparkled as they walked into the store. Arlo and Lucas had stopped to stare at all the Christmas decorations.

"Meet us in the paint section in five minutes," Gin said to the kids. Maybe that would distract Shane, but no. She was still smiling.

"Do dish," Shane encouraged.

"Nothing to dish," Gin said sourly. "Yes we have a history. Not a present."

Shane cocked her head. "Riley's over the moon her brother's home. She said that you and Lucas had joined them to get Christmas trees on their ranch."

"For Harry's House and the annex," Gin said clutching her dignity with her fingernails, and conveniently forgetting how she'd ogled Rohan sprawled on her floor setting up the Christmas tree last night.

"Hmmmmmm." Shane grabbed several sets of color swatches. "What are you thinking, blues?"

Gin wanted to kick herself. She wanted to make friends again. That meant opening herself up a little.

"Rohan and I were high school sweethearts," she admitted. "And friends before that. I thought we—" She broke off. "We went to different colleges." She strove to sound casual. "Rohan stopped off at the annex because he had a letter for my dad from one of his fallen brothers," she admitted.

"Jace McBride?" Shane's beautiful eyes lost their sparkle.

The silence felt like it had a form, like a wet sheet blanketing her.

"I didn't take it," Gin admitted and the coffee felt like acid in her tummy. "I…" She blew out a breath. "I'm angry still," she admitted. "And hurt. And mad at Rohan for giving up on us and for giving up on his dream and his family so…completely and with no explanation. He dropped me, his scholarship, his rodeo dreams, college, his family, the ranch just like that." She snapped her fingers. "And I know I'm being ridiculous. It was years ago. But now he's insisting I take this letter like it will make a difference." She huffed out a gigantic sigh that had her wanting to kick herself. "He didn't even return home to see me. He was looking for my father. Jace wrote him. And yes, I know it's stupid for me to be hurt and pissed so many years later."

"Feelings are rarely logical."

Gin scowled. "He came back and started calling me Ginny like fourteen years and a whole lot of awful never happened." She sucked in a deep breath.

She needed to reel it in. She had wanted to show Shane that she could dish a little, not throw a whole kitchen sink of dirty dishes at her. And she definitely didn't want to be the woman crying in Big Z's paint aisle at eight in the morning.

"And I'm mad at my dad for working so hard and helping so many people and then dying so suddenly just as he kicked off this whole annex dream that I'm now in charge of," she admitted, revealing herself to be as selfish as she'd accused Rohan of being.

"You're not alone on the annex," Shane said sincerely.

"I know," Gin said. But she felt alone. And she could swing the finances. She could make it work, especially with the part-time job at Miranda's store. Those earnings would go straight to college savings for Lucas.

"I need to let all this anger and hurt go. I *know* that," she said fiercely. "But I don't know how and I don't even know who I'd be without it."

Shane hugged her. She felt so warm and fragrant whereas Gin felt so rigid, like a block of wood.

"I don't even know where to start," Gin said tearfully.

"Maybe start with the letter, and maybe that will lead to an honest conversation with Rohan about your feelings."

Could she take the letter and read it? It just felt so fraught.

"A letter from a dead man to a dead man," she muttered. "That's got future written all over it. And no." Gin ripped the swatch of various light blue shades from Shane's hand and stuffed them back into the numbered slots. "We are not going with various shades of light blue. We need bold colors. We need to make a statement."

Shane smiled. "Copy that, ma'am."

"I DON'T UNDERSTAND why you're doing this," Boone said for about the fourth time since he'd arrived at dawn to find Rohan already feeding the horses and acquainting himself with the new residents.

Two Great Pyrenees had been sleeping in the barn when he'd arrived, full thermos of coffee in his hand. He hadn't been able to sleep on the couch, even with one of his mother's quilts smelling of lavender—too many memories, most of them about Ginny.

After he'd bonded with the horses, and Boone had introduced them, Rohan climbed up the stairs to the studio apartment, Boone following him, peppering him with questions like he had as a kid, only this time Rohan didn't have the answers. Rohan dimly remembered that the apartment had been used as a bookkeeping office when he'd been a kid, but once it had been an apartment for their lead horse trainer.

One wall was stacked with labeled totes. The only furniture he could see was an antique, roll-top desk, with what he thought was a yoga ball tucked under it.

"Why not just stay in the guest room?" Boone fretted. "Petal can bunk with Riley, and Riley can dismantle her studio. Witt's house should be repaired in another six weeks or so."

"It's organized," Rohan noted, dismay filtering through as he walked farther into the room. This room too was in use. Or maybe not—he opened the totes and looked at the dates on the files. Nothing looked current.

"C'mon," Boone groused. "Let's go for a short ride. Have breakfast. Catch up."

"I need to get this done. I don't mean to inconvenience you and the family."

"Inconvenience," Boone echoed.

He paused, closed his eyes and tried to recenter.

You walked away, not Boone.

He couldn't resent his little brother who'd dogged his

footsteps always for living the life he'd imagined for himself. Wanting to escape his thoughts, he walked farther around the apartment that looked more like a storage room than a functioning living space. Did it even have a kitchenette anymore? He'd have to clear out more things to find out.

Seems to be a theme.

The toilet worked. And there was a functioning shower.

Boone's boots were hard on the rough wood plank floor as he stalked after him. "What the heck is wrong with you? You're my brother. How could you ever be an inconvenience?"

Work-roughened hands seized his shoulders and spun him around. Instinct kicked in and he swung hard. His fist connected with Boone's cheek, and he was already rocking a follow-up uppercut before his brain kicked in.

Boone blocked the shot and held his fist in his hand. "Feel better?"

"No." Rohan was horrified. "I feel worse," he admitted. "Everything's wrong. I'm all wrong."

His shoulders slumped. His brother's cheek was stark white, then red as the blood rushed back. Rohan swore under his breath.

"Boone, I'm sorry. It was instinct when you grabbed me," he explained. "I'm sorry." The only thing that could have made this better was if Boone had swung back.

But no. Boone didn't even look pissed. Wary. Confused, yes. Rohan felt sick. He hadn't hit his brother ever—they'd never fought. Boone had always been sweet, good-natured, eager to learn, adoring, following Rohan and their father around, often bringing their little sister, Riley, in tow.

"Let's get you some ice."

There was going to be a bruise. He hadn't even pulled the punch. His own brother. In his family's horse barn—somewhere that should be totally a safe place.

"It's better if I move out here for a while. I need space," he admitted as he walked down the stairs.

"A thousand acres isn't enough for you?"

"It's not mine."

"You do a body and soul swap in the army I'm not aware of?"

"Funny." He looked at his brother, bruise rising fast, his sky-blue eyes nearly a match.

"This is the Telford Family Ranch. You are Rohan Telford." Boone faced him, eyes fierce, expression hard, every line in his honed body hard. "You are home."

When had his brother become such a total cowboy? He could have been cast in that *Yellowstone* show he'd heard about but had never seen.

"Doesn't feel like it," he mumbled feeling the role reversal—Boone the man, him the sullen kid.

The silence pulsed between them. Their stares clashed—two cowboys at high noon, waiting for the last chime of the church bell.

Then Boone's expression shifted a little. "I'll help you

trick this apartment out if you still want it—later. Follow me."

After the punch, Rohan didn't have the stomach to refuse Boone anything. He still felt like he was about to puke.

Boone's idea clearly was that saddling up could cure anything. And a long time ago it could. But Rohan hadn't been that man for a while.

They were silent as they rode out. The wind sliced icy even through the borrowed barn coat lined with fleece. There wasn't much snow yet in this part of the ranch. And as Boone closed the gate behind them, the sky was just pinking over the Absaroka Range. The cold felt good, numbing his body and brain so he couldn't think anymore. The horses settled into a rhythm, and Rohan let his mind blank out—only his eyes quartered the landscape, the stark beauty of winter barreling down.

He breathed in deeply, soaking in the cold, the sound of the creaking leather, the hooves, the horses' breaths steaming up. They rode along an offshoot creek of the Yellowstone River for a while, and it took Rohan a moment to realize where Boone was going. Of course. The outcropping of erratic rocks—originally from the seabed—that tumbled over the land six hundred million years ago when an ice dam burst, flooding through Montana all the way down to Oregon's Willamette Valley. The argillite was large and flat, and he and Boone had jumped off it many times and made forts around it as kids during the summer, bringing a picnic lunch their mom packed while they pretended to be gold miners or outlaws.

"Huh." Rohan dismounted, dropping the reins, assuming that the horse was ground-tied trained.

He climbed up the rock, which was a little icy. His boots slipped, but he easily balanced. Boone was already on top, looking out across their land. He made his way across the slippery surface to stand beside his brother. Cowboy boots didn't keep him nearly as sure-footed as his combat boots had on every terrain, but yet they felt right on his feet.

"You still come up here," he said, breaking the silence.

"Often when I want to think," Boone said. "It's peaceful. Beautiful. Lots of memories. Made me feel closer to you." Boone slanted him a look that Rohan felt like a fist to his face. "Made me feel like we were still connected, like I could somehow keep you safe so far away."

Damn. His brother. "Whatever happened to the strong, silent cowboy?"

"You're rocking that myth enough for the both of us."

Yeah, he was.

"You're home, brother. And if I have to say it every day three times a day for fifty years, I will. You are home."

"I'm trying to get there," he confessed, touched by Boone's words.

To his surprise, Boone smiled his slightly crooked smile, and his eyes crinkled and for a moment he looked so much like the kid Rohan remembered that he had an unexpected urge to hug him.

"I get it," Boone said, his voice oddly amused. "A few years ago at the seventy-ninth Copper Mountain Rodeo, I was coming home to compete and bringing Piper with me. I was all messed up, thinking I had to achieve something I couldn't even define in order to deserve to work the ranch with Dad."

Rohan's head jerked back so that he could look at his brother instead of the unfolding landscape dusted with snow and cradled by the Gallatin Range on one side and the Absaroka Range on the other. Snow was deeper on this part of the ranch, but not enough to prevent riding yet.

"What the—" He broke off because even after years in the military and hearing more F-bombs spewed in a variety of situations both good and bad, he still felt guilty if he cussed. "Why would you feel like that?"

"Why not?" Boone's gaze was clear. "Dad was a rodeo king. All-Around Cowboy so many times. He brought his family's ranch back from the brink. I never measured up to him at the rodeo. I didn't go to college like he wanted. I was walking into a job, a legacy by luck. I felt a strong need to prove myself, but everything I ever wanted was right here. Everything I ever wanted to be—a cowboy. A good son. Good brother. Good husband. Good father. It's all here."

Boone made it sound so easy.

Maybe it was.

"I didn't go to college like Mom and Dad wanted either."

Boone, always quick with his mouth was silent. That too was new, he thought without humor.

"I screwed up with Ginny, bad," he admitted. "'Bout as bad as a man could mess up."

Boone's eyes bugged and his mouth dropped open, but he said nothing.

"No, I didn't cheat," he said as if he could read Boone's mind. "But it was bad, and…" He stopped, not really sure how to explain the rest. And he needed to explain himself to Ginny first.

"It derailed my life," he summed up. "I'm proud of what I did in the military, I wasn't sure how to come home or when, but Boone, I'm home for good this time."

By Boone's quick intake of breath his brother understood the significance. "I realize it's going to take me time to settle in. Figure out my next steps. And I think it's best if I have a little space of my own where I can decompress."

Again, Boone's lips parted, words clearly ready to escape, but instead Boone pressed his lips together and nodded. They stood there surveying the land for several moments, and Rohan felt the peace begin to settle.

"Anything you need, brother," Boone said. "Anything."

They didn't speak again for a while. Two cowboys. Blood brothers when for so long, he'd only thought about his brothers in arms—his Coyote Cowboys. But Boone had not been built for silence.

"But I will help you trick out the apartment, and I won't miss handing off the duty of mucking out the stalls and a.m. feedings." A ghost of a smile touched Boone's lips. "And you'll be in a perfect position for foaling this spring. And catching the cows on the overnight shift."

Give Boone an inch, and he took off at top speed, but Rohan wanted to have a job and to be busy. Winter was slower at the ranch so he'd need to pick up a job or more chores to keep out of his head.

"I'm helping at Harry's House again each afternoon this long weekend," Boone said as if he'd added mind reader to his skill set. "I'm going to do some regular volunteer stints at the annex, along with my foundation work I do with at-risk youth in the county over the spring and summer." He looked sideways at Rohan. "I'd love some help with that in the future if you're interested. I enjoy teaching kids, especially teens. I've even volunteered to teach the first class on mechanics—machine repair over the vacation break."

"Ginny told me," Rohan said. "You'll be great."

"When you left, I started learning more about how to repair engines and different farm machinery. Would even get call-outs to different ranches when I was still in school." Boone smiled at his accomplishment, and Rohan tried not to think that he too had been in the same position.

"Dad signed me up for a certification course at the community college, but I knew as much as the instructor and ended up helping him. Then I hit the rodeo circuit."

He was a selfish idiot leaving for nearly a decade and a half and then returning home and feeling bad because things had changed. His brother wasn't supposed to stay fifteen forever. His family wasn't supposed to wait around for him to show up. He'd have to jump into the flowing river that was his family and the ranch and relearn how to swim.

Boone rubbed his hands together, excitement lighting his eyes.

"For the annex, I went to an estate sale over in Livingston and bought a 1950 Ford F-150—blue, well, it *was* blue." Boone's voice rang with its usual enthusiasm. "I'm planning to have a drop-in restoration project going in the new year in the shop behind the house where there are three bays. That's going to be the vocational skills area.

"Gin's father spearheaded the annex purchase to use for the new teen center. He bought the property and donated it to the Harry's House board. Gin's taking over the project and his board position," Boone said. "And I…"

"That's one of the reason's I'm home," Rohan interrupted, tired of feeling useless and playing catch-up. He just needed to jump and keep swimming. "I'm fulfilling a vow I made to my team leader who died on a mission. I'm taking his place, fulfilling his intentions to help Ginny with the annex project."

Boone rocked back on his heels. "You?"

Rohan's determination solidified. He had no idea what Jace's intentions had been. He hadn't read the letter. But he didn't care. Sometimes out on a mission, a soldier had to adjust.

"Yeah, me," he said looking his brother in the eye, and it felt good.

Chapter Twelve

GIN DIDN'T RECOGNIZE the phone number, but she hoped it wasn't another volunteer cancellation. She hated relying so much on others. How had her dad maintained his cheery optimism?

She steeled herself. Where was her inner cowgirl? She used to run so many activities and committees in high school—newspaper editor, yearbook editor, senior class VP, National Honor Society. Now she always felt exhausted, anxious and drained.

"Hey, it's Gin," she answered.

"Hey. It's me."

She wished her heart would hop back in her chest and behave. Of course Rohan knew he didn't have to use his name. Even if she hadn't seen him yesterday, she'd know his sexy voice anywhere.

Not sexy! Distinctive.

"Who?" His voice was mild, but she caught the thread of amusement—an invitation that the game was on.

The memories of how much he could make her laugh were bittersweet. He'd had bone-dry humor and had been so much fun. His confidence and intelligence and drive had utterly seduced her.

"Are you going to tell me you're my problem next?"

"Arriving out of the blue did that for me," he said wryly.

"I can't argue that." She was surprised that she had to bite back a smile. While she was tired of hurting, she wasn't ready to forgive, was she?

"Why are you calling?" She hoped she didn't sound snarky. Rohan had done so much for her yesterday and had given Lucas a precious Christmas memory.

"I'm heading to the project site. Do you need anything from the store?"

Rohan was coming here?

Panicked, Gin looked down at her ancient sweats, already streaked with a color called Winter Wheat that Shane had picked because it was a soft golden yellow with a honey undertone.

"Ummmm." Brilliant. A master's in education and that's what her brain kicked up.

"Food? I can get a to-go order from Java Café or the Main Street Diner. Any supplies from Big Z's?"

Rohan was coming here. Soon. And she was wearing sweats that she'd slept in in high school. And her hair. She reached up and patted the messy bun—curls exploding out.

"Rohan, thank you so much." She hated to admit that she did need his help. "But doesn't your family…"

"I'm already on my way. Boone's looped me in and will head into town in about an hour. I'll be there in ten minutes unless you need supplies."

Her heart's happy skip really should have her draped on a therapist's couch.

"Let me check with the boys." She walked out to the garage, clutching her phone at Rohan's combination of a snort and a laugh.

"No one would look at Colt and Cross and think, boys," he observed.

True. And even though Rohan lacked the muscle bulk and several inches above six feet of the other two men, no one would look at Rohan and not appreciate the man's man, soldier, cowboy. He effortlessly wore his masculinity, no posturing necessary.

Focus.

"Hey." She walked out of the house, shivering because she hadn't grabbed her coat on her dash to the detached garage. "Rohan's on his way. Does anyone need supplies or food or anything?" She hoped she sounded calm and professional.

Colt and Remy were installing open shelves while Lucas handed them the screws and the drywall anchors. Colt instructed Lucas in a slow, low voice, and Gin was impressed that Lucas's attention remained on the task.

"Tell him to get his lazy cowboy a…behind here. It's half past ten. Sunup was hours ago," Remy said.

"Did you hear that?" she asked Rohan.

"Yeah. Cross is hard to not hear. He informed me last

night that he was married, so he shouldn't be noticing or mentioning my ass."

Gin covered her mouth with her free hand, holding back the unaccustomed laugh.

"What about you, you need anything?" The words were polished gravel, and heat curled so inappropriately in her belly.

"Ahhh, no, I'm good." Why was she acting so fan-girly? He was a volunteer, not her boyfriend anymore.

Yeah. Right. That's why she couldn't sleep last night— she'd been kept awake thinking about all his many assets as a volunteer.

"Drive safe." She ended the call and fumbled her phone. That's what she'd always said when he'd been driving into town to pick her up for a date or an activity at the school.

Ugh. She didn't have time for this. Tucking her phone back in the pocket of her sweats, she returned to finish painting the bathroom while Shane and Arlo finished the second bedroom. With the space heaters and the fans, the smell wasn't so bad, and the paint was drying quickly enough that they'd be able to do a second coat tomorrow.

She painted, singing softly to Chris Stapleton, determined to not listen for Rohan's arrival. She wanted him to work, not chat. Gin was so focused on painting and imagining how the wall decals she'd ordered—a mountain range in earth tones for the main room, and various vines or dandelions and even a light-up ivy vine for the other classrooms—

that she jumped when she heard the deep rumble of her name.

"Ginny."

Of course she was squatting and angling precariously to achieve the last few brush strokes around the plumbing on the toilet. She would have overbalanced, spilling the small jar of paint she'd been using, but Rohan lifted her up to standing, no paint spilled.

"I brought your favorite," he said.

She was up against his hard body, and Gin tried to not think of what had once been her favorite everything.

She turned and tried to step back from all that cowboy potency, but he held her in place.

"Careful, you don't want to ruin all your work." He smiled, but his eyes searched hers, clearly looking for something she was not prepared to give.

But why couldn't her stupid body get on board with the plan? Rohan had been in town one day and she was fixated like a late-blooming buckle bunny.

She spied the large coffee from the Java Café he held. "Is that for me?"

"Of course. It's your favorite."

"How would you know my favorite?" she asked, desperate to drop herself back into reality. "The Java Café opened after you left, and a lot of my favorites have come and gone."

There. She'd put him in his place.

"Gone, being the operative word," Rohan said, a hint of

a smile creeping in. "You've had some eclectic favorites over the past couple of years."

"Well those days are over for a while," she said without thinking. She took a long swallow and held back her moan of pleasure. "Chestnut praline," she breathed happily. "A holiday latte. Rohan, this is a treat."

"You've alluded to money problems a couple of times, Ginny."

His smile was gone, and his eyes were filled with concern. Darn it. She swallowed. "Nothing I can't handle," she said crisply. Her worries were her own, and she definitely didn't want to stress Lucas or have anyone feel sorry for her. She was going to see her father's legacy come to fruition. "I'm fine, Rohan. Really."

He didn't look convinced. "Is it because of your father's passing?" His voice was low, inviting her confidence, and for a moment she almost caved and told him—crazy because she hadn't even told Shane or Miranda or any of the board that donating the annex was going to be a financial stressor on her. Her father had planned to pay the mortgage even as the annex was rolled into the foundation. But she didn't want to tarnish his memory. With careful money management, she could make it work. And Lucas was doing so well, now. She no longer felt the need to research every potential therapy and run him into Bozeman for treatment that insurance rarely covered.

"Thank you for asking," she said. "But I'm okay."

His green eyes searched hers, and she did her best to hold steady.

"I know we are a long way from where we were, Ginny," he said. "And that you don't yet trust me."

She had a hard time swallowing because she was beginning to fear that he was wrong—she was beginning to trust him. But if she didn't have her hurt and betrayal to clutch, how would she protect herself?

"And that's my fault." He straightened up as if offering himself up for inspection. "I've thought about this for years. And last night I stayed up most of the night thinking, and if you're willing, I'd really like to tell you something."

His eyes were the alpine green of Miracle Lake in the summer.

"Okay, tell me." She owed him that. She knew she did.

The hum of the space heater and the fan seemed ominous now, but it was worse, much worse, when he unplugged both pieces of equipment and nudged them out the bathroom door. Then he snicked the door shut.

ROHAN LEANED BACK against the door to give Ginny space. He should have picked a more conducive spot, and his timing sucked, but he had to say his piece, and he likely only had a few minutes to mea culpa before they were overcome with fumes or interrupted.

"That bad?" she whispered, her blue eyes as deep and wide as the Pacific he'd only seen when he'd been in Washington during early trainings.

"Yes," he admitted. "Worse. I want you to know, Ginny, that every day of the past fourteen years I have deeply regretted the grotesquely selfish way I acted and the words I said, when you shared the news of the miracle that we'd created a life."

Her breath whooshed out as if she'd been holding it. She paled, and afraid she'd fall, he lifted her onto the newly installed double vanity. He wrapped his fingers around hers as she clutched her coffee drink.

"I failed you," he continued. "I failed our child. I failed myself. I failed my family. But what kept me up most nights was that I hurt you. I betrayed your love and your trust, and for that I have never been able to forgive myself."

He wasn't sure what to expect at this late date. Not forgiveness. But he felt that even if they couldn't start over, he wanted her to know that she'd been deeply loved. Heck, last night as he'd stared at the ceiling, his aching body not soothed by the comfortable couch, he'd fully owned that he still loved her. But he loved the girl she'd been. He wanted to know the woman she'd become. But they could only start over with a clean slate.

"I am deeply ashamed that I ran from being a man."

He waited, in case she wanted to say something. Or hit him again like she'd tried to yesterday. Or douse him with hot liquid.

Instead, she looked him in the eyes. Her lips trembled but Ginny, who had always had a lot to say, remained silent. Her eyes were such a beautiful blue. He'd often remember them when he'd been trying to fall asleep somewhere far from home.

"I selfishly wanted it all—you, college, the rodeo team scholarship, but I wasn't willing to pay the price of my actions. I was only thinking of myself—of everything I'd lose and how disappointed my father would be with me when you told me our news. I know it sounds dumb. I was a kid, playing at being a man, and I let you down."

He drew a deep breath. "In retrospect, I can't believe I was such a selfish, stupid idiot. I was so focused on how everything was going to change for me—it didn't occur to me how much I would gain."

"It was a lot to take in," she finally said. "We were both young and hotheaded, and I've always been too stubborn to negotiate, my dad always said."

"You shouldn't have had to," Rohan said. "I should have just held you and asked you to marry me, or maybe asked what you wanted to do." His brow furrowed. "I was so shocked because we'd always been careful, but when you told me you were expecting, my mind just raced with how I'd failed everyone. My dad wanted us to wait—get an education and see a bit more of the world and meet more people, as if that would have changed my feelings about you."

He huffed out a breath and raked a hand through his hair. "Your dad wanted me to give you freedom to explore your dreams of writing and traveling before we settled down too quickly on the ranch."

She blinked. "I didn't know that," she said.

"I was double-teamed by the dads the Christmas before we graduated. They both, in different ways, said we were too serious too quickly. They wanted me to get my rodeo ya-yas, as your dad called it, out so that I could mature. My dad pushed for a degree so I'd have a bigger perspective on the world before I decided on the ranch. He hadn't had a choice. He wanted me to have one, but I didn't want one. I wanted you and me on the ranch. College was to make my mom and dad proud and to poke a stick a bit at Witt, who was such a brainiac—always acting too good for us."

He shook his head at his young self and slid his hands on either side of her hips as he watched her. She clutched her coffee but didn't drink. His mouth was dry as chalk dust so he took a sip of hers. She let him.

"Man that's sweet."

Humor sparked in her beautiful blues, giving him the courage to continue.

"I wasn't all that keen on college, but you were going, and I didn't want to not be with you, but both of the dads really put the heat on me, and they were right to do it. You were so bright. You had so many options. I didn't want to hold you back. So I took the scholarship out of state to give you wings and hated every minute, but when you told me we were expecting, I knew the dads would think I didn't respect you. That I hadn't respected their wishes, and I panicked. And so I'd let everyone down including my rodeo team."

"That's a lot of pressure." She spoke slowly, as if seeing the situation differently.

He shook his head. "Your dad had so many plans for you. He wanted you to meet others who matched you intellectually. He wanted you to have the opportunity to date other guys before settling on a cowboy, which just about gutted me. He said a semester abroad was in your plans. He didn't want you trapped in a small town like your mom had been—history repeating."

Ginny's bow-shaped lips formed a perfect O, and he pinched his thigh to center himself enough that he would not succumb to temptation and kiss the shock off her face. This was an apology, not a seduction or romantic reunion.

"I let you down. My father warned me condoms could fail ever since I was twelve. That's how he had Witt. He'd been a rodeo cowboy who'd hooked up with a college graduate who was heading out to med school in the fall. She traveled with him a month or two over the summer and fell pregnant, only she refused to marry him. Still, he manned up. Put aside money each month for his son, even though she didn't want the money or a cowboy screwing up her kid. And he made a scrapbook of photos, notes and letters to give to the son when he grew up so he'd know he was wanted and that he had another family who loved him."

Rohan's lips twisted at the memory. "One more way my father proved he is the better man."

"Rohan," she began.

He captured her fingers in his. "I froze up. I just told you we'd figure it out during the winter break because I had some competitions coming up and a huge chemistry test." He closed his eyes and laughed harshly at what a dumb idiot he'd been. "Then it was too late."

"You were relieved. Said it was for the best."

"Hell no. I was devastated. Handled that like an idiot too. I didn't want you to see me cry."

She stared at him. Dang, he'd actually said that out loud. The coffee cup tilted and coffee trickled out of the sipping hole in the lid and onto her figure-hugging sweats. Ginny didn't even flinch.

He righted the cup.

"Anyway, Ginny. I know it's fourteen years too late, but I don't want you to think that you once gave your heart to a man who didn't treasure it. You were my world. The only woman I ever wanted, even though I trampled on it like a bull bucking out of the chute. I handled everything badly. Spoke when I shouldn't and didn't speak when I should. I hurt you. I didn't take care of you, and I was so eaten up with shame, I couldn't find a way back to you or my life. I didn't feel like I could go on as if nothing had happened so after the first semester, I dropped out and joined the army."

Ginny stared up at him, unblinking, while his heart thundered in his ears.

"Like it was a punishment?"

He was quiet, thinking her question over. "Yeah. I wanted to escape myself and my mistakes and become a different man."

He'd nailed that at least. The moment felt like a discovery. "In the army, I became a new man, a different man, a better man. I was on a team. I was necessary like I'd never felt necessary before. There were rules that I understood. Clear expectations. I'd been good at the rodeo, but total truth talking, I was never ever going to be as good as my dad. The army gave me a way to redefine myself and to stay far away from you so I wouldn't mess up your life any more than I had. We'd lost our child so I wanted to leave you so that you could be free—travel to Spain or Paris. Write in a café overlooking some river I can't pronounce."

"Wwwwhat? Wait. Rewind." Ginny popped off the vanity, all aggressive energy and in his face. "You abandoned me after I lost our baby so that I could go write poetry in a café? You put your life in danger so you wouldn't try to come see me and get back together with me?"

She made him sound like a melodramatic martyr. Or an idiot put like that. He'd thought he was being noble all those years ago—fixing himself, atoning for all the people he'd hurt, doing some good in the world, becoming a man. Even when he was trying to explain, he still fell short in Ginny's eyes.

"Never mind," he said wearily. "I just wanted you to know you were loved. I screwed up." He kept screwing up. "You deserve a good man, Ginny. You deserve to be loved."

He tried to memorize her face—the creamy complexion, the faint pink across her cheeks; the deepest blue of her eyes and the velvety black specks in her irises; the long, feathery lashes, which she'd always complained she couldn't make curl up like his little sis, Riley's, did naturally.

"Get off your high horse. What are you really telling me here? Where are you going with this?"

He wasn't totally sure. He'd wanted to explain the past and then…

"I wanted you to have closure, Ginny. You deserve that."

He just needed to take a step away from her. Get some air. Get away from all her crackling energy and the temptation of her lips and soft skin.

"Hey." The bathroom door swung wide, smacking him in the butt. "What's going on in here?" Boone blinked. "Are you painting?"

The way he stretched out the syllables in the word made it sound dirty. And then, Boone, never subtle, waggled his eyebrows and Rohan tamped down the urge to smack his baby brother in his smirking face.

"We're done." Rohan bobbed his head at Ginny like he still had his hat on. Geeze. One day back in a Resistol, and he was cowboyed up.

"Oh." He reached in his back pocket and handed Ginny the letter.

Vow complete.

"Men suck," Gin announced, plunking on a barstool at the Graff Hotel bar while Shane restocked the shelves.

"You are just discovering this now?" Shane turned around, her eyes brimming with amusement. "And you're wrong." Shane waved a platinum band with aquamarines inlaid in it. "Not all of them suck every day, but who is sucking particularly at the moment?"

Shane tapped a long finger—nails plain and cut short and free of the paint from this morning's work—on her lower lip. "A certain long-absent cowboy perhaps?"

"Ugh," was Gin's eloquent reply. Elbows rudely spread on the Graff's historic gleaming bar, she cupped her chin in her hands. "I planned on despising him until I died."

Shane turned fully around. One raised eyebrow invited her to continue.

"And now he's apologized. And he's being nice. And honest. And making sense."

"So sucky."

"Don't laugh." Gin narrowed her eyes at Shane.

"I'll try." Shane turned around and continued to stock the shelves. "Do you want to talk about it?"

Gin looked over at the gift shop where Lucas was with Petal and Arlo, setting up the holiday crafts in the kid craft area. Her heart warmed seeing him get sweetly bossed by the slightly older, but sisterly girls, who were former students of hers. She'd never seen Lucas truly engage with kids very often—except with his scouting activities, but with her father gone, she wasn't sure how she was going to manage keeping him in Scouts.

"No. Yes. Rohan and I had a thing in high school." That sounded lame. "We were friends in school as kids and then freshman year of high school the whole dynamic changed—you know what I mean."

"Dratted hormones. Mine messed me up too many times to count, but I finally got it right with Remy."

Gin felt a little pang of what felt like envy, and she shoved it aside. Rohan's confession and reframing of their history still had her unsettled.

"I'm keeping you from your work." She eyed Lucas again, who was busy figuring out how to attach drawing paper to a roll at the end of the table.

The girls looked like they were counting out markers.

"How is it possible that Rohan's even hotter now?" Gin demanded. "And I'm a wreck."

"If Snow White could be considered a wreck." Shane deftly cut up apples, oranges, pears and cherries. "You're aware that the opposite of love is not hate," Shane said wryly. "Wanting to 'despise' someone until death indicates a lot of passion remains."

"Ugh. I don't want to talk about it."

"Maybe you should—let it out."

"No head-shrinking."

Shane laughed. "Bartender and your friend. Your head is safe from professional interference, although Colt and now Remy have me contemplating getting my licenses updated."

Gin smiled. Friend. She loved the sound of that. "You're thinking of helping Colt and his organization."

"Remy and Huck are on board, and I think I've beat myself up enough about my past."

"Rohan's return reminds me of the past."

"Maybe you're realizing that you finally need to address it."

"Probably," Gin admitted in a burst of honesty. She frowned and looked down at her glass of water. "He's reawakened feelings that I didn't want to deal with, and now I'm just trying to make sense of everything."

"Give it some time. It's important to process, and if you had a falling-out when you were still teens, it's likely that logic and deliberation played very little role," Shane admonished. "Men's frontal lobes are baby-butt smooth until their mid-twenties."

"I'm a teacher and a mom. I know all about the frontal lobe or lack of it." Gin snorted a laugh thinking of Rohan's brain as a baby's butt, and it hit her that if she could laugh about such a thing, maybe she was closer to understanding than she realized. And if she had compassion, could forgiveness be far behind?

"Still that's a bit harsh," Gin noted.

Shane smiled. "It's that kind of a day. If you stick around long enough, I'm mulling wine with a new recipe."

"I have Lucas."

"You can take a sip like a wine tasting if you want," Shane said. "But Miranda has the kids making sugar cookies to decorate for tomorrow's ornament-making party for the trees at Harry's House and the annex on Sunday. They'll be there a while."

Gin nodded.

"You can help me wrap these twinkle lights around the bar's columns while we talk about Rohan's apology." Shane put several small boxes of lights on the counter with stick-on hooks.

Gin pulled the strands out carefully. Did she want to talk about Rohan's apology or the past? Would it help or hurt?

"You're not alone, Gin." Shane lightly touched her hand. "You don't have to be an island."

It wasn't an unexpected thing for Shane to say, and yet, her words hit deeper than Gin had anticipated. To hide her emotion, she retrieved the footstool from behind the bar.

"I know." She finally spoke, climbing up and plugging in the lights at the top. The golden glow immediately lightened her heavy heart. She began to wind the lights down the column close together, using a few hooks for support. "I think I'm finally realizing how much I've shut myself off."

She hopped off the stool and finished the first column and then repeated the process on the next one.

"When I was a teenager, I was crazy in love with Rohan. We went to separate colleges, and I was devastated. He didn't seem as upset as I was. He wouldn't really talk about it, just said we'd reassess at Christmas, and then I discovered I was pregnant."

Shane was clearly listening, but focused on her mulled wine recipe, adding brandy to the fruit in the pot along with some spices from one of her homemade blends. She switched on the commercial hot plate and shot a look at Lucas.

"No Lucas isn't Rohan's," Gin said, feeling the need to defend Rohan in a way she hadn't felt warranted in so long. She'd always felt abandoned. Now, after this morning's full explanation, she felt their parents had interfered far more than she'd realized.

She finished stringing the lights on the second column of the bar's entrance. Already it looked more festive.

"Shall I wrap the beams above the bar?"

"Knock yourself out. It's the season to twinkle."

Already a delicious smell was beginning to waft her way.

Gin slipped off her boots and climbed up on top of the bar. This was probably violating more than one health code, but she'd seen Shane in socks on the bar decorating the highest shelves and beams and lights for a holiday. They were alone at the moment, but she still looked across the lobby at

Lucas, who appeared to be rolling out dough for the sugar cookies, his tongue stuck out at an angle, and her heart turned over with love and happiness that he was participating in a holiday ritual.

Maybe he'd have the patience to help her make a wreath tonight for their door. She'd planned to make it when he was in bed, but maybe she needed to try to include him more—create new traditions, new challenges, things they could do together or do with other people. Gin knew that Shane created elaborate wreaths—she'd taught her how to make them a few years ago.

"I was excited about the baby," she admitted. "I loved it already. I thought we'd quit school, return to his family's ranch and start our own family. He'd work with his dad, and I'd write poetry and raise our child. Hearing myself say this, I sound like a self-centered, dreamy idiot mooning around the soundstage of *Oklahoma* or something—a woman who never heard of feminism." She flopped her head on her arms on the counter.

Shane laughed. "There's nothing wrong with wanting to be a mom and have a child with the man you love and working the land. Look around—plenty of cowboys and women chasing them and tourists who pay a lot to see the whole show."

Gin plugged the strings of lights together to check them, and then began to loop them through the hooks she'd stuck at the top of the bar. She had enough to layer the lights, or would that be too much festiveness?

"You were young and in love. Definition of self-centered." Shane stirred the pot, and more fruit and cinnamon and something else wafted up toward her.

"I am definitely going to want a taste of that," Gin decided, hopping off the bar to check her work.

"I feel like it's officially the season now." Shane joined her and they both looked at the bar. Gin's embarrassment over her confession eased.

"When I told Rohan, he didn't react the way I'd imagined. He was…" She thought back to that day when she'd skipped classes, borrowed her roommate's car and driven all day to Reno, Nevada. She'd pictured him being thrilled. Picking her up and spinning her around and proposing.

"He was stunned," she recalled. "Super quiet. I don't think he even said anything. He just sat down on his bed and stared at nothing and asked me if I was sure. I was so…" Gin winced. "Hurt. Shocked. Angry. I'd expected him to be thrilled, which now as I say this sounds utterly stupid." She made a face at her self-absorbed eighteen-year-old self.

"I said a lot of things. I had more of a temper then, and I accused him of being selfish and not loving me. He'd said that he'd trapped us." She shook her head, realizing that that was exactly what he'd said—not that she'd trapped him, which was how she'd remembered it at the time. "Then he had to go to a class and said we'd talk when he got back. He told me to wait in his dorm room, but I was so upset, I just drove all the way back to college. Total drama queen. It was, like, a twelve-hour drive, and I ignored his calls and blocked his number."

"You were young, scared, confused, likely hormonal," Shane began.

"Rohan was young too," Gin said. "And until this morning, I never really thought of it from Rohan's point of view. I'd a few days to think about the baby, prepare. I just dumped the news on him and expected him to play hero, ride up on his white horse and whisk me off to get married, and when he didn't, I was so self-righteous, shutting him out. I thought we'd live happily ever after, college scholarship and rodeo dreams be damned."

Gin groaned. "Thank God I don't have a daughter. I was ridiculous."

Shane laughed. "I do have a daughter, but our kids will make their own mistakes, learn from them and thrive." Shane gave her a quick hug and returned behind the bar to open three bottles of red wine that she added to her concoction.

"When I lost the baby a month later, I was so devastated. I felt like I'd lost myself and definitely Rohan," Gin recounted but without the usual hard stab of pain. "I called Rohan with the news. He didn't say anything, not even sorry, for a long time, and then he said it was 'probably for the best.'"

Shane winced. "I lost a baby too, and it's shocking how many people will say that and think they are helping."

Gin stared at Shane. She'd had no idea Shane had lost a pregnancy, but then she'd never shared her grief, not even with her father.

"I really have been bottling a lot up and living in the past," she admitted.

"Easy to do, hard to let go, but necessary," Shane said.

The added wine began to warm and layered in a darker, delicious fragrance to the bar. Shane shook out a couple of cinnamon sticks and several star anise to add to the pot before placing the lid on it. She handed one star anise to Gin.

"Keep that to remind yourself that there is magic in life's process."

Gin definitely needed that reminder and tucked the spice in her pocket.

Chapter Thirteen

Rohan worked the hinge of the wall bed he'd designed and built yesterday, finally satisfied that it would work smoothly and be durable. He'd ordered a mattress and bedding online, along with a couch and a wingback chair and ottoman—early this morning, actually. He just needed to build the shelves to surround the king-size bed and he'd be ready to attack the bathroom—tile, new shower and tub, vanity, shelving. Mystery looked up at him, tail wagging.

"You've been busy." His father leaned against the doorjamb of the spacious studio apartment.

"Yeah." He straightened, wary.

How had he not heard the barn door open? His father's boots coming up the stairs? A few weeks off active duty should not have dulled his senses to this extent, although he had been working with a drill.

"You trying to outwork us?" his father asked mildly, his perceptive gaze quartering the room. Yeah, the man knew his ranch, his animals, his land, every outbuilding and everything in it. He would have noticed the new shelves with the fresh-cut wood scent downstairs near the tack room and office, which Rohan had built to store the totes that had been stacked in the former apartment.

"Can't sleep," Rohan admitted.

He'd never been able to slip anything past his dad except his disaster with Ginny, although it was likely his father had suspected something monumental had gone down to send him careening into a new life direction without warning.

"So your answer is to remodel a studio that hasn't been used in over a decade?"

Rohan's disquiet grew. Was his dad pissed that he was making modifications to the studio? True, he hadn't asked, but it was clear it hadn't been touched in a long time—the electricity, water, septic and propane for heating and cooking had all been turned off and some of it needed an upgrade, which he would accomplish this week.

"Not much of a vacation." No question inflected his father's statement. Rohan had been avoiding this moment, just as he'd avoided his come-to-Jesus with Ginny for years, holding his shame tight.

"Not a vacation."

The silence hung like a curtain between them.

"You quit the military?"

Rohan felt like his dad had just called him a loser, something he'd never once done. His father treated everyone, including his kids and staff, with kindness, respect and patience. Why was he so defensive?

"Didn't re-enlist this time," he muttered.

His father's face lit up like the town Christmas tree, and

he took two quick steps forward before he faltered to a stop.

"Isn't that great news, Rohan?"

"It was time," he said, and he looked around the room. Nothing but wood and his tools. He'd cleared everything out yesterday afternoon and had been working nonstop except to feed the horses and muck out the stalls this morning and help Boone when he asked. "Still getting used to the idea."

"You're home then?" His father's voice resonated with excitement. "For good this time." His father's eyes glowed with happiness, and yet held a hint of worry.

"It doesn't feel like it." Rohan's legs weakened like they wouldn't hold him anymore.

"What do you mean?" His father took two more steps into the room.

Rohan blew out a breath, and without planning to, sank down on the floor to his butt, his legs sprawled out. His head fell back against the closed wall bed. He liked the rough, wide floor planks, and wondered if he should refinish the floor or leave it rustic after scrubbing and sanding away the years of dirt, dust, and who knew what else. Mystery sat at his side, her head pressed against his palm, and he stroked her silky ears and neck. The dog moaned a little in pleasure, and Rohan felt his own frayed feelings soften at the sharp edges.

"Rohan. Why didn't you tell us, your mom and me, your plans?"

Bewildered, barely banked hurt colored his father's voice,

and that about killed him. His father was a good man. Strong and smart, he'd do anything for family. Always jumped in to help others.

Rohan had run.

"It didn't seem real," he finally said, breaking the silence. "The guys in my unit. We were all coming up over the next year or so for re-enlistment and Jace McBride, our team leader, was mustering out. He wanted to come home to Marietta, save his family's ranch, have us join him, start a business together. Build new lives together."

His father was silent. His brilliant blue eyes—so like Riley's—bored into his. His father had always been an excellent listener. Something else Rohan knew he could improve on.

"He…he didn't make it home."

Taryn Telford sat down on the floor, his movements slow and careful as if he were trying to coax a wild animal.

Rohan wanted to laugh at his father's careful handling of him, but really, there was nothing funny about any of this.

"He had a to-do list. To make amends to his friends and family, things he wanted to accomplish when he arrived home before he started a new chapter."

His father waited, even though he must have heard about Jace.

"So all of us—the Coyote Cowboys…" He waited to see if his father remembered what they'd been dubbed as he'd risen in the military and had formed friendships and a tight unit. But his father didn't change expression. Maybe he'd never told his dad. Most of his career had been classified. He'd known his parents hadn't wanted him to join the military. His mom had cried. Begged him to resign so many times, but he couldn't leave behind his men, and his mission. He was good at what he did. His skills were needed.

"We will carry out his wishes, and then have a final send-off for him."

"And then?" his father asked after Rohan stopped speaking.

"I don't know," he admitted.

"Rohan. You always have a place at the ranch. This is your home."

He knew that. But intellectual knowledge and heart knowledge were different.

"I don't know what I want to do," he conceded. "Though I can't imagine living in a big city."

"You have time," his father said. "I'm sure it will be an adjustment for all of us. Communication helps."

He winced.

"And if you want projects—" he looked around the empty space that spoke of many pending projects as well as a few checked off "—the ranch is full of them."

"I have money saved," Rohan said.

"Keep it. Give yourself time. It's a luxury a person doesn't often get."

He nodded. Waited. Wondered if he should say more. Explain what he was only beginning to understand.

"You are always welcome in the main house, Rohan. Riley and your mom cleaned out your old room. Witt, Miranda, Petal and Cannon will be moving back to their house in January. Boone, Piper and Reid will be back in their home in April or May."

"This is better." He finally admitted it to himself. "I don't sleep well." Massive understatement. "This gives me something to focus on."

"Seems like you are taking on more than your share of ranch chores. You don't have anything to prove, Rohan. You are my son. Your mother and I will always love you no matter what. You'll always be Boone's older brother he measures himself against."

Rohan nodded but kept his head down, blinking back the moisture.

"Boone has his own small spread that he works along with our cattle business and a foundation for at-risk youth. Your mother and Riley board and train and breed horses. If you're looking for work, it's here. Boone had the same trouble adjusting after the rodeo a few years back. He had some mythical marker he felt he needed to hit to prove himself to me. The only goals a man should set are his own."

His father stood and held out a hand. After a moment, Rohan took it, and his father pulled him to his feet. His dad was still cowboy fit, not surprisingly. He hadn't yet hit sixty.

"The answers you seek are here, Rohan." His father tapped his palm on his chest. "You just need to listen."

He nodded, too choked up to speak.

"But, son, your home is with your family. We're always here for you."

Rohan looked around the barren space. Could he turn this into a temporary home while he figured out his next move? There were a lot of things he could do. Colt had texted him about opportunities. So had Remy. And now his dad. But he couldn't quite let go of the hope that Ginny and Lucas could be a part of his future. Yesterday, he'd told himself that he should let her go, even as he intended to help her fulfill her father's dreams for the annex. And he wanted to help her with money if she needed.

But the tendril of hope had grown, unfurled until he was choking on it.

"I'm such a different man," he admitted.

His father, in the act of walking out, turned back. "We all are. It's been nearly fourteen years, son. Who you were at twelve wasn't who you were at eighteen. Who you were at eighteen isn't who you were at thirty. Who you are today is not who you'll be at fifty-seven. We're all growing and peeling layers. Nothing's static except death."

Rohan thought about that. "The onion," he said. Jace had said something similar a few weeks before he'd died.

"I'd like to think we aren't evolving underground." His father smiled. "I try to live in the light. But the storms come. We weather them as we can. Days shorten and grow dark, but spring returns. We can only do our best each day."

"My best's not always good enough."

"But if you're lucky there is another day."

He swallowed hard and wanted to hug his dad. When was the last time he'd done that?

"Did you finish your task for Jace?" his father asked curiously.

Rohan thought about. "Yes, but no," he admitted. "There's a lot more I could do."

"Then do it," his father said and left.

"C'MON, BUD. LET'S bust it," Gin called out to Lucas on Sunday for what felt like the tenth time. It wasn't yet noon, yet she felt she'd put in a full day, waking at five to finish grading the last of her eighth-grade history honors papers, then running three miles on her treadmill, and then cleaning the house before climbing up to the attic to pull down Christmas decorations. She'd been dreading the last bit—Christmas without her father seemed an insurmountable chore, and yet she had Lucas to think of. And the annex.

It had felt like such a millstone, and yet it kept her vertical and moving forward. Today was the ornament-decorating party at Harry's House. If that didn't put her in the Christmas spirit to come home and tackle her and Lucas's tree then she had a serious case of the Scrooges.

She'd yet to jump in the shower, but she and Lucas

needed to shovel the driveway and walkway after last night's snow dump. She hoped one of the volunteers would clean up the walkway of Harry's House, but she'd bring her shovels just in case.

"Lucas." Her voice rose despite her intention to not get frustrated. He was very sound-sensitive and having him shut down wouldn't make him move any faster. "Lucas, sweetie. We need to shovel the driveway." She didn't offer a bribe like stopping off for a hot chocolate from the Copper Mountain Chocolate Shop. With her dad gone, she needed to watch her dollars as much as her time.

She stopped short. Lucas wasn't in his room.

"Lucas?" He wasn't in the kitchen or living room. Would he be in her father's room? She reached out for the handle, dread pooling in her stomach. She wasn't ready. Not at all. But she needed to get there. So many people in Marietta and Paradise Valley could benefit from the donation of her father's clothing and the bedroom furniture.

A rhythmic scraping sound cut through her worry. Was Lucas already shoveling? Wonder coursed through her. Not worrying about a coat or her boots, she rushed outside. Three pair of eyes met hers. Rohan shifted his weight, one arm bent, resting on the shovel. Lucas mirrored the pose. Even Mystery sat and lifted both paws in an uncanny imitation of Rohan and Lucas.

"What are you…?" She paused. It was obvious what Rohan was doing. But not why. Yesterday, he'd shoved a letter at her, and it seemed as if he'd gone all tough-guy, mission-accomplished, tipped-hat goodbye.

"Thank you?"

Ugh. That wasn't a question. Why did this man, this cowboy, this soldier turn her into a stammering teen—something she hadn't been even when she'd been a teen?

"Thank you, boys," she said.

"Boys?" Lucas objected. "We're men."

Gin swallowed an unexpected laugh.

"Manly men," Rohan said, straight-faced, and she was too far away to see if he was laughing at her. Rohan's eyes had always given him away. She'd never had to wonder where she stood. But this version of Rohan was more mercurial. Gin took a couple of steps toward them. Her slippers slid on the ice.

"Careful now." Rohan put down his shovel and started toward her.

"Mom, you're not dressed appropriately for the weather."

She stared at Rohan conscious of her sweatpants and sweatshirt. "He sounds exactly like me," she said. "Totally annoying."

Rohan barked a laugh, and she couldn't help her answering smile. He closed the distance between them, his green eyes lighter with amusement. And his sexy mouth tilted in a smile that did something sinful to her tummy. She took another step toward him, remembering how his hands had always felt on her tucked-in waist that had for some reason obsessed him when they'd been together. He'd spent a lot of time kissing her waist, abs, belly button and marveling at the swell of her hips when she'd thought she was pretty standard. Slim, muscular for a girl, but nothing remarkable from what she'd been able to see in the high school locker room. And now? She didn't even think about how she looked. She just tried to get at least midway through her to-do list every day.

"I'm…um…going to take a shower." She could barely say the words because she couldn't breathe.

"Need any help?" He seemed to feel the same pull.

"No?" What the heck was she doing? How was this body-thrumming attraction even MORE potent than it had been when they'd been teens? She certainly hadn't felt it again with anyone else.

"Rohan," she breathed, feeling her body go liquid.

His green eyes darkened, the yellow flecks sparking to life. He took another step toward her, his hand resting on her waist, and the chill she'd just started to acknowledge dissipated. "We can't," she breathed, and even she heard the failed protest in her voice.

The scrape of metal on cement was obscenely loud.

"Almost there," Lucas's voice shattered the space between them, and they both jumped back.

"Shower," Gin whispered, more to remind herself than to inform him.

Almost there. Truer words had never been spoken. But

where exactly was 'there,' and did she want to go there with Rohan?

"Rohan, I don't think..."

"Lucas invited me. He said something about spiced apple cider."

Rohan lifted the shovel out of the back of his truck. Mystery jumped out, and he felt a pinch of pride. The dog was getting stronger just in the couple of days she'd been with him. She no longer seemed so tentative, though she still dogged his every step, unless she was following Lucas around.

Ginny gave him a look, and he hid his smile. Since his talk with his dad this morning, he felt lighter. Now that he'd mentally committed to getting the annex ready for the teenage clients, and to remaking the apartment in the barn into something that would feel like a home rather than just be functional, he felt more settled.

His dad had said to take his time figuring out his next steps, and he'd decided that he wouldn't worry about figuring out a role on the ranch, continuing his education or a career until after the New Year. Putting off his feelings for Ginny for another four weeks wasn't possible. But he promised himself to proceed slowly. He didn't want to hurt her again.

"It's not that I don't appreciate you coming to the annex today to help," Ginny said. "It's just that you already shoveled out my driveway and…"

"And now I'm shoveling the Harry's House driveway before the families start arriving."

He hated that she looked at him so cautiously still. Yesterday, he'd gutted himself open. But he was determined to earn her trust. It took time and effort to earn the trust of a wounded horse or farm dog or feral cat. Ginny deserved his patience to earn her trust, but she'd likely brain him if she thought he was comparing her to anything four-legged at the ranch. He smiled at the idea.

"You don't want me to get out of shape."

She laughed as he'd hoped. "I can't imagine that happening ever," she said, and the way her gaze skimmed over his body made the temperature, in the high twenties, seem balmy.

"So Mystery and I will get to work."

Gin went back into Harry's House to prepare for the ornament-decorating party. Setting up for a party might stretch his skill set, but he could definitely shovel the walkway to the annex next. Colt drove up with his family, and he grabbed a shovel and joined him.

His wife, Talon, exited the truck and two older kids popped out carrying totes of decorating supplies.

"Parker, come back for the apple cider. Montana you bring the platters of cookies," Colt's wife said.

She helped a younger child out of a booster seat and walked over, holding the child's hand, and introduced herself. Rohan shot a quick look at Colt—how had such an aloof, silent giant of a man landed such a warm, lovely woman?

"Hold on, babe." Colt rested the shovel against a bare tree.

"Oh, are you going to carry me into the house?" She laughed and stood on tiptoes, even though she was quite tall, to kiss her husband's cheek. "Pregnant not helpless."

"Still…" He slung the two totes of supplies she held over his shoulder and, holding her hand, walked her to the front door. "Humor me."

She glanced back at Rohan. "This is progress. With our first baby, he tried to run all the errands and when I did escape the house, he tried to carry me everywhere. Don't try to pull that on Ginny."

Her blue eyes laughed at him, as he choked on his spit.

"Small town." She answered the question he hadn't asked.

"You are a wicked woman," Colt said.

"Lucky you," Talon said before disappearing inside the house just as Parker and Montana barreled out to bring in the cider and drinks. Cross and Shane arrived with their daughter Arlo and more food and drinks.

"So it's a party." Rohan watched as another Crock-Pot was carried inside, along with a large carafe of something steaming.

"The women know all the dads work for food so there's plenty," Colt said as Cross joined them, hefting a shovel out of the truck.

"I'm working, and I'm not a dad," Rohan commented.

"Yet," Cross said.

Rohan kept his mouth closed. Ginny was just beginning to look at him with that sexual awareness, and he didn't want to jinx anything.

Chapter Fourteen

"I DON'T HAVE a dad."

Gin checked the enchiladas in her oven as she continued to dwell on the flat way Lucas had delivered that truth this afternoon at the ornament-decorating party when several of the other children had been talking about their dads. Arlo had sweetly said that Lucas might get his own dad—she recently had, and he'd stared at her as if she'd announced she'd flown to space, and then he'd demanded how. Several girls had launched into hypotheticals, which had made her cheeks burn. Even Parker had recounted how Colt had adopted him when he'd been seven.

They'd made getting a dad sound as easy as getting a puppy—something else Gin had been avoiding.

Then Parker had asked Lucas who was taking him on the Boy Scout snow-cave-building camping trip at the start of winter break. Lucas's dismay had been devastating enough, but the sympathetic looks cast her way by a few of the moms had been worse. She hadn't even thought about the camping trip—not her scene at all, especially in snow. Her father had loved all the Scout outings. She'd been contemplating how to gracefully slide Lucas out of the one activity he'd seemed to enjoy and that's when it had hit her. She was going to have to big-girl panty it up and become a Scout mom.

Then Colt, Remy and Rohan had walked into the annex during the scouting conversation. She'd hoped they'd missed her deer-in-the-headlights moment as she'd bustled around like a nineteen-fifties housewife setting the menfolk up with hot cider and sandwiches.

The rest of the party had been less emotionally fraught, although more than a few times she'd caught Rohan looking at her speculatively, which had made her heart do crazy things, rendering her embarrassingly breathless.

Was it too soon to hope that they might have a second chance? Did he want that? Could she risk it?

Gin tried to put the afternoon and Rohan out of her mind—hard when he was helping Lucas set up the train set while she focused on preparing dinner. The enchiladas were almost ready, and the scent of a homecooked meal combined with their still-naked Christmas tree and the evergreen boughs she'd collected was mouth-watering and evocatively seasonal. Gin checked on the rice and grilled vegetables she'd made and dished out the salsa that she'd canned from last summer's veggies.

See, I'm not a total washout as a mom.

Great she was reduced to giving herself pep talks to counter her own narrative. She took a deep breath. She could do this. Have Rohan for dinner as a thank you for all his help over the past few days, and not read too much into it. Or jump him.

She went out to the living room to tell them dinner was ready, but her mouth stilled into a circle of astonishment. Lucas and Rohan sat side by side, snapping pieces of track together, while Mystery watched intently. They had Rohan's phone out, and were looking at something on it, Rohan asking questions in a low voice. Lucas's face was scrunched in thought as Rohan scrolled through whatever was on the phone.

It was so sweet. So natural. But the homey scene packed an emotional punch. Lucas had lost her father too, the one male who'd truly cared about him. She'd thought she and Lucas would just have to struggle on alone. But what if they didn't?

She was so startled by the thought, she backed into the kitchen and stood by the stove, gulping in deep breaths.

She wanted to play it safe. She needed to. But everything inside her wanted to jump in feet first. But if things didn't work out, she wasn't sure she could trust herself to hold it together for Lucas. She'd fallen apart after her miscarriage and their breakup. Spun out of control and there was no dad to pick up the pieces.

But she was older, wiser, a mom. Maybe she could trust herself just a little—dip her toe into the possibility of something more with Rohan. She touched the star anise that she'd put in the pocket of her jeans. Maybe she could find a little magic once again instead of just worry and drive to prove herself.

Giving herself a mental and physical shake, she walked back out into the living room to tell Rohan and her son that it was time for dinner.

THE MEAL WAS simple, but delicious, yet Rohan couldn't help the heaviness in his heart. He'd been so determined today to keep looking forward, let go of the past. He'd felt more confident after the conversation with his father, and he'd enjoyed the camaraderie of putting the finishing touches on the garage today with Colt and Cross, and organizing the donated tools and purchasing more to complete the workshop with Boone.

But putting together the model train set this evening with Lucas, coaxing memories and ideas out of him, had felt transformational. While he enjoyed working with the kid— Lucas was unique, unexpected—but it had really hit him then the loss that he and Ginny had suffered. Their child never got a chance to be read a story, make a Christmas ornament, go to a party, pet a dog. Before, the loss of their baby had been abstract, not a boy with a personality, quirks, likes, worries.

The sense of loss had expanded over dinner as they'd eaten as if they were a family, discussed the day, school starting back up. And he couldn't help thinking about the snow-cave camping trip he'd heard mentioned. He'd asked Lucas about it, and the kid's face had lit up, and then dimmed because Gramps was gone and couldn't take him.

The family dinner, the camping trip, working on the annex had all filled him with a sense of purpose he'd thought lost when he'd left the service. But he could have it again—with Ginny and Lucas and maybe the ranch. He wanted that so much it hurt. And as he ate, he'd started to plan. He'd need finesse, strategy. A lot was at risk—not just his heart, not just Ginny's, but a young boy's as well.

"Can I try the train out after dinner?"

"Yes," Ginny said. "Ten minutes, but then you will need to do your reading for thirty minutes, and then we will go over your backpack and school supplies for tomorrow."

"Twenty minutes for the train?" Lucas bargained and quickly stared back down at his plate.

"Ten minutes. Tonight is a school night. Did you thank Rohan for helping you set up the track?"

Lucas nodded. "Thank you for setting up the train tracks with me," he said woodenly. "When will the new pieces arrive?"

"Wednesday," Rohan said, and he could feel Ginny's scrutiny. Hopefully he hadn't overstepped, but buying the bridge, the lake piece with the little ice skaters on it, reminded him of so many winters driving up to Miracle Lake after school, holding Ginny's hand and whipping across the lake, the other skaters, or pickup games of hocky fading into oblivion.

"You'll have to ask your mother when it's okay to set up the extra pieces since you'll be having schoolwork each night," he said. There. He hadn't invited himself over, and he thought he sounded deferential enough.

But of course he pushed. "You still ice-skate?" he asked, catching her staring at him.

"Um, no." She looked down at her half-eaten meal.

He stared at her. She'd loved to ice-skate. She'd been fast, graceful, and she could do all the tricks—spins, jumps; she'd practically danced on the ice. He'd just been fast. He'd had to be to keep up with her.

"We went with class last year," Lucas said. "But I didn't skate."

Ginny made a quick movement to get up.

"Why not?" Rohan asked, figuring that the reason might be important, offer clues how he could work with him, maybe.

"Other kids' feet had been in those skates."

"Hmmmm," he said. "True." He and Ginny had had their own skates, but there was a shed that rented out skates and sold hot chocolate and apple cider even when they'd been kids.

"Was that the only reason you didn't try it?"

"Too many holes. Hard to lace and kids would laugh. I don't know how to skate and have bad balance. And the music was loud, and I didn't have my earphones."

Rohan problem solved. New skates. He could google to

see if they made them with Velcro straps. Learning to ride a horse would help Lucas with balance. He could purchase some noise-canceling earbuds that would look more natural than headphones. Rohan ticked off each issue.

"Petal, Parker and Arlo and their gang are going skating next Sunday the day after the Stroll," he noted, and by Ginny's launch to her feet, he knew he'd pushed too far and likely too fast.

"Lucas, I'll do the dishes, and you can run the train," Ginny said. "Set your timer."

Both Ginny and Lucas set the timers on their watches, and Rohan felt a curious combination of wanting to laugh and cry.

"I'll clear and help your mom," he said softly.

She marched into the kitchen. Rohan gathered plates, cups, cutlery just as Lucas switched on the train set's motor. He returned to gather up the serving dishes and asked about Tupperware.

"Wasn't sure a man like you would know about Tupperware," she said into the silence.

"A man like me," he murmured. He'd definitely pushed it with her.

Too bad. He'd backed away about as far as a man could go, and he wasn't playing it safe anymore.

"Did you read the letter?"

"Not yet," she said over the rush of warm water in the sink. She filled the casserole dish with the warm suds, and then began to wash the dishes. He scrubbed the casserole dish and the pot and pan.

"Too painful still?"

She lifted a shoulder.

"I enjoyed putting the train set together with Lucas. He's a funny kid."

"You think something's wrong with him, right?" She spun toward him but left the water running. Ginny had always been about conserving resources, even when they'd been teens, so he figured she didn't want to be overheard.

"It's none of your business."

"I hope to make it my business." He'd put it out there.

"What's that mean?" she whispered.

"You know," he prompted. "There's always been this fire between us, Ginny. Not just sexual attraction." Although spending time with her the past couple of days had reawakened his libido to off the chart bright red. "This simpatico, understanding, talking without talking."

He expected her to disagree. Make excuses.

"Yeah." She turned back to the dishes. "We still got it." Her smile held no humor. "But I have to think of Lucas, Rohan. I can't just do what I want."

That made his heart leap. So she did want to try.

"Lucas is…" She paused. "As a parent, I hate labels, but as a teacher, I find they can be helpful if the educator is able to look beyond the label, to use it as a tool to guide, not define the child by their label."

Label. He felt his heart drop to his boots.

"Lucas developed asynchronously. He didn't talk until he was nearly four. He was delayed with every milestone, especially language and muscle tone. Hypersensitive to light and sound and touch."

Rohan's protective instincts jumped to his throat as he feared where she was going.

"But then he responded so well to different therapies—OT, PT, speech, tutors that the neurologist thought perhaps he'd been over-diagnosed. The last language specialist he worked with said that middle school would be critical as the social and language pieces really rocket to the next level, as do academics. And social interactions have more nuance, which is not Lucas's strength."

"That's why money's tight," he guessed. "I'd imagine therapies are expensive. Don't teachers have…"

"Teachers do have amazing insurance, thank God." She kept the water running and her hands under the stream even though all the dishes were clean and he'd dried the last one.

"But a lot of the therapies were not covered for one reason or another." She laughed bitterly. "And while Lucas would often qualify for services through his elementary school, he'd improved enough after six months that he'd no longer be a large enough standard deviation from the norm so I'd have to drive him to Bozeman or he would do specialized camps during school breaks geared for kids who had a wide array of diagnoses.

"But also, full disclosure…" She turned toward him, her expression fierce, and her eyes shining with tears. "Money is tight because my father refinanced this home to get a home-equity loan to buy the house next door to Harry's House so he could donate it for the teen center, and no I am not in trouble or in need of a white knight," she said. "My father planned to continue working with kids even after his retirement. He wanted teens to have access to a wide range of experiences and opportunities and mentors even though they lived in a small, rural town. He started something important, and I will see his legacy through."

"Of course you will," he said softly, no longer able to accept the physical distance between them and pulling her into a hug. She held herself so tightly. So brave and determined to face life head-on and alone.

But he didn't want that. "You're not alone, Ginny. I'm right here, determined to re-earn your trust. And so many people in the community support Harry's House. Big Z's gave me and Boone a huge discount on the tools and other equipment we purchased. Monroe's Grocery Store did the same for the food staples in the kitchen. The volunteers who've been showing up—I'd forgotten how much people in Marietta step up for each other."

"They do," Ginny said, resting her head briefly on his chest, and he felt like he could breathe again properly. Her palm was on his chest, and for a moment, he felt invincible.

Then she sighed and wiped her eyes. "I have to pull myself together and go into mom mode," she said, then she paused. "Do you want coffee? It's a long ride back to the ranch."

"I probably shouldn't," he said. "I've been having trouble sleeping." He made it sound like no big deal, but he couldn't remember the last time he'd been able to relax enough to sleep properly. His mind kept racing, but he knew at some point he'd finally collapse.

The timer on her watch beeped.

"But maybe I will." He felt sleep pulling at him, and the ranch was a good twenty-five minutes away. "I'll make it; you get Lucas squared away."

GIN WAS SURPRISED that Lucas had already turned off the train. He pointed out the spot to her, where he and Rohan were going to put the lake and add in the bridge.

"That will be really beautiful," she said. "Something new."

"I told Rohan Grandpa and I added something new each year," Lucas reminded her. "The tradition continues."

"Yes, it does. Time for your reading."

"What about dessert?"

Dessert. She'd forgotten. She'd made brownies this morning for the ornament decorating, but had saved a few for dessert tonight and Lucas's lunch tomorrow.

"I'll bring you a brownie and a glass of milk so read at your desk first."

He nodded. Gin returned to the kitchen. The coffee was brewing and smelled heavenly. She'd started skimping on a few things, but her coffee beans were not one of them. She grabbed three plates, cut a small brownie for herself and a bigger piece each for Lucas and Rohan. She brought Lucas's to him with milk and then took the two other desserts into the living room, expecting to see Rohan sitting on the couch.

Instead, he was sprawled out taking up the entire couch and fast asleep. She stared at him, finally drinking in her fill, noticing the things that were so familiar—the long, feathery lashes; high cheekbones; strong, square jaw; golden-brown hair springing back from his forehead. And the things that were different—his body was longer, more muscled, his facial expression more shuttered. He smiled less, and while his vivid green eyes were still beautiful, they were haunted in a way they hadn't been.

He was a man.

Question was, what was she going to do with him?

Her smartwatch buzzed with a text. She reached into her pocket for her phone, but it wasn't there. Instead she pulled out the star anise. She looked at the intricate spice. A little touch of magic. She felt the ghost of a smile start in her chest and climb up to her lips. Finding Rohan and forgiveness for them both felt magical.

Then she read the text on her watch, frowning as she scrolled.

Gin. Family and work issues. I can't teach the class the first week of the school holiday. Rohan's free. Sorry. He taught me everything I know with my dad. You'll be in good hands.

Was the universe plotting against her? Or were Rohan and Boone colluding?

If so, Rohan had better come through. Gin gently laid a blanket over him.

ROHAN WOKE UP, disoriented. He blinked. He saw a fully lit and decorated Christmas tree and a cheery gas fire still blazing away. The house smelled amazing, like a pine forest with a sprinkle of cinnamon. One old-fashioned lamp with a red silk beaded lampshade that hung over a large cherry wingback chair was on, but the rest of the lights were off. Had he fallen asleep at Ginny's? What time was it?

He stared at his watch. That couldn't be right. It was nearly five in morning. He'd slept for ten hours or so—dreamlessly. He sat up, surprisingly well rested and relaxed. But he needed to get home before Boone came to run the chores with him. And Witt headed into the hospital after his six-a.m. workout. He did not need his family speculating about Ginny and him, especially when he'd done something as lame as fall asleep on her couch before her kid even went to bed.

Totally innocent, but he had no doubt Boone would blow it up and tell their parents they were engaged before noon.

That jackknifed him off the couch. He was sliding his feet into his boots, when he heard a door open behind him. He turned around. Ginny stood there in leggings and a tank top and trainers.

"Good morning, Sleeping Beauty."

He felt his cheeks heat. "Sorry about that."

She waved her hand airily. "You said you'd been having trouble sleeping. No way was I going to wake you when you might finally catch up a little."

Her dark hair tumbled down her back in a thick ponytail he wanted to touch.

"I was thinking..." he began, trying to get his brain in gear. It had been something about Lucas and scouting. Something that Colt had talked about.

"No thoughts before six in the morning," she said, and he couldn't tell if she was joking or not, but he also didn't want to take a shot at some serious persuasion and boundary crossing when his brain wasn't fully awake.

"But you can make it up to me," she said, a mischievous smile touched her lips and she held out her phone with a text.

"Huh?" He read the text from Boone.

"Did you coordinate with your brother about the class?"

What the heck? "Class?" He still felt half asleep.

"Car maintenance and beginning mechanics."

"Me?" he sputtered.

"In two weeks. One to four, four afternoons the first week of break at the annex. Eight kids are signed up. Better buckle up, Romeo. Looks like your little brother just threw you under the bus, and you'd better get yourself back in the driver seat.

Chapter Fifteen

"I don't know if I should thank you or slug you," Rohan said mildly as he barely made it back to the barn after making coffee at the main house before Boone entered ready for chores.

"Thank me," Boone said, holding two thermoses of coffee. "Thanks for getting this started."

Rohan nodded. He'd bought his own coffeepot and supplies, but also went over each morning to the main house to start the coffee. This morning, he'd already heard people stirring upstairs so he'd been extra quiet so they wouldn't realize he was late.

Boone pulled two breakfast sandwiches out of an insulated bag and handed one to Rohan, who hadn't even realized he was hungry.

"Mom's still getting up and making biscuits and breakfast?" He guessed he shouldn't be surprised. It wasn't like anyone who lived on a ranch slept in. Winter hours were much shorter and the workload lighter, but still there was never a lack of things to do.

"Piper made the biscuits." Boone smirked and bit into the fluffy offering.

"I did the scramble, ham and cheese and spinach. Piper always insists on something green."

Rohan stared suspiciously at the sandwich, but the smell was so tantalizing he couldn't resist.

"You used to hate vegetables. Mom had to blend them up in stews and soups."

"I grew up," Boone said around a second mouthful. "Piper traveled with me on the rodeo for a summer, and she loved to cook—veggies. She got me hooked."

"On more than veggies," Rohan teased, relieved that conversation with his youngest brother was starting to feel more natural.

Maybe he was beginning to relax.

"Piper changed my life." Boone took another bite and chewed thoughtfully. His side-eye was anything but subtle. "You and Gin?"

"Is that why you dogged out of teaching the mechanics class at the annex and volunteered me?"

"Yup." Boone grinned and took another bite of the sandwich.

"Subtle as a horseshoe to the head."

"What's the holdup?" Boone was unfazed. "You and Virginia Lane were destined for each other since middle school. Probably before. Don't you think you've wasted enough time?"

Rohan tried to be offended, irritated by Boone's interfering, but it was so Boone—good-hearted, impulsive, solving what he perceived to be a simple problem.

"I've only been home three days."

"And? You can't take your eyes off of her," Boone said good-naturedly. "And she's got it just as bad. Sometimes history is not all that historical."

"We have some serious issues to work through," Rohan said, hanging on to his patience. "And she's got a son."

"Lucas is great. Get on the horse and ride, Cowboy," Boone said. "Although today we're taking the ATVs. We can talk about the class if you need some tips while we're loading up the feeders."

"Since you texted Ginny that I taught you everything you know, I think I can figure it out."

"Teaching teens takes skill, brother," Boone said. "I've been working with them a few summers now." His blue eyes cast a crafty glint. "Can't wait to see what you bring to the party. Wouldn't mind your help with my foundation if you discover you have a gift turning surly, distracted teens into useful citizens." Boone finished his sandwich.

"Were you always this manipulative?"

"It's my new superpower," Boone joked.

Muttering something that felt like a desperate prayer, he took the stairs down to the main floor of the stable and grabbed his thickest barn coat with the fleece. Boone clattered down behind him.

"Maybe you should text Ginny and invite her to dinner at Rocco's or Rosie's or maybe Main Street Diner if you want to be more subtle about it to discuss the class," Boone offered helpfully as they rolled back the door and headed across to the large equipment barn. "And Monday night Lucas has Scouts so you have a clear field tonight."

"Maybe you should stay in your own lane and mind your own business," Rohan said without heat. He hid his smile, enjoying the back-and-forth with Boone, but why let him know that?

MONDAY, LATER AFTERNOON, Rohan walked down the main hall of the middle school. It didn't look all that different from what he remembered—maybe a little brighter and smaller. Ginny's room was down toward the end. He kept his steps quiet out of habit, and looked at the student work posted outside each of the classrooms and lining the bulletin boards down the halls.

Ginny was up at the whiteboard, spraying something and wiping the board clean.

"Hey," he said, feeling like a creeper since he'd been transfixed watching the long, graceful lines of her body as she moved.

She spun around. "Hey yourself."

He suddenly felt absurdly shy. Ginny looked so effortlessly stylish and professional. Her hair was pulled back in a thick braid, and she wore a royal-blue pantsuit with black details and a black blazer. He didn't remember any of his teachers looking so beautiful, and he wondered how any of the boys in her class focused. Every dumb cliché about hot for teacher danced in his suddenly adolescent brain.

"I was hoping we could…ah…catch an early dinner and discuss the class at the annex."

Her shoulders relaxed and her breath whooshed out. "You'll teach it?"

He'd been questioning his sanity the entire drive into town, but her obvious relief and sparkling eyes had him metaphorically mounting his white horse.

"Yes," he said. "After I had my moment kicking my little brother for interfering."

"You and Boone always got along so well." Ginny smiled. "And you were always so inclusive and kind to Riley. I was always envious of your family—your mom, your siblings," she said wistfully.

"I was lucky," Rohan said, not wanting to think about all he'd given away, but instead about all he could reclaim and rebuild.

"So." He swallowed and soldiered on. "Main Street Diner sound okay? Will Lucas be okay with that?"

"Lucas has his Boy Scout meeting right now." She winced. "I really should be there. It's not mandatory, and Colt is one of the assistant leaders, but my dad used to be one as well," she finished softly, and her eyes closed. "But yes, we have time to walk over and get something. I'll order a to-go meal for Lucas at the end. The mechanics class is important to the kids and to the annex and my father's legacy so, thank you, Rohan."

Her voice tightened and her eyes shimmered, and he felt a little choked up himself. This was what he'd wanted—a life with meaning.

"Welcome home, Soldier," Flo, who'd worked at the diner for as long as Gin could remember, greeted them, two menus in hand.

"Good to see you, Flo," Rohan said, but Gin could feel his rising tension. Rohan was a hero, but he didn't want public acknowledgment. He'd do the work, but not crave the kudos.

"Seems like old times." Flo smiled again. She looked up at a hanging sprig of mistletoe and winked.

Gin's shock at the obviousness had Flo winking again. "Just in case the spirit of the holidays sings to you," she said cheerfully and led them to a booth. "Can I start you two off with something to drink?" The long-time server pulled a pencil from her blast-from-the-past beehive hairstyle that Gin felt was a Marietta institution. "No Lucas?"

"Just us today," Gin said, striving not to blush. Flo knew pretty much everything about town, but she was fairly discreet, far more than pharmacy owner Carol Bingley.

Gin ordered a Diet Coke. Rohan ordered black coffee and water.

"Did you read Jace's letter yet?"

"No," she said. "But I did tuck it in my purse." She tilted her practical black cross-body bag toward him to reveal the slip of red. "I haven't had time really, but it is weighing on me. I've been thinking so much about my dad and wanting to ensure his legacy, and yet you are trying to do the same for Jace, and I haven't respected that." She lowered her gaze to her hands on the table as her fingers plucked at the napkin. "I've been selfish, Rohan. I'm sorry."

He covered her hands, and she welcomed the warmth and his innate tenderness.

"Nothing to apologize for. I didn't account for the emotional toll the letter might take on you," he admitted.

"Wow." She stared at him. "Not many men, especially cowboys, will admit so easily they're wrong," she teased him to lighten the mood. They were going to talk about a mechanics class, not write a dirge.

"This cowboy's been wrong a lot."

"You also were right." She owed him that. "I think subconsciously I was really happy about the baby because I wanted us to marry and be together. I didn't want us to be at separate colleges so while I didn't set out to trap you, I think I was glad on some level," she admitted softly.

"Water under the bridge," he said. "I wanted us to be together too, but I was trying to do right by you, do what your dad and mine wanted, not be selfish." He wiped a hand down his face. "But I don't want to talk about the past. I want to talk about the future."

She nodded. "Yes, the class."

His gaze assessed her, but he said nothing about mechanics. Flo returned. Rohan ordered the meat loaf. Gin went for a half of a Reuben sandwich and a small salad. That would hold her throughout the night.

"One more thing bothered me, which I'm not ashamed to admit, but then I want to let it go." He looked up at her, his green eyes clear. "It hurt how quickly you replaced me."

"Replaced you?" That was such an unexpected comment that she could only stare.

"Just doing the math in my head. In less than a few months, you were expecting another man's baby, and I…I couldn't let go of you for a couple of years to even look at another woman. Felt like I was cheating—no judgment," he said quickly. "It's just that you fell in love again so easily, and I hate that he hurt you, that he didn't do right by you and his son."

She could barely swallow around that softly spoken conclusion.

"I had to say it, and we don't have to speak of it again unless you want to." Rohan picked up the coffee Flo had quietly dropped off as if she realized this was not a casual, friends-meeting-up meal.

He took a swallow. "But I don't like the fact that you are

worried about money. I think Lucas's father should be chipping in for all of the therapies that have helped him. Isn't that the law?"

She stared at the bubbles floating up along the straw in her Coke.

"Ginny?"

She still couldn't meet Rohan's steady regard, but she owed him the truth. He'd been honest. Put himself out there. And if they were going to take another shot at this, she had to hold up her end.

"Am I overstepping again? Perhaps he has already made payments and started a college fund." Rohan's voice was humble, and he took another swig of coffee as if trying to stop himself from speaking again.

"No," she said. "You are not overstepping." She squeezed her eyes shut, gulped in a breath and forced herself to straighten and look him in his beautiful eyes.

"I don't receive any support because," she whispered and looked around, "I don't know who Lucas's father was."

He stared at her, utter incomprehension on his face. And then he half rose out of his seat, fury blazing in his eyes. "You were raped?" he hissed, fists balling like he was going to go out and seek vengeance.

"No, no, nothing like that," she said quickly. "I just... Please sit." She noticed a few people looking at them. She blew out the breath she hadn't realized had stuck in her throat. "When I lost the baby, and you, I could barely get out of bed or make it to my classes. I was a mess. Then when I pulled it together, sort of, I did a complete one-eighty. I still didn't go to class much, but I became the life of the party, especially at the frat houses." She scowled in distaste. It was such a humiliating cliché.

"I started drinking a lot and doing other things, and I just sort of threw myself at other guys and good times, hoping to forget you and losing the baby."

Now he'd know she'd acted slutty.

"If you'd been drinking, that's not consent." Rohan's voice sounded like a bass string stretched too taut. "Those frat boys should have helped you back to your dorm, not taken advantage."

Rohan was so outraged on her behalf, not at her.

"They were drunk too. Nobody was at fault. I was just as stupid. Careless. They were too. We were dumb kids."

"Why didn't you come to me?" he asked. "I tried to call so many times. Text. Email. I called your dad, but he said if you weren't answering me, it was because you didn't want to and had moved on."

"I was so lost," she admitted. "And ashamed. And then you joined the army, and we were over, and I was pregnant again."

Their food arrived, and neither of them made a move to eat.

They just stared at each other. Gin had no idea how much time had passed.

Rohan slapped his hand on the table hard enough to startle her. His eyes glittered with determination. "I want us to go to the Stroll together this weekend. You. Me and Lucas."

She stared at him. It sounded like a declaration. And perfect. She'd thought her explanation would disgust him. Instead, she felt free.

"And I want us to take Lucas ice-skating on Miracle Lake—let him try it. No pressure."

Excitement soared through her. Rohan didn't blame her for her lapse of reason. She tried to temper the balloon of joy soaring but failed. "I'd like that, Rohan," she admitted. "But doing things that we loved in the past won't necessarily wash us clean so we can start over, blank slate."

"I don't want a blank slate. I want us. I want you. Me. Who we are now, not who we were."

She could hardly object to that, and as if making his announcement had suddenly freed him, Rohan cut up a piece of his meat loaf and held it out to her. It was something he'd always done, shared his food with her and she with him. Gin stared into his eyes and took a bite.

"How's your food." Flo appeared, smiling again. "Definitely like old times. Enjoy, you two."

ROHAN PAID, AND as they walked out, he paused by the

front desk and looked up, his hand on Ginny's hip. Flo looked over at them from where she was putting in an order.

"What?" Ginny paused, confusion in her gaze.

"Mistletoe. It's a Christmas tradition." He spoke softly but with intent as he slowly leaned into her and gently kissed her lips in front of the entire diner.

They drove back to the school in his rental truck, and Rohan felt so keyed up he had a hard time not letting his leg bounce. He'd kissed Ginny—very innocently but publicly. No way that wouldn't get around, and he wanted it to. He was beginning to think his father and Boone were right. He needed to buy a truck or use one of the ranch trucks emblazoned with the Telford Family Ranch logo.

Ginny was quiet. She'd pulled the letter out of her purse and had turned it around and around in her hands.

"Thank you for bringing this home to me," she said. "I feel like Jace, even though I didn't know him well, has helped us both to heal."

"He was like that."

He pulled into the parking lot. He could see a classroom full of kids of different ages wearing tan shirts with lots of patches. Ginny smiled sadly.

"Scouts was the one thing Lucas seemed to enjoy like a mostly regular kid," she said, and he heard that wistful note in her voice again. "He didn't seem as out of step with his peers as he did when we tried sports or other things. Part of it was because there are so many different age levels and lots of parent support. Lucas got more acceptance there than in the classroom."

"I never did Scouts," Rohan said, thinking back. "Too busy on the ranch and then with 4-H and the rodeo. It's goal-oriented, right? Different skills? Things to master? You get badges or something?"

"Yeah, merit badges. Lucas likes that. The check marks. The specific skills. Working at your own pace. I found it overwhelming—one more thing I had to keep track of, but my dad started him in Cub Scouts in second grade, and they just kept going to the meetings and moving up."

"Is it just dads?" Rohan looked through the windshield at the fifteen or so kids sitting around different tables with adults working in small groups.

"No, some moms do it too, but more dads—it's a big bonding experience." She sighed. "With my job, Lucas, and being on the Harry's House board and getting the annex up and running, I don't get much free time, and camping just seems exhausting," she admitted. "So much to organize and so many contingencies to prepare for, and I hate to be bad at anything."

She shook her head and rolled her eyes. "But I think I'm going to have to get over myself. I was trying to weasel out, but since Scouts is something Lucas enjoys, I'm going to suck it up. My dad was the fun one with him. I was always the taskmaster."

She made a face. "But I want him to see a little of the

world. I remember when I was in high school, I'd imagined traveling."

He'd been all over the world.

She stirred restlessly. "Not practical now, but no big deal. Lots of people dream of it. Lucas has a campout coming up when break starts. He's finally old enough, and he was excited. Snow camping." She shivered. "They snowshoe and sled, track animals, do owl walks at night and build snow caves." She laughed. "Sounds like my version of hell, but this year I've decided I'm going to big-girl panty it and take him."

"Big-girl panty," he repeated, and was pleased to see her blush.

"Somehow it sounds dirty when you say it."

"I hope so. But the 'big' kinda spoils the mood. Panty implies small, lacy and peeking above jeans just a little bit so men lose any higher level cognition."

"You've given this some thought."

"I am now," Rohan confessed.

Pleasure rushed through him at her throaty laugh. Again she palmed the letter.

"Ginny, let me take Lucas snow camping."

"What?" She stared at him. "That's not why I told you that. I was trying to talk myself into it with my public announcement."

"I want to. I practically carved a career out of camping in places with no amenities—this will be fun. I'll get to know

Lucas a bit and try my hand at scouting."

Her eyes were wide, and he could practically hear her ticking off reasons to say no.

"I'd have some experiences working with a variety of ages, which might help me with the class you and Boone maneuvered me into teaching."

He couldn't tell if he was getting through to her or not. And usually when he'd been camping, he'd been trying to infiltrate the enemy and not get caught so perhaps his skills would not be of much use, but he found himself really wanting to go, and he didn't stop to question why.

"It will be fun. I'll be careful with him."

She nibbled on her thumb.

"What are you afraid of?"

"Everything," she finally said, her shoulders sagging.

The boys started lining up and two boys retrieved the American flag and two others the Montana state flag, while they watched through the classroom window. Boys started lining up in small groups, and the adults were rearranging the furniture back to where it had been.

Lucas still sat working on something. Colt crouched down next to Lucas, saying something. Lucas ignored him and then when Colt touched whatever Lucas was working on, he stopped and looked up at Colt before glancing away.

"Lucas has troubles with transitioning," she said. "And he can be stubborn."

Rohan thought Ginny could give anyone a run for their

money with her stubbornness, but he kept his mouth shut hoping she'd talk herself into saying yes.

"He hasn't had a meltdown in a couple of years, and he's familiar with the adults and the Scouts," she said.

"So, it's a yes?"

"I don't know." Her gaze was troubled.

"Maybe we could practice one night in your backyard."

She smiled. "Rohan, I don't think you have to practice at anything," she said. "The problem is that you're perfect."

"I'm not but hypothetically, why is that bad?"

"I'm afraid Lucas will get attached to you, and we're so…new, maybe. Lucas has already lost my dad, and someday he might wonder about his father, and I still haven't figured out how to explain that to him."

"Think about it," Rohan urged, trying to keep a lid on his triumph. "We can maybe bring it up at the Stroll this weekend."

"You're still persistent," she noted.

"I need to be."

Chapter Sixteen

ROHAN PULLED INTO her driveway and turned the truck off. His hands played with the keys. The clink of the metal dragged more memories backward out of her brain. She could see her homemade wreath on the door—the greenery, twigs, pinecones and holly leaves and sprigs from the Telford Ranch. She'd built the wreath last night at the dining room table, while watching Rohan sleep. Part of her had hoped he'd wake up, while another part had been thrilled he was finally getting some rest.

"We're not in high school anymore." Gin meant to sound facetious, but her smile felt forced.

No father waited for her. And Lucas and Mystery sat on alert in the back seat.

"You used to do that when you'd drop me off in high school," she said. Her father had always been at the front door, protectively waiting.

"Yes, I did," he said quietly, and the way he looked at her stole her breath. She could see longing there. Regret. Hope. A mirror image of what she felt.

"Lucas." She handed him the keys to the house. "Why don't you open up the house, get the gas fire going, plate your food from the diner and you can read while you eat if you want."

"Mystery, we need to do our reading." Lucas opened the door and slid out of the truck.

"Do you think I coddle Lucas too much?"

She hadn't planned on asking the question. She had bristled when her father had pushed and winced when friends would nudge her. She knew, absolutely, that she couldn't protect Lucas from every bump in life, but it was so scary to let go. And scarier still to open him to the pain, isolation and ridicule she feared might be coming in middle school and high school.

"You think I should give him a phone and a dog."

Rohan was silent for a moment, and she braced herself for his answer.

"He's your son, Ginny. You love him. You want the best for him."

And would it be best for her to let another man in their lives? Rohan was the only man she'd ever wanted, and his large, loving family was a seductive bonus. But could she trust him to stay? Could they finally have their happy ever after?

So tired of running on the hamster wheel of her thoughts, Gin leaned up and kissed him.

THE PRESS OF her lips, her hand on his thigh, her body moving into his was heaven and hell. Rohan's groan felt wrenched from his soul, and he speared his fingers through her hair, the silky, fragrant fall amped up his body even more.

But it was his slamming heart and ragged breath and the feeling of finally being home that had him slowly releasing her after a long battle between his brain and body.

His breath sawed in and out, and he rested his forehead against hers, realizing that during the kiss, she'd tossed his hat off.

"Sorry, not sorry."

He laughed, even though his body was on fire, and the press of his erection against his zipper had him nearly unzipping as there was no discreet way to adjust himself. He breathed in her scent, absorbing the pain and pleasure, even though some things needed to be said.

"No." Ginny's eyes were a blue he wanted to drown in. "Don't say it. I know."

She pressed her fingers against his still-throbbing lips, and he captured her hand to stay it, kissing each finger.

"I may have many regrets, Ginny," he said and kissed her closed eyelids.

"But kissing you will never ever be one of them."

She looked up at him, her smile tentative, and with his lips, he traced one graceful dark brow that had always reminded him of a raven in flight.

"I want us to be friends again."

"Friends?" She pulled away from him.

She adjusted her clothing although he hadn't pulled anything askew during their passionate kiss that still had his blood thrumming through his body. He hadn't felt so alive since he and his team had been pinned down during one of his last few missions, and time had slowed, and his focus had honed with deadly intent.

"Friends?" She reached for the door handle.

"We were friends for years before we were lovers."

"You're right. Friends. Friends is good. Safe. Makes sense." The smile she hit him with was cardboard and had disappeared before her feet hit the ground. "Thank you for taking on the class at the annex. Boone wrote a course description for the parents, and I'll text that to you." She practically sprinted up the walkway.

"Ginny, hold up." Dang, how did she move so fast?

She wobbled on the ice but caught herself before she fell. Even so, he wrapped his arms around her and pulled her into his body.

"Don't run," he whispered, her hair tickling his lips. "We've both been running."

She was still in his arms, her heart slamming against his forearm.

"I said friends," he reiterated, wanting her to be clear as to his intentions. "We need that. We had that once. I want that again. A lot of time and changes since we were eighteen, and you and Lucas are too important to me. I don't want to be selfish and risk messing up again."

"What are you saying?" Her voice was a puff of air in the night.

"I want to regain your trust. I want to be your friend. I want you to know you can always count on me. And I want to figure out my place at the ranch and with my family. And I want to work on all of that with you by my side. I want to learn how to work with Lucas, gain his trust, be a support for him and you."

He felt like he was holding his breath waiting for her answer. The tension in her body eased.

"Rohan, that sounds so…so perfect, but I'm not sure how we get there?" She turned in his arms. Worry and hope tugged at her expression.

"Together."

THERE WAS NO reason to be nervous.

None.

So why was she walking back and forth between her kitchen and the living room inventing jobs for herself? Lucas peered out the front window, face pressed against the glass. It was cute and heartbreaking all at the same time—not that she thought Rohan wouldn't show up, but Lucas's excitement was sweet yet scary.

Give Rohan a chance.

"He's here," Lucas shouted out, but then he ducked out of the window and curled up on the couch. "He saw me. He saw me. He saw me."

"Isn't that the point?" She kept her voice light, even, hoping to ease Lucas through his embarrassment. "Rohan's coming to walk us to the Stroll."

"I know. I know. I know." Lucas wombatted and Gin walked by, lightly brushing her hand through his hair. "I too am excited to see a friend."

Lucas didn't answer.

"I'm going to open the door for Rohan. Make sure you bring your noise-canceling headphones. There will be a lot of people on Main Street and there will be caroling and some musicians busking at the stores."

"Will Parker, Petal and Arlo be there?" His eyes were scrunched shut.

The hope in his voice hurt, even though she knew that it was a good sign that he was showing an interest in other kids. But even though she was friends with Shane and Talon, she didn't want to overpromise.

"I hope so," she said.

She opened the door before Rohan could knock.

"I brought hotties," Rohan said, holding up a fistful of the small packets that when shaken, heated up.

Replies swam through her head—a few of them even G-rated, but after a moment of drinking her fill of the cowboy—new Wranglers, buckle from a college rodeo roping event, Henley shirt, flannel over it and a black Carhartt barn coat lined with pristine fleece, black Resistol and newly shined black cowboy boots—she swallowed all of the slightly suggestive replies.

"You bring a lot more than that, Rohan Telford."

His smile made her happy.

"You and Lucas ready?"

"Yes." She had to forcibly remind herself to stop staring. "Lucas, it's time."

He bounced off the couch and careened outside. "Will Petal be there?"

"Likely we will run into my family," Rohan said, not sounding completely happy. Gin could relate except she felt the opposite. As much as she wanted to spend time with Rohan, the idea of experiencing the Stroll with his close-knit family held a lot of appeal.

"That will be nice. Coat," Gin reminded Lucas brightly.

Lucas spun around and ran back into the house and jammed his hands into mittens before pulling on a knit cap and then shrugging into his coat. "Ready."

"One more thing," Gin said gently.

"I don't want them." Lucas's bottom lip stuck out.

"Bring them just in case." Gin kept her tone even.

Lucas kicked at the snow, and then slouched back into the house and returned with a pair of noise-canceling headphones. His body drooped and he moved like he was crossing a river of molasses.

"Those are sweet," Rohan said. "I wish I'd had those when I was strapped into the jump seats of cargo planes. Probably fewer headaches."

"Really?" Lucas's mouth dropped open.

He nodded.

"No. You wouldn't wear them. They're weird."

"To be comfortable and safe, I definitely would," he said, as Gin locked the front door. "All soldiers wear and use safety equipment. Cowboys too. Cops. Medical professionals. Construction workers, seat belts in cars."

"Safety first," Gin said, amused to hear Rohan—a man who had embraced adrenaline-laced, dangerous pursuits—mouth a public service safety statement.

Lucas slipped the earphones over his head. Rohan pulled off one glove with his teeth and crammed himself next to Gin and Lucas.

"Marietta Stroll," he said, taking a selfie. Then he looked at the dark roofline of the ranch house behind them.

"I should have gotten some lights up on your house," he noted. "Your dad always went all out with the lighting displays."

"It was a vision quest for him," Gin said, sadness bleeding through. "He loved Christmas, and he loved lighting up the dark, and I haven't even hung the ornaments on my tree."

Rohan reached for her hand, his gloved fingers threading

through hers.

"Lucas, you and I have a colorful mission."

"Yes, sir." Lucas did a little salute. "Where's Mystery?"

"Town will be too crowded for her. She's in my apartment in her new bed."

Gin tucked herself closer to Rohan as they walked down her street, joining a few more families heading toward the tree lighting.

"Thank you for suggesting this, Rohan," Gin said. "I feel like we are refinding some happy memories."

"Tonight, I want us to make new memories," he stated.

"I'd like that," she said, her reply so simple considering everything banging around in her heart wanting to fly free.

HE'D FORGOTTEN THE feeling of community. Rohan breathed in deeply through his nose, counting, breathing out again on the same count. During his multiple deployments he'd had to be so hypervigilant. Now he had to continually remind himself to relax.

"You doing okay?" she asked.

He looked at her, warmed by her awareness and concern, even when her son was hunching up, trying to avoid people touching him.

"Feeling good," he said. "Lucas, what do you think about finding a place off to the side toward the back so it's not so crowded at the tree lighting," Rohan suggested, parsing the crowd slowly filing out onto Main Street and heading toward the large tree in the park near the courthouse.

Main Street looked beautiful lit up. Garlands and lights were wrapped around every lamppost, and each store window had a charming seasonal display. He also saw trees in many of the stores decorated by local businesses to be auctioned off to be given to families in need as part of a fundraiser. More trees were on display in the Graff. He knew that because he and Boone had delivered the tree his family had decorated. Harry's House was keeping their trees on site, though they were part of the auction. Rohan had already bid.

The town seemed to have grown in the past ten years.

"I was reading about new earbuds that are also noise-canceling," he said softly to Ginny. "Maybe those would be more comfortable for Lucas if he thought they wouldn't make him look different since almost all teens seem to wear earbuds."

"Tell me about it." Ginny rolled her eyes. "I heard about them too. It's a nice idea, but they're really spendy."

"Christmas is coming."

"That's a lot of money to spend on a kid you just met."

"Lucas is more than that," he said softly. "You are far more to me than that." He stared into her eyes, wanting to stop time and ensure she saw him for who he was now—the man who learned from his mistakes. "Tell me you know that."

"It's starting to sink in," she replied, but kept walking, her focus on Lucas.

"It's time. Did you bring them?" Lucas demanded.

Ginny pulled three red pillar-style candles from her backpack.

Lucas reached for one.

"I even put in new batteries. Give one to Mr. Telford."

Rohan choked on a laugh. Mr. Telford. That still sounded like his dad.

"Here you go, Mr. Telford. It's tradition."

"You can call me Rohan. I used to attend the tree lighting when I was younger than you and then with your mom when we were a bit older."

"Did you know my dad?"

Ginny fumbled her votive. He caught it and handed it back. "No," he said calmly. "I never had the opportunity to meet your father, Lucas."

"I wonder if he was tall like you? With so many muscles. I'm small. Tenth percentile for my age. Weak and skinny too."

"Your mom's got some height so I bet you'll grow, and if you eat healthy food and stay active doing something you love, you'll build muscle in your teens. There are advantages to not being tall."

"Like what?"

"Being on the smaller size is an asset for a rodeo cowboy. I struggled to keep my seat on the bucking broncs and bulls once I shot up to six feet."

"Why?"

"Center of gravity is higher. One inch makes a huge difference. If you look at the stats of top-rated bull riders most of them are rangy like me, but several inches shorter. They have an advantage."

"Really?" Lucas lifted one hand up in the air and undulated his body back and forth. He made a fist with his other hand. "I'd never be able to hold on. I'm not strong."

"You can get stronger if you work at it safely over time and watch your nutrition. But you tie yourself into your grip on the bull and use your body—legs, core, arms, flexibility and intelligence to move with the bull. You can't outmuscle a two-thousand-pound animal no matter how much weight you lift. But your body is the body God gave you. You can always improve on nature with work and care, but building muscle is genetic."

Rohan unzipped his coat and spread out his arms. "I've always been lean. No matter how much weight I lifted when training as a soldier, I never bulked up like a lot of my brothers—you've met Cross, ummmm, Remy—Arlo's, ummm, dad." Wow that was going to take time getting used to. "And Colt, Parker's dad. I could never build muscle like them, but I'm good with that. You take what you get and work to make yourself the best you can be."

"I've always wanted to ride a horse," Lucas said mimicking the motion of riding. "Dr. Z said it would be good for balance and movement, but we don't have a horse and Mom and Grandpa didn't have time to take me."

Lucas looked and sounded devoid of guile, but Rohan wondered if he was being manipulated and couldn't be happier.

"Really." He pretended to ponder, and nearly laughed at Ginny's frustrated sigh. "I have horses. A lot of them." It hit him then, how he'd already started integrating back into ranch think—what was his family's was also his. "I practically sleep with them—my new apartment's in the barn."

"Does it stink?"

"We keep the horses pretty clean, but yeah, to an outsider it's probably odiferous. But if your mom agrees—" he looked at her to make sure he wasn't stepping too far out on a thin limb "—I will teach you to ride as long as you are keeping up with your schoolwork, chores, Scouts and other obligations."

That sounded parental.

"But don't pester your mom. Now." He wanted to get back on safer ground. "How do I turn this on?" He showed his candle to Lucas, hoping to distract him from thoughts of his father and his size, which were clearly bothering the boy. Maybe the self-awareness was good, but Rohan knew little about children and didn't want to step on Ginny's parenting toes.

"Thank you," she murmured to him as they made their way down Main Street. "Lucas has wanted to learn to ride for a while now, and his neurologist recommended it when he was younger, but the only horse therapy barn was too far away and insurance didn't cover it, so I tried yoga with Lucas. We both sucked, but it was kind of fun." She smiled at the memory.

"A lot of people still think Lucas is much younger." She bit her lip. "The pediatrician says I shouldn't worry, but…"

He gave in to his desire to hold her, no longer willing to rein in his feelings and play it cool, cautious. He put his arm around her shoulders and pulled her close to him.

"When someone tells you not to worry, I know it often seems like impossible advice to take, but you are paying the doctor for their expertise. I'd be happy to teach Lucas to ride. I taught you."

"I think you had an ulterior motive then, Cowboy."

"Absolutely." He kissed her cheek, savoring the velvet feel, her closeness and this second chance. She stopped walking and looked up at him.

"Thank you for the reminder," she said, her tone and gaze serious. "You may need to pinch me a few more times as a prompt when I fret about Lucas's skewed milestones."

He tried to tamp down the thrill at her words that pointed to a future. She meant to give them a chance and she wouldn't regret it.

THEY GATHERED IN the park, staying a little to the back of the crowd. Gin had her arms loosely around Lucas, as he stood in front of her, rising up and down on his tiptoes, likely trying to see Petal, Arlo or Parker in the crowd. Usually he shrugged out of her touch, which was so hard as Gin had always been so tactile.

So had Rohan. She'd loved the way he'd always held her hand, stroked her hair or skin. Now he stood next to her, his arm around her shoulders, his hand casually playing with her hair tumbling down her back. She'd been planning to skip the Stroll this year. Her father had always been one of the volunteers so they'd always gone as a family, and he would help to keep Lucas grounded.

She didn't think she'd be able to face all the bittersweet memories, but tonight she was creating new ones. And she tried not to think too far ahead about future problems.

She heard someone call out Rohan's name. And then a shriek of excitement and a shouted 'Lucas.'

"It's Petal." Lucas strained against her hold. "And Arlo and Parker. Can we go? Mom, let go."

She saw Rohan's whole family and the Wilders closer to the tree. It would be louder there. More people. But before she could express her concerns, Rohan brushed his lips against her ear, so that she forgot how to speak.

"Do you mind hanging out with my family a little bit tonight?"

No. She'd love to. Gin had always fantasized about being

part of a big family as a kid—she'd loved Rohan's, and even as an adult when she and her father would walk to the Stroll and join in, she'd often wished she was part of a larger group welcoming the holiday cheer.

"I did want you to myself," he admitted. "Well, the both of you," he said a little ruefully. "My family can be overwhelming, but they are really trying to help me settle back home."

"We definitely should join your family, and if Lucas gets overwhelmed, I'll slip away."

"With me," he said firmly.

They made their way toward his family where everyone greeted them, and Gin immediately felt that she and Lucas were easily accepted.

Lucas slipped away to stand with the group of kids. Rohan, learning that Witt was on call at the hospital, and Miranda was at her store working a few last-minute decorations for the open house during the Stroll, picked up his nephew Cannon and put the boy on his shoulders so that he could see the tree.

And now she was fangirling over her cowboy in a dad-like role. She really had it bad. He hadn't been ready at eighteen. That didn't mean he wouldn't be ready now.

You are way out in front of your horse, girl.

But it was hard not to let herself get caught up in the fantasy. Rohan. A life partner. A man in her bed and her home. Someone to share and build a life. A father for Lucas.

Another baby?

That thought brought her to a stop.

Rohan would probably want to have a child—his child. And with their history, that would be a sweet, full circle. Did she want another baby? Would she still have the time and energy for Lucas? Would he enjoy a sibling? He wasn't the most nurturing of kids, but he'd been gentle and sweet and helpful with Mystery. And then there was the financial element.

Stop.

Tonight was their first date as adults. She didn't need to invent problems or think babies. Rohan was behind her, his body strong and warm, and his hands loosely rested on her hips.

A single note from a triangle rang out in the night, and the crowd pushed a little closer, quieting.

A group of high schoolers filed up on the makeshift stage, and Chelsea Crawford Collier Flint—the mayor—took the mic, welcoming them to the annual tree-lighting ceremony. She spoke briefly about the evening's activities and how the town's businesses would be open, many of the shops offering specials, and she entreated everyone to shop local. And then the music teacher began to play the electric piano and the choir and the crowd broke into 'Oh Come All Ye Faithful.'

Gin's heart soared. This could be the best Christmas ever.

Chapter Seventeen

TWO WEEKS LATER Gin turned a full circle in the Harry's House Annex's living room, which was the hangout and meeting area. "This is amazing. I can't believe the transformation. I just can't believe it. I wish my father—" Gin broke off, tears threatening. "I keep taking pictures for the social media sites Arlo and Petal set up for the annex and then I want to send them to my father."

Piper hugged her. "I didn't know your dad, but I'm sure this was beyond his wildest dreams too. The first couple of days I volunteered for cleanup, Boone wanted to put me in a hazmat suit. The transformation is amazing."

"We probably should have had the suits," Talon Wilder agreed. "Colt wouldn't let me come inside until all the carpets and fabrics were pulled up and hauled out."

"Can't be too careful," Gin agreed looking at both women's baby bumps.

"We didn't get to paint, but I did help with the shelving installs and the decoration," Talon said. "I'm getting quite handy with power tools," she said. "And I'm thrilled with the science lab. I love that one room is dedicated to science."

"Talon, I'm so happy you've agreed to teach some science workshops over the summer for all age groups and that you will write the grants for more equipment," Gin said. "The annex is not only coming together, but it's also functional and beautiful."

She looked around at everyone. They were volunteers and now becoming friends. "We already have so much planned—the machine repair class will launch the annex, and we have a wait list, but now we're developing the spring catalog offerings online, and we already have a music recording studio and jam nights." She looked at Riley. "Science and cooking and gardening and mixology." She looked at Talon and Shane. "Sky Wilder's going to teach welding and a sculpture class; Boone and Rohan have an open afternoon and evening time for classic auto restoration; and there's yoga and meditation." She smiled at Piper. "My heart's so full. I can hardly believe it's happening so fast. We need to set a date for the grand opening."

"Leave the party planning to me and Miranda," Shane said. "You are finally on break from teaching for two whole weeks, and you should enjoy them."

"Although this weekend I heard she's flying solo." Talon grinned, and Gin felt her cheeks flush as the four women pivoted to look at her. "Colt has taken over being one of the assistant leaders of Parker's Scout troop since Mr. Lane's passing, and he said that Rohan will be taking Lucas on the snow camping trip this weekend, so two days and one long Saturday where you can sloth out."

"Or sample my new Christmas cocktails," Shane said.

"That sounds lonely," Piper said, straight-faced. "Whatever will you do—listen to music at the Graff or FlintWorks? Dancing at Grey's after a couple of pink drinks? A night of self-care? I could set you up with a massage or personal yoga class so you'd be really limber and relaxed when Rohan came back."

"Yuck." Riley made a face and covered her ears. "That's my brother, and I don't want to hear it."

"Your mind." Gin felt a little shocked by Piper's insinuation, but also excited. They were teasing her like friends did. She hadn't really had that since high school. She'd cut herself off to focus on raising Lucas and being the best teacher she could be.

"Maybe a couples' massage," Shane said, "on Sunday night to relax Rohan before he teaches his first group of teens."

"Still ew." Riley stuck her tongue out.

"Actually, Boone and Rohan are going to teach it together. Brother bonding, but Rohan insists he's playing lead. Older brothers." Piper laughed. "Those two are hilarious to watch together. Boone's always trying to outcompete Rohan on everything including how many flapjacks they can eat at Saturday family breakfast, so Rohan is probably not as nervous since Boone's worked with kids and planned out the curriculum."

"They also compete over chores. Who does that? I swear

they act more like besties than brothers," Riley said.

"I'm happy because I think Rohan's going to help Boone with his foundation. I overheard them planning out an obstacle and ropes course and camping site on our property and building some massive tree house using one of Colt's plans. But," Piper drawled out and winked at Gin, "I'm sure after camping in the snow for a weekend with a group of Scouts, Rohan will need some serious thawing out—cozy fire, belt of whiskey, a warm and willing woman…"

"I had no idea you were so racy," Gin said.

"I should buy you soap for Christmas," Riley said.

Piper just laughed.

"We learned that pretty quickly," Shane and Talon chorused.

"She looks sweet, but her mind…" Shane said.

"It's the cowboys," Talon said. "They bring out your inner naughty."

"And the soldiers." Shane nodded. "They raunch us up, but it's probably been challenging to find alone time with Rohan considering you have Lucas and the annex."

"If you need creative time-managing tips for hot cowboy-soldier sex, I have them," Talon said. "When I met Colt, Parker was only seven, and I was working and going to school, and Colt was building Parker a tree house and bottle feeding a runt-of-the-litter pup, and we still managed plenty of horizontal and not always horizontal time."

"Now that's a brag and a challenge," Piper said. "Tips?"

"Have you and Rohan…?" Shane trailed off suggestively.

"I am not having this discussion with any of you," Gin said, laughing and pressing her hands against her flaming cheeks. "We are keeping things G, very G."

"Yes, please," Riley chimed.

With her history, she didn't want to jump into anything too quickly. "I have to think of Lucas."

"This camping trip will be good for both of them," Talon said, losing her teasing tone. "The way Colt was with Parker—watching his baseball practices, going to his Cub Scout meetings, building the tree house with him, just won me over. Rohan seems like the same kind of man. This camping trip speaks of commitment."

Gin nodded. "It does seem huge. I'm going to be on pins and needles this weekend, hoping it goes well. I've been…" She paused and then plunged ahead—just as she was trying to be more open and take risks with Rohan, she had to open up to new friends as well to forge the deep friendships she wanted.

"I've been afraid to hope for love," she admitted. "I thought I'd lost Rohan forever and opening myself up to trust again has been hard but wonderful. I never thought I wanted to be in a relationship again."

The four women nodded, their teasing expressions creased to sympathy and interest.

"I felt like I'd missed so much becoming a mom so young. I'd gone away to college but instead of thriving I made a lot of mistakes, acted destructively, let myself and my father down. I basically failed out of college initially and came home pregnant, no degree, no job. And I stopped writing. I just gave up all my dreams." Her voice cracked. That hurt the most—that she'd given up on herself.

"I turned my life around." She looked at the four women. None of them showed any shock or judgment. They listened with open expressions and hearts like friends did. "And I'm happy, but I can't help but feel like I've missed so much. I've never traveled. I've never even left this state."

"Where do you want to go?" Riley asked, looking alarmed.

"I don't know. I haven't even thought about it. Lucas needs so much structure it never occurred to me that I could leave. Plus my father was here. But he's gone. And Lucas is doing well in school and more willing to try new things—even to make friends, so I feel like there might be the light of opportunity in my future. He handled the Stroll well. He's excited about camping with Rohan. He even wants to learn to ride. I feel like so much more is possible for both of us."

She stopped. She worried she was confessing too much, but everyone seemed to be listening. "I have hope now, like I can live a bigger life. I've even started thinking about travel and writing again. Writing was once as big a part of me as breathing, but now I just do the daily freewriting assignments in the first ten minutes of my language arts classes with my students."

"That's writing," Piper said, touching Gin's hand.

She shrugged, not wanting to get too maudlin. She was happy. She had hope for the future instead of just trying to make it through each day.

"Maybe buy yourself a journal at the bookstore and take this Saturday night to freewrite," Shane said. "Write for yourself. See where it takes you. Just as Rohan will be having a moment with Lucas, you can have a moment with yourself."

"I haven't had any freedom in thirteen years," Gin said slowly. "I don't even know what I'd do with it."

"Whatever you want," Piper said. "You just have to seize those moments for yourself. Savor them. Fill up your well of you."

"I don't even know if I know how," she said. "I've got Lucas, my job, the annex, bills—" She broke off. She sounded so negative. She also had hope now that she wouldn't have to do everything alone.

"You also have us," Shane reminded her. "We'll help you shine your light and blaze your trail and all that jazz." She spread her fingers and waggled her hands.

Gin heard a sound in the front room of the house and went out to investigate.

"Oh, you're early." She smiled at Rohan and walked up to him, expecting a kiss.

"Yes," he said, looking a little spacey or sick.

"You okay? You don't have to take Lucas if you don't

want to. I can…"

"Yes," he said firmly. "I want to take him camping. I want you to have a couple of days for yourself."

"Okay." Gin wished he'd kiss her, but he stood in front of her rigid as a block of wood. What was wrong with him? Everyone seemed to be pushing her away, and alone time and freedom didn't sound as appealing as everyone was trying to make them sound.

"I'M DOING IT. I'm skating." Lucas's eyes were huge, his arms stiff and awkwardly angled out from his sides. His knees were locked, but yes, he was moving across the ice, Rohan's hands parallel to Lucas's waist for security. Ginny skated backward facing them, a smile on her beautiful face.

The afternoon was like something out of a dream. He and Ginny were at Miracle Lake. The weather was crisp and clear. Not too many people were on the ice yet. The sun hadn't yet set behind the mountains but the lights strung up in the trees surrounding part of the lake that was open for skating had already winked on, turning everything a rosy gold. A jazzy version of 'Silver Bells' played over the loudspeakers. The crisp air was redolent with scents of evergreen, kettle corn and roasting nuts.

The moment was perfect. The whole past three weeks had played like a movie of the life he'd been supposed to lead—the life he wanted to lead. He was home on the ranch, finding his footing. Connecting with his family, old friends and two of his brothers from his unit.

Ginny once again looked at him like he had some magical superpower when he knew he absolutely didn't.

The camping trip with Lucas had been eye-opening. Lucas had been eager to try everything, but he'd required more explanation about certain activities and Ginny had packed him a lot of his own foods, though Rohan had encouraged Lucas to try what everyone else was eating, even though it required so much patience and encouragement and often ended in failure.

The other parents and Colt had helped when he'd felt a bit lost. Parker had also stepped in as a bigger buddy. He seemed to be one of the most popular and accomplished kids in the troop and by taking Lucas under his wing, Parker had helped smooth the way for Lucas.

Rohan had had fun and Colt had even reminded him that Scouts started up again the first week of January, and he'd added his cell and email to the parents roster.

It should have seemed like a huge step, and yet looking at Lucas, struggling under the weight of his duffel bag, determined to load it into Rohan's truck at the trailhead parking, Rohan had felt like the step was a no-brainer. He wanted to take Lucas to Scouts in the new year. He wanted to be involved in Lucas's life.

Was it too early to think of himself as a dad?

The way he'd started researching stones online indicated he didn't think so. He definitely wanted to marry Ginny, but ever since he'd overheard her talking to her friends and his sister at the annex, when he'd arrived a little early to pick up Lucas's camping gear, he'd been on the fence—not about his feelings or hope for a shared future—but more about what was best for Ginny.

He'd had a career that had taken him across the globe, but her quiet explanation about how small her world had become after Lucas's birth, how she'd abandoned her dreams and writing, brought all of Ron Lane's fears back.

What would marriage to him offer her other than another tie-down to a small town? He'd certainly love her until he died, but was love enough?

For the past almost fourteen years Ginny had lived in her childhood home, raising her son. Next year Lucas would be in middle school. In seven years he'd graduate, and Ginny wouldn't even be forty. She'd be free to pursue another career, travel, move to a different state, write. The possibilities were endless, but if she married him and they had a child or two like he wanted, she'd be trapped all over again—living in Marietta, tied to him, the ranch and motherhood.

He'd been set on buying her a ring for Christmas. Now he worried it would be more of an albatross than a blessing. Was he once again being selfish?

She was right—she hadn't had much chance to live, to explore and to carve her own path. He didn't want his love and his dream to clip her wings again.

"I'm skating." Lucas made a weird whistling sound and flapped his arms. "I'm flying like a bird."

"Yes, yes you are, Lucas. Continue to fly."

He looked at Ginny. Her eyes shone with pride, and her smile included—he felt—both him and Lucas.

He felt the warmth to his toes, but the ring, the proposal would have to wait. Ginny too needed her chance to fly.

"Both of you," he choked out.

LUCAS SAT ON a bench, carefully untying the skates that Rohan had purchased for him as an early Christmas present. Lucas's fingers faltered, but when she bent to help him, Rohan was already talking Lucas through it.

Instead of feeling irritated, she felt a rush of relief as Lucas struggled but then got it. His smile was quick, but there. "I did it, Rohan."

"I knew you could."

"Do you want to come to dinner?" Gin asked, feeling a little shy.

She and Rohan had been spending so much time together over the past few weeks that she figured he'd say yes. She already had Moroccan stew in the Crock-Pot.

"Dinner with you and Lucas is always a treat," he said softly.

Something in his tone seemed a little off. And his normally fluid movements were stiff. And it wasn't a yes. Alarm bubbled in her tummy.

They left Miracle Lake and headed back to town, Gin racking her brain as to what could be bothering Rohan. Lucas stared out the window, likely exhausted and overwhelmed from the skating.

"Are you going to do it tonight?" Lucas asked.

"What?" Gin asked, turning around, but Lucas's focus was on the back of Rohan's head.

"Mom, I can't tell you."

"Excuse me?"

Lucas avoided her gaze and question.

"Lucas, I asked you a question." Beside her Rohan stiffened.

"It's a secret."

"We don't have secrets, Lucas," she prodded softly.

He turned away from her, a scowl marring his face.

"That's okay, Lucas," Rohan interrupted her next question. "Lucas and I made a little something for the tree to commemorate our trip, and I also asked his opinion about a Christmas present for you when we were camping."

"Oh." She nearly slapped her forehead. She hadn't even thought of that. "Sorry," she said to Lucas. "I didn't think about that, sweetie. I overreacted."

Her cheeks heated. "I'm sorry." She touched Rohan's arm.

"No worries," he said, but his tension seemed to have increased.

It hadn't occurred to her that Lucas would have a secret from her, but now with Rohan in their lives, and with Lucas finally having a few budding friendships—fingers crossed—he might eventually have some, and she'd need to reconsider their rule—one of those shades of gray he didn't intuitively understand.

Rohan pulled up to her house. Gin smiled at the Christmas lights wrapped around the evergreen, the candy cane lights lining the sidewalk and the white icicle lights along the roof. The house looked welcoming and happy.

"It looks so beautiful. Thank you. I'm still in awe that you and Lucas did this as a surprise. When I was out for girls' night, I never suspected you two had something like this planned."

"Rohan will have another surprise soon," Lucas said, miming zipping his lips—something he'd never done before. "Do you have it yet?"

"Not yet, bud, and if we talk about it, it's not a secret."

She popped out of the truck, surprised Rohan hadn't yet turned off the truck or come around to her side to help her out. She'd always thought it was old-fashioned manners, but now she missed it.

"Aren't you coming?"

He hesitated.

"Rohan?"

She tried to kick the ball of doom gathered in her belly, but it grew.

"Lucas, you can open up the house." She handed him the keys realizing that Rohan had something to say. She tried to keep her heart from pounding with dread. She'd promised herself she wouldn't always imagine the worst.

"What's going on?" she asked urgently, wrapping her arms around herself. The sun was just starting to set, and the chill ramped up accordingly.

"Let's get you inside."

"Just tell me, Rohan." Whatever she was imagining was likely far worse than what he was about to say.

"I…I…just…we've been spending a lot of time together."

She stared at him. It was worse than even she had imagined.

"You're dumping me?" she asked incredulously.

"No. Never," he objected and drew her into his embrace. She clung to him.

"I know what I want," he said grimly, and Gin looked up at his starkly drawn features. What he wanted didn't seem to be making him happy.

"But I'm afraid I'm pushing too hard, crowding you. I shoved back into your life like a rampaging rank bull knocking everything over. I don't want to take over. I want to give you time to think about what you want, what's best for you and for Lucas. I read that you shouldn't make any major changes for at least a year following a huge life loss, and me, well, I'm a huge change."

She stared at him. What was he saying? He was breaking up with her for a year or just until next September or putting on the brakes? She wanted to scream in frustration.

"You've never had the time to travel or explore or have the freedom your father wanted for you. I'm one more tent post."

She stared at him feeling sick and utterly mystified by his change of heart.

He squared his shoulders, his jaw grim and somehow managed to look even more stoic.

"I want you to have freedom to choose."

She gaped at him. "What are you talking about?" she demanded. Did he have some idea some other cowboy was stage left pointing at himself, pick me, pick me like Blake Shelton on *The Voice*? "What happened? Why are you saying these things? If you don't want us. If you've changed your mind, just man up and say it. Dump me."

Fear choked her, but anger rose to her defense.

"I don't want to get in your way again. I want to give you choices."

"Very generous," she snarked, trembling with hurt and fury and confusion. "Thank you so much, Rohan Telford, for your altruism. You traveling thousands of miles to deliver a letter for a friend, worm your way into a young boy's heart and then offer me choices in my life."

"Ginny, I..." He took off his hat and worried it through his fingers. "It's not that I..."

"Good night, Cowboy. I'm going inside to contemplate all my marvelous choices without you, and you can ride off into the sunset pleased with your generosity. You should have brought your horse. More atmosphere. Good night and goodbye."

She slammed the hat back on his head and stalked up her brightly lit path and kicked the door shut behind her with a satisfying thud.

"Cowboys," she bit out.

Lucas looked up from where he'd started the holiday train, and the skaters were already twirling on the pond. "Where's Rohan?"

"Navel gazing."

"Huh?" Lucas looked at his belly.

She half laughed and half cried as she rushed across the room to pull Lucas in for a quick hug.

It lasted almost ten seconds before he squirmed away.

"How about some stew?" she said grimacing at the mom anticlimactic offering.

Choices indeed.

Chapter Eighteen

HIS FAMILY LOOKED up startled when he entered the main house, too keyed up to face his empty apartment. He'd done it. He'd given Ginny her freedom if she wanted it, even though every cell in his body had urged him to drop, one knee down, and beg her to be his wife. Not very twenty-first-century male. And he hadn't expected her to be so angry, though in truth he hadn't really thought through how he expected her to respond.

Maybe he should have practiced his speech or something—outlined why he wanted to give her space if she needed it. He guessed he'd hoped that she'd throw herself in his arms and declare that he was her choice every single time. Probably pretty dumb. It was hard to act against his instincts. If he hadn't given her freedom to choose he'd be eating dinner with Ginny and Lucas right now, and he ached with loneliness even surrounded by family.

"You're in time for dinner, if you want," his mom greeted him. "We figured you'd be at Ginny's, just like old times, although she loved to come out this way when you two were together."

"I wanted to come home and see all of you," Rohan said,

trying to sound cheerful, even though he felt like he was drowning, but his family deserved his best efforts. They went out of their way to show him love and support every day. "The food smells delicious."

Spaghetti Bolognese with a vegetable ratatouille and garlic bread and salad."

"You trying to put Rocco out of business?" he teased, kissing her cheek.

"Where do you think they got their recipes from?" she shot back. "Go wash up. You can help me serve and say grace tonight."

Dinner was delicious, though he had no appetite. His entire family was there, talking, teasing, sharing their day, but he could barely bring himself to speak. Although Boone and his mom kept shooting him some confused looks, everyone politely let his sulk go unremarked.

At least he didn't dim their fun. He wondered what Lucas would make of the boisterous meal. Would he need the earbuds Pro to help him cope? He'd ordered them yesterday as Lucas's Christmas present. Even if Ginny kicked him to the curb, realizing that she'd rather have her freedom, he still intended to teach Lucas to ride and to help him in Scouts if she'd let him. He could be like a mentor or volunteer in the Big Brother program. He could spend time with Lucas while Ginny wrote or… There he went trying to manage her life again for her.

She was still grieving her father. As far as he knew she

hadn't even read the letter yet. He had no business trying to propose to her so quickly. They could take their time. See each other more casually. He hated the idea of that, but it was considerate toward her.

He dogged out of playing Scrabble, unable to hold up even a modicum of appearances by this point, although he did pull Boone aside to ask him a favor.

"You want me to teach Lucas to ride? Something wrong with your legs or hands?"

"No. I promised Lucas I'd teach him to ride, and tomorrow was to be the first lesson, but Ginny and I talked about slowing things down a bit and…"

"Ginny dumped you?"

"No, shshshsh." He looked around as if suddenly one of their family members would decide to walk a hundred yards in the icy cold to visit the barn. "She didn't dump me. I just…"

"You dumped her?" Boone was incredulous.

"No, I love her," Rohan declared. "I've always loved her. I just…she…" He raked his shaking fingers through his hair, wanting to pull it out by the roots. He felt wrecked, off. "I want to marry her."

"So you slowed things down." Boone crossed his arms and rocked back on his heels. "That's stupid and you aren't stupid. Explain."

"It's complicated."

"No, it's dumb."

"Thanks for your support."

"Why should I support you when you're being an idiot?"

"I'm trying to give her space, okay? She's hasn't had a lot of choices. When we—" He broke off, not able to discuss the past with Boone who looked like he wanted to hit him, and a big part of him wished he'd take a swing. "She had Lucas when she was young, and has been raising him and going to school and now teaching, and she's doing the annex because it was her father's dream. She's all heart and doing things for other people and if she marries me, she'll be tied down to the ranch, and hopefully a mother again, and she'll have even less time to herself to write or travel or…" He made a helpless gesture.

"Does she want to do those things?"

"Of course. I heard her talking about not having any freedom, not even knowing what it would feel like or what to do with it when I went to pick up Lucas for the camping trip."

Boone blew out a hard breath.

"Please. This is hard enough," Rohan said.

"Fine. I'll teach Lucas to ride. I'll pick him up tomorrow."

"Thank you."

"But I still think you should explain your reasoning to Ginny. Knowing you, you just sacrificed yourself stoically and mumbled something about giving her space or freedom, which probably pissed her off."

She had slammed the door on him.

"I'll leave you your freedom to figure out how you're going to dig yourself out of this hole you dug." Boone stalked off.

"WHAT'S THAT?" GIN asked half-heartedly after she didn't manage more than a couple of bites of her dinner, and Lucas had picked around the vegetables to eat a little meat and rice.

Lucas stood at the Christmas tree, gently touching an ornament that she hadn't seen before.

"It's an igloo. Rohan and I made it at the gift store at that hotel. It's to commem…coment…no…remember our first snow camping trip. He also bought me a horse ornament. He's going to teach me to ride tomorrow."

Helplessness and confusion poured through her. What was going on? Why would Rohan make all these plans but then bail on her?

"It takes more than one lesson to learn to ride, and ahhh the lesson might not happen tomorrow, bud."

"Why not? A promise is a promise."

Her father used to say that, and with her father it was true. She would have said the same about Rohan, but she was feeling too emotionally battered to trust anyone at the moment. No. That wasn't true. She trusted herself.

"We'll make sure you learn to ride," she promised. Plenty

of stables around Marietta, and she was not going to let fear hold her back anymore. If Rohan wanted to get squirrely, then he could just keep collecting and hiding his nuts. She was not playing games with anyone's emotions.

That night before she settled into bed, she paused and then pulled the red envelope from the drawer of her nightstand and opened it.

Dear Mr. Lane,

I wanted to thank you for never giving up on me. For never giving me a pass to just hang back and squander the time I was given on earth. You called me on my attitude every single time. You never let me turn away or blink. You constantly held a mirror up to me and exhorted me to be the best version of myself, never the easiest.

Maybe you thought your advice and attention went unheeded. I know many days I was just so tired of being me, of trying to drag myself and my family across an imaginary finish line that just kept moving, but you were right. I did have better inside of me. It took your unwavering belief in me and my army training and years of leading other good men to find that man you saw so many years ago. I'm keeping him.

I'm coming home soon. I'm bringing five lost brothers with me. Six eventually, I hope. They will need homes. They will need hope. They will need guidance to rebuild their lives. I think togeth-

er we will have much to offer the community of Marietta. I intend to rebuild my family's legacy, not in the same form, but in a kinder, healthier image. I hope I can continue to reach out to you for inspiration and guidance. I too want to live my life in the light and be of service and never shirk from duty or what's right because I am afraid.

You encouraged me to push myself hard and then harder. You urged me to take risks, to face what I fear. You have always been a strong pillar in the community. I hope to stand beside you, lending my strength and my voice to others to help pull them into the light. I have often thought of you when I've been leading men on missions. Your faith in me has helped me to have faith in myself and others.

Best wishes,
Jace McBride

"No fear," she whispered. Her father had always said to face fear, not run from it. Jace had taken his advice to heart. She should do the same.

Was fear what had stalked Rohan this afternoon or something else? He'd talked of freedom. So had Shane and the others that day in the annex, and it had sounded so nebulous and lonely. Had Rohan overheard more of their conversation than she thought? Was he trying once again to be noble like he had been in college?

She dropped the letter in her lap and scowled. Seriously? That sounded more believable than he'd just changed his mind about them and wanted to slow down. Rohan hadn't done anything slow in his life and since he'd arrived home less than a month ago, he'd barged back into her life, thrown himself into renovating the annex, practically becoming Father Christmas taking them tree hunting, sleigh riding and to the Stroll. He'd decorated her tree and house with Lucas and had taken him camping and had even made a frickin' ornament with her son to commemorate a camping trip. Then he'd bought Lucas skates and offered riding lessons.

Who did that and then poofed out of the picture?

Rohan? Mister hero. He was probably afraid he was going to hold her back from some imagined destination she wasn't even keen on going to.

Last time she'd run away, desperately hurt. She lacked the courage to fight for them, but she'd blamed her fear on him—he should have fought for her.

She looked down at the letter in her lap and traced the word *fear*. No fear. She had to face her fears and fight for what she wanted.

She was going to fight for Rohan, and if he wanted freedom, he'd have to earn it with an explanation because like her father and Jace, she was a fighter, and she would no longer live in fear.

"Thank you, Jace," she whispered, putting the letter back in the envelope. She kissed it and placed it back in her nightstand drawer.

"Hey, buddy." Gin handed Lucas a fluffy pumpkin pancake with a smidgeon of shredded zucchini. "What do you think if we head up to the Telford Ranch for your riding lesson in a little bit?"

That piqued his interest.

"I thought you said I might not have a lesson."

"I've decided that if Rohan promised you a lesson, you are going to have a lesson."

"You called him?" Lucas turned his plate around, lifting the edges of the pancake to look under it.

"I thought we'd surprise him."

He stared at her. "You don't like surprises."

Fantastic lesson for her already anxious kid. "Sometimes surprises teach us something we don't know about ourselves. Like Gramps said. It's good to sometimes step out of our comfort zone."

"I'm not that scared of riding."

"Good because we're leaving in ten minutes."

Gin wished her bravado had lasted the entire drive, but no, with each mile in their rearview mirror, she seemed to have some new physical reaction to showing up unannounced and confronting Rohan at his family's ranch. She was so not femme fatale material.

"Walk with fear, don't let it lead," she reminded herself, gripping the steering wheel.

She pulled into the long drive of the Telford Ranch and turned left to drive up to the horse barn. It suddenly occurred to her that there were hundreds of places Rohan might be other than the horse barn. He wasn't expecting her at nine a.m. on a Wednesday a few days before Christmas. His family could also be around to bear witness to what had become in her mind an epic showdown that had her palms clammy.

"So be it." She reached for some of that cowgirl swagger Marietta was so famous for.

Just as she exited the truck, the barn door swung wide and Rohan, Boone, Riley and Sarah and Taryn Telford strolled out of the barn.

She stared. Not exactly private. Still she was going to speak her mind and tell Rohan what she wanted in front of her son and Rohan's family. Actions speak louder than words. Her father had said that. She told her students that.

"Good morning." Gin sucked in a deep breath, stomped down her nerves and hopped out of her car.

"Rohan Telford," she said clearly. "You need to explain yourself."

ROHAN STARED AT Ginny. She was here. He'd been trying to get Boone out of the barn and on the road and dodging his parents' questions about why he wouldn't go pick up

Lucas if he was going to teach him to ride, and then, like magic Ginny appeared, beautiful in her dark denim jumpsuit and a cream, blue and yellow plaid, fleece-lined flannel.

He hadn't slept last night and had started on the coffee before the sun came up. Lucas slid out of the car looking adorably awkward. Mystery barked once and ran over to Lucas, who then crouched down to pet the dog, utterly absorbed in the moment.

He had no idea what to say. His mind was an utter blank and all he wanted to do was pull her into his arms and tell her that freedom was highly overrated.

"You don't have the right to tell me what I want." She walked toward him, eyes blazing, her body taut as a strung bow. "You don't have the right to give me freedom. If I want it, I'll seize it with both hands."

She stopped in front of him, and he was aware that everyone else was eerily silent, and the silence felt expectant.

"You told me to think about what I wanted," she said eating up the silence before he had a chance to speak. Her hair danced around her face in the morning breeze, and all he wanted to do was run his fingers through her curls, kiss her stupid and hold her until time ended.

"I want you. I've always wanted you. Your turn. What do you want, Rohan?"

"You, Ginny. It's always been you." The words came easy. "I've loved you forever," he vowed and stared into her ocean of blue. "I always have. Even with all the years and miles between us, I loved you. You have always been and will always be my one."

"So why the brush-off last night—nerves or did you eavesdrop last week when I was talking to Riley, Shane, Piper and Talon?"

"I wasn't trying listen in," he said. "But yeah, I heard them urging you to take time for yourself to explore, and that was something your dad wanted for you and you never had time. I didn't want to hold you back."

"So you concluded, without asking, that I had some fantastical fantasy about traveling to Paris on my own sipping champagne out of a Chanel shoe and then writing about it?" She rolled her eyes, and he heard Riley stifle a giggle.

"I didn't exactly picture that," he said.

"I once had a man sip champagne out of my boot." Riley laughed. "Go rope your cowboy, Ginny."

"I intend to."

"Finally," Boone cheered. "Thank you, Ginny, for putting this idiot out of his misery. Hey, Riles, let's get Lucas tricked out with riding boots and we'll start him on Sugar."

"No. Everyone stays for a moment." Ginny sucked in a breath. "When Rohan and I had problems before, I ran away and blocked his number. I blamed him for everything. This time I'm declaring myself publicly. My father always encouraged others to live their best lives and to challenge themselves and look fear in the face. I am my father's daughter."

Rohan felt so proud of her in that moment. He was the

luckiest man in the world to have a second chance with Ginny Lane. He wanted to look up at Heaven and thank Jace for this miracle, but he couldn't take his eyes off of her.

She walked up to him and cupped Rohan's cheeks between her icy hands. "Rohan Telford, I love you, and I'm not going anywhere without you, not even Paris."

"Ginny Lane, I'm home to stay and I want you and Lucas to be my family."

He pulled her to him and kissed her, finally feeling whole again.

"Let me break out the champagne," his father said. "I bought it a few weeks ago after the sleigh ride. We definitely have something to celebrate this morning after Lucas's riding lesson."

"Why wait?" Rohan said. "I think thirteen years is already far too long."

"I have a boot." Lucas kicked off one snow boat. "That's sort of French."

"Oui." Riley grinned.

"But since this is a special occasion, we'll toast with glasses." Rohan couldn't let Ginny go, not even when his father brought champagne and orange juice on a tray along with some fluted glasses that Rohan had no idea his family owned.

"To love and second chances." Rohan held up his glass with a small amount of bubbly.

"To the future." Ginny clinked glasses with him and smiled.

Rohan didn't need champagne to feel like an effervescent sun was rising in his soul to spread out and encompass his entire family in a golden light.

"To us," he whispered against her lips.

Epilogue

A FEW DAYS later, it was Christmas Eve, and Rohan couldn't remember feeling more content. He had Ginny curled up next to him on her couch while Lucas tied a bow around Mystery's neck. The train traveled around the brightly lit Christmas tree and Lucas was looking at a list of songs Petal, Arlo and Parker had compiled and listening to samples of the music before downloading then onto his phone.

He had no idea what Lucas's taste in music was because he was wearing the earbuds and despite Ginny's concerns, they were a hit and didn't irritate his ears.

The gas fire danced, cheerfully emitting warmth and holiday atmosphere. Symphonic Christmas music played softly in the background. He and Ginny had made dinner together, and then Lucas had joined them making a braided Christmas bread for Christmas dinner with his family tomorrow.

"You've only been home a month and our lives have changed so much," she said softly.

He kissed the nape of her neck, allowing his fingers to play in her hair.

"For years I dreaded coming home. I didn't feel like I'd belong, and now I can't imagine being anywhere else."

"Same for me," Ginny said and linked her fingers with his. "It's like we were never apart except now we're deeper and better at communicating."

"I still have a ways to go in that department," he admitted.

"That's okay. I have some new cowgirl boots with a seriously pointy toe." She lifted up her leg to admire the boots he'd given her for an early Christmas present. "I can give you a kick if you slide back into martyr role and start deciding what is best for me again."

"Maybe we shouldn't have opened any of the gifts tonight," he mused, but couldn't stop smiling.

He'd wanted Lucas to have the earbuds for tomorrow and the phone made sense so that Lucas would have some music or games to enjoy and could consult Petal about some apps to download. Rohan knew they'd have to supervise his phone use, but he hoped that it would help Lucas navigate the social scene better as he grew.

"I'm excited about tomorrow," Ginny said. "I've felt lonely for a long time but didn't know it, and I finally feel like I'm where I'm supposed to be, where I've always wanted to be—with you, but also part of a big family."

His heart skipped a beat.

"If you really feel like that, there's one more gift you could open before we celebrate Christmas with my family tomorrow."

She turned around in his arms so that they were facing. "Rohan?"

"I don't want to wait," he said. "Not even one more day."

Her eyes searched his. He hoped she saw everything he felt and all his intentions to be the man she wanted and needed and could count on in their future.

He texted Lucas.

Can you bring the special present we talked about over?

Lucas looked up, his eyes round. He popped to his feet and reached for the igloo ornament. He brought it over, his eyes lit up like a light bulb.

"Mystery, it's happening."

Rohan sat up and slid to his knees. Lucas also knelt beside him. Mystery sat next to Lucas and raised one paw like she wanted to shake. Ginny's breath came in quick gasps, and one hand was pressed to her heart, but she was smiling.

Rohan reached into the igloo and pulled out a tiny red velvet bag.

"Part of me wishes I'd done this thirteen years ago, but I'm happy with the man I am now, and I love the woman you are today even more than I ever thought possible, and our lives would never feel complete without Lucas, so I think tonight is the perfect night. No more past, only future."

He handed her the small bag.

"Yes," she said, tears spilling down her face. "Absolutely

and forever yes."

She wrapped him up in her warm embrace and Rohan felt that this was the best moment of his life.

"You're supposed to open it," Lucas said. "And wear it forever and ever. A promise kept."

Ginny laughed and cried and fumbled with the bag. Rohan ended up untying the strings and slipping the ring on her finger.

"Do you like it? I helped pick it," Lucas stated proudly.

"I love it. I love you," she said to Rohan. "I love both of you forever and ever."

And Ginny wrapped her arms around all of them, including Mystery, and pulled them close.

"Best Christmas ever, and it's not even tomorrow yet. I can't wait."

"Best Christmas and best family," Ginny said, and Rohan also wrapped his arms around his family.

"This is a new beginning," he vowed. "But let's just savor the now."

The End

If you enjoyed *The Cowboy's Christmas Homecoming*, you'll love the next books in…

The Coyote Cowboys of Montana series

Book 1: *The Cowboy's Word*

Book 2: *Marry Me Please, Cowboy*

Book 3: *The Cowboy's Christmas Homecoming*

Book 4: *Coming soon*

Book 5: *Coming soon*

Available now at your favorite online retailer!

More Books by Sinclair Jayne

Montana Rodeo Brides series

Book 1: *The Cowboy Says I Do*

Book 2: *The Cowboy's Challenge*

Book 3: *Breaking the Cowboy's Rules*

The Texas Wolf Brothers series

Book 1: *A Son for the Texas Cowboy*

Book 2: *A Bride for the Texas Cowboy*

Book 3: *A Baby for the Texas Cowboy*

The Wilder Brothers series

Book 1: *Seducing the Bachelor*

Book 2: *Want Me, Cowboy*

Book 3: *The Christmas Challenge*

Book 4: *Cowboy Takes All*

The Misguided Masala Matchmaker series

Book 1: *A Hard Yes*

Book 2: *Swipe Right for Marriage*

Book 3: *An Unsuitable Boy*

Book 4: *Stealing Mr. Right*

Available now at your favorite online retailer!

About the Author

Sinclair Sawhney is a former journalist and middle school teacher who holds a BA in Political Science and K-8 teaching certificate from the University of California, Irvine and a MS in Education with an emphasis in teaching writing from the University of Washington. She has worked as Senior Editor with Tule Publishing for over seven years.

Writing as Sinclair Jayne she's published fifteen short contemporary romances with Tule Publishing with another four books being released in 2021. Married for over twenty-four years, she has two children, and when she isn't writing or editing, she and her husband, Deepak, are hosting wine tastings of their pinot noir and pinot noir rose at their vineyard Roshni, which is a Hindi word for light-filled, located in Oregon's Willamette Valley. Shaandaar!

Thank you for reading

The Cowboy's Christmas Homecoming

If you enjoyed this book, you can find more from all our great authors at TulePublishing.com, or from your favorite online retailer.

Made in United States
Troutdale, OR
08/01/2024

21687796R00190